THE NECROMANCER'S DANCE

THE BEACON HILL SORCERER BOOK ONE

SJ HIMES

THE NECROMANCER'S DANCE

SJ HIMES

The Necromancer's Dance
The Beacon Hill Sorcerer Series Book One
Copyright © 2016 SJ Himes
All rights reserved.
Edited by Miranda Vescio

Cover art by Sleepy Fox Studio

No part of this book may be reproduced in any form or by any electronic or mechanical means including information storage and retrieval systems, without permission in writing from the author. The only exception is by a reviewer, who may quote short excerpts in a review.

This book is a work of fiction. Names, characters, places, and incidents either are products of the author's imagination or are used fictitiously. Any resemblance to actual persons, living or dead, events, or locales is entirely coincidental.

Digital piracy directly impacts the financial resources of authors, whether traditionally published or independently. Please don't pirate my books.

CONTENT ADVISORY: On page alcohol abuse, mentions of sexual assault, violence and gore.

CONTENTS

1. Smoking Can Kill You ... 1
2. Tastes Like Chocolate ... 17
3. Even Demons Need a Break ... 33
4. Family of Choice ... 44
5. Mourning Sickness ... 67
6. Dearly Departed ... 78
7. Felonious Conversations ... 108
8. Making Alibis ... 119
9. The Master ... 147
10. Unexpected Festivities ... 168
11. Love in Death's Embrace ... 189
12. New Beginnings ... 212

Afterword ... 216
Also by SJ Himes ... 217

About the Author ... 219

DEDICATION

To the family we make.

1
SMOKING CAN KILL YOU

"Elder Simeon begs you attend an urgent matter most delicate. Elder Simeon wishes to inform you our Master is holding to your behest in regards to Gregory Doyle, and bids you come with all speed."

It was well past eleven at night when Angel Salvatore got a knock on the door and the summons that dragged him out into the cold night in nothing but thin silk pajama bottoms. He'd slid a pair of sandals on and followed the two blood slaves out of his apartment complex and into the Master's car, idling at the curb.

He usually would've told the Master to stick it where the sun won't shine, seeing as how the old vamp would burn to a brittle crisp if even a smidgen of daylight touched that porcelain delicate skin of his, but it took one name to get Angel out of the relative safety of his apartment and grabbing his work bag. And that one name was always mentioned in conjunction with another, one annoying and dear to Angel, so out he went.

Isaac Salvatore and Greg Doyle lived in each other's pockets, and that applied in times of trouble, too.

Fucking idiots.

They managed the short drive across town in silence, after the two blood bags of minimal thinking refused to answer Angel's questions, and he rolled the window down as far it could go, propping his arm on the open frame and breathing in the moist night air. Angel could see downtown across the bay, lit up in bright gold and sunset orange lights, the skyscrapers and high-rises burning like medieval torches in the far distance. The briny water gave the air a heady, damp and earthy taste, the recent drenching from autumn rains soaking the banks and keeping everything slightly squishy with retained water. It was really too cold to have the window open, seeing as how he was just in sleepwear, but he was more concerned with why his brother's best friend decided to break into the local vamp headquarters. And of course he got caught, seeing as how most of the bloodsuckers in residence at HQ were older than dirt and could hear a pin drop in a crowded football stadium during a Sunday night game.

His brother Isaac was a loner, or he had been after their family died. The summer of their funerals was when he met Greg, and the loner status became instead that of sidekick to the recent addition to their tiny corner of Beacon Hill. Things used to be quiet when they were kids, and their parents were still alive, but things changed after the massacre and the Blood Wars ten years ago. So after that horrific spring and the bodies were buried and families were trying to patch themselves up around the gaping holes left in them, which was the summer Isaac decided he wasn't going to be a good boy and go to school, and tagged along behind Greg. And that was just the first summer of misadventure, with Angel coming along to fix his brother's mess, one disaster after another. Just like tonight.

The car came to a halt in the narrow alley behind vamp HQ, and Angel was out of the car and slamming the door shut before the blood slaves even moved, heading for the back door. Angel slapped it open with the flat of his hand, the sound sharp enough to get every eye on him as he stormed into the storage room just off the kitchen. He ignored the vampires growling and hissing at his entrance, and pushed through the humans crowded along the back wall, and went straight to the idiot sitting alone in the center of the killing horde.

Greg, Isaac Salvatore's best friend and Angel's worst nightmare, was sitting at a small wooden table under a single bare bulb hanging from the ceiling, and he flinched when he saw Angel storming across the room. Angel took a quick look but didn't see Isaac anywhere. There was a lessening of the tension in his shoulders. Angel was cautious though—just because he didn't see Isaac, that didn't mean his idiot brother wasn't around somewhere. Angel just hoped he had a pulse and wasn't feeding an enraged master vamp.

"Someone want to tell me what the fuck is going on here?" Angel demanded, throwing his dark green linen satchel down on the table, clanging and clashing as the contents protested at the rough handling. Greg flinched away, opened his mouth, but Angel snapped his fingers at him, and Greg stopped before he started. "Someone who won't lie to me, if you would?"

Angel skewered the crowd in the small room, glaring at everyone brave enough to meet his eyes. The shadows hid most of them from Angel's gaze, but there was a ton of shifting and ducking of heads as most of the occupants tried to pretend they weren't there.

Most, not all. One man stood tall and proud, unafraid to meet the stony eyes of a necromancer.

Tall, broad-shouldered, and with dark auburn hair, Simeon met Angel's eyes fearlessly, his dark green orbs catching the light as the bare bulb above their head swung with the breeze of Angel's entrance. Simeon gave Angel a simple twitch of the lips, as close to a smile as Angel had ever seen the four-hundred-year-old vampire get. Simeon smirked; he never smiled. Angel thought Simeon was that old, as the tattoo on his right upper arm dated back to Ireland at about that time period, and Angel had heard the lower ranked vamps and blood slaves call him the 'Celt'. Vamps can't get tattooed after their resurrection, and the tattoos on his body could only have been placed there while he was human. It made sense to Angel. He couldn't tell for certain though, but Angel knew that right now he was the oldest vamp in the room, so Simeon had the authority to tell him what was going on.

"Simeon. Care to share? Wanna tell me why I was dragged outta bed and driven across town to find my brother's boyfriend locked in your storage room?" Angel growled at the old vamp, and Simeon's lip twitched again.

Angel had something of a temper problem. Just a bit. And Simeon loved to poke at it, like a fool hunter nagging at a bear with a stick after a long cold winter. "And if anyone says Isaac was involved with this stupid endeavor I'm about to hear, I am gonna start handing out hexes indiscriminately."

"Mr. Doyle," Simeon said, tilting his head at the man cowering at the table, "decided he was going to take a job to burglarize the place of business of our Master. He was caught," Simeon continued, a calm veneer over a well of tension. Simeon's voice was accented faintly, and had a lilt to it that could seduce the clothes off a nun—which Angel was certain Simeon had done at some point in his long life. Simeon was one slick bastard. "He refuses to tell us who hired him. As per the arrangement you have with our master, we did not get the information from him as we usually would. That is why you are here, Sorcerer Salvatore."

He's *breaking out the title, he must really want to know what's going on, and he's being very careful with me.* Never mind Angel hated being called that, as it sounded like the name for an online sex-worker. He wasn't going to complain though, because he'd never hear the end of it from Simeon if Angel confessed why he didn't like his name.

And those methods of extracting information? That usually comes with the extracting of blood from unwilling blood donors. Crap. Thank heaven for small mercies, Greg hasn't been drained. Now all I can do is pray silently that Isaac wasn't involved.

"And my brother? Was he involved as well?" Angel asked, finally looking away from the Irish vamp and at the idiot stinking of booze and stale cigarette smoke. Greg was the same age as Isaac, but no one would ever be able to tell. Greg had been chain smoking since he was a pre-teen, and drinking for nearly as long. While both Isaac Salvatore and Greg Doyle were in their early twenties, Greg could pass for a man in his late thirties, worn out by life and bad, bad choices.

Thankfully, Isaac had the family genes, and hard living had yet to leave its mark on him.

"Mr. Doyle was caught alone, within the confines of the building. He has yet to speak, aside to tell us that it wasn't his idea, he was being paid to do it. We asked politely what he was after," *yeah, I'm sure they did*, "—but he has refused to speak more on the matter. We then recalled his connection to you, and the arrangement you have with our Master. We would like to know what he was sent here to steal, and by whom."

"So would I." Angel grabbed another chair, and pulled it back from the table, sitting heavily with an exasperated sigh. He sat across the table from Greg, who was doing his level best not to make eye contact with Angel.

Think a room full of pissed off vampires is scary? Try pissing off a sorcerer with anger management issues and an affinity for working with the dead and dearly departed.

Angel stared. Silence. More staring. Angel was letting this fool see every single time he regretted not hexing his ass over the years—and it was only because Isaac loved this poor excuse of a man, and once upon a time, he helped Angel's little brother get over the deep depression he'd fallen into after the death of their whole family. Greg wouldn't make eye contact, and he was sweating, a drop running down his left temple and dripping off his jaw to land on his stained shirt. There were a few bruises and abrasions on him, but Angel didn't see any apparent bite marks, or anything serious. Angel could take his time on this if he had to—he was already up, and Angel was not going away until he got some answers.

"I'm not talking," Greg finally burst out after what felt like hours of silence, mumbling defiantly down at the scarred tabletop. What felt like forever was really only a handful of minutes. Angel waited, quiet and motionless, knowing that Greg was about to crack. It didn't take long. "It wasn't my idea."

"What wasn't your idea?" Angel asked, sounding bored, when inside all he wanted to do was bash in Greg's skull and dig around for his one last remaining brain cell. *The poor thing needs to be rescued, all alone in that empty head.*

"Comin' here. Not my idea. Just needed the cash." Sweat ran down his temples, his hairline soaking wet.

"I can see that. You're always bumming money off of Isaac. Who paid you?" Angel asked calmly, picking at one of his nails, the corner jagged. Angel wasn't looking at him directly, but could still see the way Greg's eyes darted around the room, ever mindful of the numerous vampires and fanatically devoted blood slaves surrounding them. Though Greg really didn't need to worry about them, he needed to worry about the man sitting across from him.

"Not telling."

Gawd, that's mature. *Sounds like a five-year-old being asked if he did something wrong. And this guy is Isaac's bestie? I'm really hoping they aren't sleeping together. I'm pretty sure Greg's gay, and I don't want to deal with any STDs that Isaac may get from him.*

Angel was watching his face when Greg replied to his question, so he saw a tiny twitch of his head. To most normal people, that wouldn't even register to them, and if someone did see that twitch? Angel knew most people would dismiss it out of hand. *Just nerves or something, right? Nope.*

It was a good thing Angel was there, and not a cop or another master vamp. If they'd tried draining Greg to get their answers, Angel would have had a five-story building full of very old and very sick vamps to deal with. This was a compulsion. Magical compulsion. When magic was active and running its course through a human, the blood would make vamps ill if they drank it. Which was another reason why Angel was cool sitting there in a relatively skimpy outfit and not worried about becoming a snack. Angel's kind didn't taste good to vamps.

That particular head twitch was common across the board for humans compelled by sorcery, and it usually took a practitioner of the arts to recognize the signs.

Not making eye contact. Extreme sweating. Refusal to speak when it would save your ass, behavior contrary to personality. Greg should be tattling so fast right now yet he's not. Mental faculties diminished the longer the compulsion is in place. Yup. He's been hexed.

"Clear the room please," Angel said softly, and Simeon made no sound, but the vamps blurred as they darted out of the room, the blood slaves moving at a comparatively leisurely pace after their masters. Simeon remained, and two blood slaves, and a couple of vamps Angel didn't recognize stayed in the shadows along the far wall. For them to stay they must be older masters and the humans who belonged to them. Simeon stared at one in particular for a long moment, face unreadable, expression frozen, but the Celt said nothing to the vampire in the shadows, so he or she was probably another Elder. Angel shrugged, unperturbed by the remaining witnesses. It was the whole mob of lesser masters and symbiotic slaves that couldn't keep a secret and gossiped like old ladies at bingo.

"What... what are you gonna do?" Greg asked, eyes darting between Angel and the door over his shoulder. *Sorry hun, you're not fast enough to get outta here.*

"I'm going to get you talking. So shut up."

Angel heard Simeon snort quietly at that, and sent him a sneer. It was almost midnight on a work night, Angel was sleeping an hour ago, and his grownup behavior was left on his pillow. Simeon grinned at Angel, all cocky attitude and rippling muscles, and Angel had to force himself to look back at the ruin of human potential sitting at the table. Angel was floored Simeon was smiling at him, since he had never seen the master vamp actually smile. *Maybe it's the outfit I'm barely wearing. Simeon is eye candy for certain, but that's a whole-bag-full-of-pissed-off-cats kinda trouble there.*

Angel dug into his bag, and pulled out his smartphone, waking the screen to see that it was a few minutes to midnight. Had he really been in this dank and smelly storage room with the world's biggest idiot for forty minutes?

Angel pulled out a small silver dish, once part of a serving set that their Grams used to have, but the pieces had all steadily disappeared over the years. Probably thanks to Isaac and his bad habits. It was small, and ornately etched, blackened from long years and zero polishing on Angel's part. It was going to serve its purpose tonight well enough. Angel kept digging, but couldn't find what he needed. Angel sent a look at Greg, and considered bumming the bum for a cigarette, but he wrinkled his nose at that thought. *I'd rather not pollute my lungs with anything he's carrying around.*

"Anyone got a smoke?" Angel asked the room at large, and unsurprisingly, Simeon materialized next to him, a slim gold cigar case open in his pale hand. Angel cocked a brow at the old vamp, and got another dazzling grin in return. Angel leaned over, and picked out a thin cheroot that smelled like rich green things and cinnamon. He ran it under his nose, breathed in deep, and smiled, eyes closing for a moment in appreciation. For an undead bloodsucker, Simeon had fantastic taste in human vices. Angel send Simeon a wink and grin of his own, too angry and fed up to worry about encouraging the vampire. "Thanks, babe."

Simeon backed away, arranging himself on Angel's right and a step back. Simeon would have a front row seat to Angel's spell, and he would also be out of line of sight. Simeon was accustomed to magic users. *Smart fucker.*

Greg was watching Angel, sweat still running from the top of his head and down his face. His hands were shaking, and he was gripping the edge of the table as if the room was spinning. The compulsion riding Greg was set sloppily, and it was unraveling fast. Whoever hired Greg to break into the vampires' restaurant-cum-apartment building was either really impatient, incompetent, or was willing to risk a man's life and sanity for monetary gain—Angel was betting the latter. He didn't know for sure what the Master had cooking around in vamp HQ, but seeing as how the Master was rumored to be over a thousand years old and was a near recluse, Angel wouldn't be surprised if the oldest vamp in Boston had some things worth stealing in the building.

Angel leaned back in his chair, cheroot in his right hand, holding it like he was waiting for a light.

"So, Greg, think you can work your way around that compulsion buried in your brain, or is this gonna get dirty?" Angel asked, conversational and relaxed.

Greg blinked at Angel in confusion, and he was guessing the answer was no. Greg probably wasn't even aware he'd been compelled to stay silent. Most humans weren't capable, lacking in mental willpower and fortitude to work themselves free from a compulsion, but it was known to happen. Angel was certain Greg was not amongst the able. Most addicts have their willpower eroded by their habits.

Magic came in many forms. Elemental magic was the province of witches, each witch with his or her own particular affinity, be it fire or air or any of the other elements. All magic users are born to it, like witches and wizards. A wizard is a beefed up witch, male or female, and can access power beyond the elements. That was the point where magical energy begins to gather, and it pushed at the veil between worlds, bleeding over the barrier to the other side. Wizards were able to access the more powerful pockets of magical energy, before it left this plane. As soon as magical energy was over there, on the other side, it joined a deep well of power that was usually beyond access by mortals. Unless the magic user was a sorcerer. Or sorceress. Once the magic bled through the veil, it was usually out of bounds. The different rankings of magic user were really dependent on the level of power a person had access to, and their ability to manipulate it.

Angel was ranked as a sorcerer. The unfathomable infinite maelstrom of magic that gathered beyond this world in a brilliant sea of light and shadows, swirling and singing... Angel could use it. He was able reach out, through the veil, and touch the infinite. And even within the three tiers of magic users, witch, wizard, and sorcerer, there were rankings. All based on the personal strength of their individual abilities, and their affinities.

Angel's affinity was for death, and he was a necromancer.

Not just death in its literal meaning; but all that lead to death and dying, and everything touched by mortality. Spirits, ghosts, poltergeists, all kinds of undead, the dying, illness, disease, poisons, and mortal injuries, and a whole mess of really nasty creatures and conditions. Anything on the other side of the veil and anything rushing towards death was within Angel's affinity, in reach of his talents. Angel got along great with demons and vampires, when they weren't trying to kill him. Nothing makes a vamp more nervous than a necromancer. The smart ones, at least.

Greg had a serious case of the shakes, and Angel figured the idiot was close enough to have his brain melted and his nerves fried that the technique he had in mind would work. He leaned to the side, and hooked one leg over an arm of the chair, kicking off his sandal, which plopped to the floor. Angel took his eyes off Greg, and held up the cheroot, staring at it. Just at the end, breathing in and out all the while, soothing his temper and thoughts.

It was never wise to perform delicate spells when mad. Horrible things tended to happen.

"Need a light?" Simeon asked softly, voice heavy with a dry irony that made the other vamps chuckle and the slaves twitter.

Angel quirked a brow at the handsome vamp without taking his eyes off the slim cigar, and let his vision blur at the periphery, focusing on the tip, and called soundlessly for fire. A tiny red ember flared to life at the end of the cheroot, and a thin wisp of smoke rose. A soft, wordless sigh echoed through the room, and the atmosphere shifted. It was as if the roof was gone and they were all under the open night sky, hemmed in by close walls, cocooned and safe. Nothing but a sensory illusion, but was powerfully present. Magic—it moved Angel in strange ways. He let his eyes close, and tipped his head back as he took that first sweet drag of freshly lit tobacco, potent and burning, hot as it slid over his tongue and into his lungs.

Angel sensed the power in the room, heard the whispers of it as it pooled and eddied around him, gray and cool and fluid. His eyes were still shut, but that was no matter. Angel could see the magic as no one else in this room was able, tangible and real and malleable. He held his breath, the smoke deep in his lungs, and called. It answered, rising from the floor and peeling off the walls, racing from the dim glow of the humans in the room. It came to him, time slowing, the magic winding about itself, roping and writhing like snakes made from liquid light and smoke. Angel held the tumbling cloud of magic in front of him, with the merest shift of his thoughts and opened his eyes. Angel dropped his chin, and looked to Greg. Angel held his breath, reality around him slow and heavy.

Angel let the smoke out of his lungs, blowing it to where the cloud of magic hovered unseen. If Angel called more magic, any one could see it, but there was no need. He had enough. Angel was not raising the dead, merely manipulating the approaching death of the compelled man, so what he gathered was sufficient. The smoke from his lungs arced through the invisible magic cloud, and thickened, becoming more substantial. It grew, and moved with the magic gathered over the table. Angel heard Simeon shift on his feet, and the other vamps stiffened. The humans all inhaled sharply, and stared. They don't often see magic performed, going by their reactions. Greg was so far gone he was barely conscious.

Time to play.

Angel gave the smoke and magic cloud a gentle mental nudge, and a thin thread of it peeled off from the mass and snaked out towards Greg. He saw it coming, and jerked, trying to escape the chair. It was the compulsion working, trying to get the compelled out of the way of the spell.

The smoke was on him before Greg even finished lifting in his seat. A thin thread ran into his gaping mouth, as if inhaled. The magic pulled the writhing mass from the air into his body. Eventually all the smoke was absorbed, and Greg stopped breathing. He slumped in his chair, hands falling from the table, and he fell over, forehead smacking the hard wood surface.

"*Mors nos tangit omnes,*" Angel whispered, releasing all tension from his muscles, relaxing fully in the chair.

Death touches us all.

He pulled in a breath, and collected his thoughts, taking his time. Though not too much time, a man was dying across the table from him.

"Life reduced to cold corpse, enslaved flame to ash. Ash to smoke, death made spirit. All is mine by first and last breath. *Potest quidem mortuum meum,*" Angel recited softly, each word pushing the smoke and magic through Greg's body.

What is dead is mine.

The tobacco was the corpse, the spark Angel called the enslaved flame, the ashes to smoke, and so on. Magic was an English major's wet dream of symbolism. Angel used the bare bones version of a greatly complicated spell, not needing the full incantation. He was not aiming to create a zombie, just get some answers and free an idiot from another magic user's influence. Technically Greg was dying right that second. Body starved of oxygen, his brain suffering under the rapidly eroding compulsion that was killing him just as fast as Angel's spell.

Until Angel stopped it.

Vision blurred again, melding the invisible with the visible. Angel watched the smoke running through Greg, filling every crevasse of his body, every artery and vein. It raced through his nerves, his muscles, and battled its way up the compelled man's spinal cord. Angel saw when the gray smoke hit Greg's brain stem, and that is where the sparks happened. Angel was able to see the compulsion, and set the smoke on it like a hound to a coon. The smoke flashed hot, and burnt away the spell buried in Greg's brain. The remnants disappeared fast, as swiftly as small embers thrown from a bonfire.

Now he is mine.

"Hear me, Gregory Doyle. Hear me, and obey. Breathe, and speak."

Angel took a new drag on the cheroot, and the tip glowed as he breathed in, and Greg's chest rose with his. Greg sucked in air and began to cough. He sat up slowly, coughing and hacking, tears running from his eyes. The scent of fire and smoke was immediately present in the room, as if they were all about to be consumed by flames. His red-shot eyes locked on Angel's, and for the first time in an hour, he saw true recognition in them.

"Angie? What the hell?" Greg mumbled, clearly not understanding what was happening. He probably didn't remember anything since he agreed to rob Boston's Master. Angel narrowed his eyes at the annoying nickname, but decided not to waste time on it.

"Seems you were an idiot, Greg. Someone hired you to rob the Master, break into his place, and steal something here. Care to share?" Angel said, a hint of impatience leaking past his control. His magic stayed steady, Greg's life ticking away by the second.

Greg blinked, lost and dazed, but Angel was expecting that. Angel sent the smoke through Greg's mind, inhaling another deep drag of tobacco rich air. Angel could almost see the individual memories flash in Greg's eyes as he burnt away the fatigue and stress, the injuries to the other man's brain left behind by the compulsion as it controlled him.

"Answer me, now."

Greg spoke so fast he startled himself. "It was some dude down at Sexy Femme in Fall River. Never seen him before. Said he would pay cold hard cash for a quick job."

"What was his name? What did he look like?" Simeon asked at his shoulder, and he spoke to Greg directly. Angel tipped his head once, and Greg breathed in time as he inhaled more smoke. The cheroot was a long one, but this was taking some time, and Angel needed to hurry this up. Only a couple of deep drags and the slim cheroot was half way gone to ash. Angel would rather not explain to Isaac why he turned his best friend into a living zombie, or a 'wraith', as the community called them.

Greg looked at Simeon, and furrowed his brow.

"I.... he called himself Deuce. Tallish kid, dirty blond hair, pale, with really dark eyes. Kinda thin. Had a leather jacket, and five thousand dollars."

"Deuce? Gawd that's horrible." Angel couldn't restrain himself, and one of the blood slaves giggled. He sent the walking blood bag a wink, and Simeon glared at him before returning his attention to Greg.

"What did he hire you to steal?" Simeon asked, his accent stronger, and Angel heard the anger in his voice. Angel didn't blame him for being upset. Someone invaded his home, and tried to steal from him and his master. Angel would have been pissed in his place, and the thief would have been turned to ash or minion in seconds. Simeon, thinking about it now, had a lot more restraint that Angel gave him credit for—or maybe that was the Master.

"I don't know. He gave me the money, and told me where to go...." Greg's face developed a seriously confused expression, and Angel took another drag, a smaller one, trying to conserve what was left of the cheroot. Angel was unable to sense any hesitation on Greg's part. There was nothing left of the compulsion. Simeon growled, and took a small step, as if he wanted to rip the answers from Greg's body.

"Simeon." The Celt turned his head to Angel, eyes vivid and striking. Angel gave him a small frown, and shook his head once. "He doesn't know. I don't think he was really sent here to steal anything; he would recall what it was. He is incapable of hiding anything from me right now."

"Explain."

"I'm thinking the compulsion was placed as soon as Greg saw the money. His greed gave that Deuce guy a mental foothold on him. Whoever this Deuce is never told Greg what he was stealing, merely that he was going to steal something here. Where to go, and what to say once he was caught." It made sense in a limited fashion, but then Angel was just a necromancer. He didn't hire people to do his dirty work, he saved that for himself. "I'm thinking this Deuce guy was either expecting your fanged brethren to tear him apart, or even me for that matter. Maybe he was just fucking around? Doubtful, but even idiots can be born gifted."

"Interesting." Simeon looked thoughtful. Well, as thoughtful as he could when he looks like he wanted to sink his teeth into Greg and rip out his throat.

"Yeah.... He got compelled. Only thing he's really guilty of is being an idiot." Angel dropped his leg from the armrest, put both elbows on the table, and stared at the end of the cheroot. It was about to go out. The smoke cloud inside of Greg was wriggling faster, settling in deep, seeking out every cell and molecule. "I gotta end this now before it's too late."

"Damnation," Simeon cursed, and Angel smirked. He would never tell Simeon, but that sounded almost British. He knew better though, and refrained.

Angel grabbed the small silver dish, and dropped the column of ash into it. He then added the end too, and lit it on fire with a flicker of thought, burning it to ash as well. Angel dug in his bag, and his hand found the lone glass vial of holy water near the bottom. He pulled it out and popped the cork, pouring the blessed water into the silver dish, the ash turning to a floating dark gray mess that suddenly stunk to high hell. Greg was shaking his head, hands clutching and releasing at the edge of the table, and his eyes were growing dull, the smoke coiling just behind his corneas. If Angel had the desire, he could let this go on until completion, and give himself a living wraith, a pseudo zombie, for a pet. A wraith was able to follow simple directions and perform tasks, and if this was a hundred years ago and Greg wasn't his brother's best friend slash lover, he just might let the spell come to its natural conclusion.

Angel had a couple minutes before it really was too late, and swirled the mixture fast with one finger as he leaned over the table, glaring at Greg. "Where is Isaac?"

"Left him.... passed out at his place," Greg gasped, and it looked like he was about to pass out himself. Angel lifted his free hand, and slapped Greg across the cheek. Greg shook his head again, and blinked at him, the smoke retreating a little in his eyes.

"He wasn't with you at the bar in Fall River?" Angel demanded, making sure. If this Deuce guy got to Greg, he might have taken Isaac too. Greg shook his head no, whipping it fast side to side. Angel exhaled hard in relief, and picked up the dish, handing it to Greg. "Drink this, all of it, now."

Greg took the dish from his hands and stared at the gray sodden mess, wrinkling his nose at the odor. Angel sympathized, as the smell was enough to make anyone say no to the concoction. Yet he must drink it, or he was dead in truth.

Angel called on the smoke inside Greg, and he lifted the silver dish to his mouth. Greg swallowed it fast, damn near chugging it like a coed at Boston College.

Angel moved away from the table, grabbing his bag and stepping swiftly to the side. Just in time too, as Greg vomited violently across the table top, spewing a vile flood of smoke, dirty holy water, and ash. Simeon swore and ducked out of the way, his vamp reflexes saving him from getting soaked.

The holy water mixed with the ash, which was the genesis for the smoke, and the two ingredients ingested neutralized the spell running through Greg's body. Angel could have summoned it out of him, but then he would have had an incomplete spell messing with his power balance. It was better to abort the spell completely than trying to pull the power back and dismantling it piece by piece. Greg gagged and coughed up the last of it, moaning and crying. Smoke rose from the table, looking like steam and smelling like ass. Angel sensed the spell evaporate back out into the world, falling apart completely, the power seeping away from his second sight.

"Well, this was fun." Angel yawned, his jaw creaking as he snapped his mouth shut and rubbed at his face. He was suddenly exhausted, and swayed on his feet, thinking longingly of his nice warm bed and soft pillow.

"You need to rest, Angel." Simeon was at his side, one cool hand under Angel's elbow. He stared at Simeon's hand, the smooth cool fingers oddly pleasant on his skin, and shrugged.

"Yeah, I know. What are you going to do with him?" Angel pointed his chin at Greg and tried not to sway anymore.

"He was not responsible for his actions. We will hold him for further questioning, and most likely let him go tomorrow," Simeon paused, and Angel turned his head to see a wry smile curve the sexy pout of the vampire's lips. It was easily the third smile he'd seen that night on Simeon's chiseled sexy face, and it was just as stunning as the first one. "It would not do to kill a helpless human."

"Oh, that's nice of you. Good—I won't have to tell my brother I let vamps kill his best friend."

2

TASTES LIKE CHOCOLATE

He was so tired Angel missed Greg's removal from the room, Simeon's hand propping him up. The vampire's fingers were hard and unyielding, covered in smooth skin that wore the illusion of being soft. A vamp's body temp was far lower than a human's, warmed only by the blood they drank and the mysterious death magic they had that animated them. Angel barely managed to throw the strap of his bag over his head, the band across his chest. Angel made sure to bend over and pick up the sopping wet silver tray. He almost spilled out flat to the floor but for Simeon's unbreakable grip on his elbow, his head spinning, and Simeon took the silver dish from Angel with his free hand. Angel's eyes were blurry now from strain and fatigue, and his head felt like it was stuffed with cotton.

Simeon was looking past him, green eyes as sharp as glass, and Angel tried to turn his head to see who he was looking at, but the attempt made him groan and wish fervently was the nearest flat surface. Simeon sent one last hard look, and Angel got a glimpse of a shadowed figure leaving the room behind the others. Must be that remaining Elder, but Angel was too tired to speculate.

"You must sleep, Angel," Simeon whispered in his ear, his breath tickling over his skin, and Angel shivered in response. Simeon smelled of copper, mint and spice, and chocolate. Simeon felt Angel's whole body reaction, and his hand tightened on his elbow. Angel wasn't sure how it happened but his head ended up resting on Simeon's solid, stone-cold shoulder. Angel's hands were on the vampire's chest, clutching at his fine dress shirt.

Angel opened his mouth to speak, to say something, but the world dropped away and his mind fell into darkness.

HE MUST HAVE PASSED OUT, too damn tired from a long day at work, interrupted sleep, and a semi-major working that consumed a huge portion of his reserves. It took power to use power, and even though Angel fueled the spell with ambient magic, he still had to control and shape the working. It was a bitch, doing magic cold like that, and he would have been better off if he hadn't gone into it stressed out and tired. Not to mention he couldn't remember the last time he ate anything more substantial than tea and a muffin. Isaac moving out meant Angel forgot to eat more often than not.

Angel woke wrapped up in his favorite blanket, his bed warm and welcoming. Something was tickling his face, and he worked a hand free from under the blanket to swipe at his cheek. Feeling cool skin and soft lips, Angel opened his eyes.

He was in Simeon's arms, laying half on his clothed chest, their faces so close together the vampire's deep green eyes were all he could see.

Angel's hand was caught up in Simeon's, their fingers intertwining. Angel's eyes drifted shut as Simeon closed the tiny distance between them, his soft and cool lips ghosting over Angel's. He pulled in a deep breath of Simeon-flavored air, the vampire's scent filling his mouth and nose.

The scent of fresh blood was in there too—Simeon must have fed before taking Angel home, the potent tang of hot metal impossible to miss. The sensation of Simeon's lips barely touching Angel's did unrepeatable things to his nervous system, setting him on fire with a cool flame.

His body jerked, just a little, freezing and alternately relaxing as Simeon's lips settled over his in a full kiss, with a hint of tongue and the nip of sharp teeth.

ANGEL HAD BEEN THINKING about kissing Simeon since the day they met, a little over two years ago. It was Halloween, and Angel was dressed in normal clothes because only humans would dress up as a witch and think it not insulting, and he was dragging Isaac and Greg out of a bar in downtown Boston.

Angel's boots wore a few flecks of vomit on them when Isaac kindly threw up before he got in Angel's car. While the two drunks passed out in the back seat, Angel had gone back in the bar to the restrooms, hoping to wipe off the sickening liquid before he drove them all home. No way in hell was he driving an hour with the windows down in autumn just to escape the smell.

At the time, he hadn't known the Master of Boston owned the bar. No one did—no one mortal, at least. All anyone knew was that it was vamp property owned by any one of the lesser masters, and a place for people to go if they wanted to flirt with fangheads and try out for a place as a blood slave. Isaac was safe from that Fate, as his blood was caustic and poisonous to vampires, and most of them could smell it up close. Angel thought that maybe the boys just wanted to go for the atmosphere or the discounted beer, not that it mattered.

His lack of a costume that night actually drew more attention than if he had been dressed in black leather and fishnets. His tight blue jeans, white tee, and brown leather boots stood out in the crowd of goth wannabes, steampunk, and a myriad of other 'vampire' fashions that made him feel bad for the people wearing them. Smoke filled the place, the dry kind that looked dangerous to breathe but is relatively harmless, humans pressed up against the bar and the tables along the walls, the dance floor packed as the DJ played some kind of rapid-fire techno-house mix. Lasers danced and blue light lit Angel up as he cut through the crowd, and he was halfway across the dance floor when a rough grasp of a cold hand caught his arm, jerking him to an abrupt halt.

Angel wasn't a big guy. He was only five-seven, about a hundred thirty-five pounds, and he was glad he was able to grow in a decent enough five o'clock shadow on his jaw or the twink label would have followed him into his late twenties. He wasn't jacked or a gym bunny, though he was lean like a swimmer, and his muscles were vaguely defined. Yet he was no weakling or pushover, so having someone yank him to a forceful stop, dead in his tracks, made his hackles go up faster than a wet cat's surrounded by aggressive toddlers.

Bodies bumped and ground, the music ghastly and obnoxious, and Angel was tired and surrounded by drunk humans. He spun to confront the fool who dared to touch him, someone with no manners and all arrogance. He looked down at the hand holding his arm, and it was pale, colder than the air outside, and the grip that of a metal vise. Angel sent his gaze up, over the black lace-covered wrist, the slim arm in black velvet, and past the black smoking jacket and black silk shirt to see a vampire, a real one, looking back at him with a decidedly predatory gaze.

It wasn't a master vamp or one of the upper-level fangheads. This vamp was a lackey, a lower-rung vamp fresh from the turn and looking to impress humans with how fucking cool he was in his faux period outfit. Angel pegged him as a few years old, still arrogant enough to think he was the new Lestat or the sparkling kid with the hair, and stupid enough to think that everyone in this bar on Halloween was a human willing to be snacked on. And definitely, an idiot, since he wasn't using his nose, ignoring the hint of death magic Angel carried on him just by breathing. Even with the hundreds of bodies pressing close in the club, a smart and experienced vamp would have recognized what Angel was immediately, and cut his or her losses and let him go.

"Take your hand off of me," Angel spoke clearly, as the music was loud and even vamp hearing started to suffer at some point. "I'm not here as a snack."

Gothic Steampunk Vamp smirked at Angel, tightened his grip, and pulled him in closer. Angel ended up pressed to the rude vamp's front, his hand so tight now on Angel's elbow he was already sporting bruises. All Angel wanted was to go wash his boots and drive his brother home. Yet he couldn't, since he now had to deal with a very forward vamp who was at that moment caressing Angel's cheek with an over-perfumed hand like he'd just been watching a really bad B-movie of a villain doing the same.

"You aren't wearing a costume, my pretty. Think we need to collect the penalty fee for coming in here without a costume on." Mr. Rude tried to pull off a purring European accent, but all Angel heard was strangling cats. B-movie villain indeed.

Angel rolled his eyes, and he began pulling in some of the ambient magic in the room, prepared to blast the vamp fucker off of him. He wouldn't use too much magic since there were humans so close to where they stood Angel could feel wandering hands in rude places.

The vampire leaned down, ignoring Angel's tugs to free his arm as the vampire sniffed at his neck when suddenly one of the owners of the wandering hands materialized into another vamp. Angel was now pinned between two vamps, the new one a female in an outfit just as campy as the male, and she looked and acted just as new as the presumptuous male.

Angel pegged her for just as stupid, too.

"Last chance, fuckers. Let me go." Angel made sure to say it loudly enough some people dancing around them heard, looking their way.

Angel felt the brush of sharp fangs grazing his skin, on the top of his shoulder, the female way too close to taking a sip. Angel lifted his free hand, energy buzzing on his fingertips when the fangheads both struck at the same time. The female got him at the top of his left shoulder, and the male attacked the right side of Angel's neck, and he gasped at the pain.

He'd been bitten before, and it was tolerable, but the double attack was too much and Angel began to freak out for a second. Pain shot from his neck and shoulder, inescapable, and his knees jerked like they were about to drop him on the floor. The vamps weren't savaging him yet. They were trying to get a good drag of blood off their bites, so they were distracted, and Angel regained control enough to keep pulling on the ambient energy around them.

Angel brought his hand up, fingertips rubbing together, charge building, and made contact with the female's temple, tapping lightly. The zap hit her like a magical stun gun, and she pulled off his shoulder, her fangs tearing the flesh as they withdrew. The female growled as she staggered to her knees at his side, knocking back several humans and a few other vamps in the process. Angel kept his hand moving, and dropped it on the back of the male vamp's head, applying the same charge. The male coughed blood and he backed away as fast as she did, falling on his ass. Angel slapped a hand over the seeping wound in his neck, feeling blood run past his fingers. Not too much blood, but he might need stitches, and the gash on his shoulder was going to leave a fucking nasty scar if he didn't get it healed.

Angel backed away, and the music stopped. The crowd stared at him, as he bled all over his white tee, one hand pressed tight to his neck, with two vamps still trying to reboot their nervous systems on the floor at his feet. Hissing came from the shushed crowd, and he saw vamps moving through the throng of humans, approaching fast.

Angel looked back towards the door, but the way was blocked by more vamps heading his way.

"Back the fuck off, now!" Angel shouted, and he got more hissing in response.

The two vamps on the floor were trying to get up. Several vamps were moving in on him, none of them looking friendly, and there were too many humans surrounding him. Angel was about to be turned into a shredded blood bag, and they would kill him even faster once his blood started to make them sick, which would be several long painful minutes into his torture.

That was when Angel gave up being subtle.

Angel was aware of his blood. Not the blood running past his fingers, warm on his shoulder and neck. Angel could sense the blood stolen from him by the vampires, coursing through their mouths and throats, in their stomachs. He was in them, and his death affinity was about to show the crowd packed around him why vampires hated necromancers.

"Moderatus mortem!" The Latin came as easily as his English, and though unnecessary, it let those hearing him know he was casting, and it was enough to make even the most foolish of observers back off. I control death. "*Ego meum corpus est corpus meum mihi!*"

I am my body, and my body is me.

Simple, and devastatingly brutal as Angel reached past the veil, and dragged power screaming back into this dimension. He sucked in every wave of power, his hair crackling with static, the air burning as it warped in the rising heat, and Angel saturated every cell of his body with the raw power that came at his call. Crude, very crude. He didn't have time for proper spell-casting, and instinctual casting was enough for him to level the building if he chose.

The vamps in the crowd were seconds from attacking, the two on the floor getting up in what felt like slow motion, death promised in their eyes.

Angel reached out to his still living blood in the vampires' undead bodies, and it gave him a foothold that he could exploit. This was why necromancers and vampires usually didn't get along all that well—a necromancer, if strong enough, could slip inside a vampire's body and completely subsume a vampire's free will. They were dead, after all.

Angel's life energy and focused will exploded through their systems and he owned his attackers in seconds.

They stopped in macabre tableaus of arrested motion, the two who bit him and took his blood. They stood, eyes wild with fear, their bodies now under Angel's control. They had their thoughts, but he owned their actions. They stepped back to Angel's side and turned to face the crowd that was now milling in confusion. The crowd was backing away and the rest of the vamps felt the power surge in the room, but still kept approaching.

"*Prohibe eos,*" Angel whispered, and the two vamps he held leashed to his will blitzed out, attacking the approaching vamps.

Stop them.

His attackers were not expecting the two vamps they were presumably coming to assist to suddenly turn and attack them—two of the other vamps ended up thrown over the crowd, landing on some tables as they fell to the ground. Drinks and screams spilled out, and Angel's unwilling defenders spun, knocking back two more vamps closing in on him from behind.

Angel kept the power pouring in, the tear in the veil held open by his willpower and nerves. Humans were screaming, confused, running over each other, pushing back against the tables and the bar, the dance floor emptying. Angel yanked on the blood in the two vamps and pulled them back to him, both of them crouched at his feet, hissing, fangs out and claws extended.

"*Necromancer!*"

Angel had no idea who screamed it, but the bar was shocked into motionlessness. Everyone froze where they stood, even the vamps in mid-stride coming back for another go at Angel and his new pets. The word necromancer raced across the room, and a hush settled that was creepier than the hissing moments before.

Whispers rose and fell in waves amongst the crowd, people looking at each other with nervous expressions. A rumble of growls, a low, nearly inaudible hum through the room made the hair on the back of his neck stand up. Angel sent out more power, tightening his foothold on the vamps at his feet, and they snarled in response.

"All I wanted was to use the restroom, and I get attacked. I want nothing to do with violence, but I will use any means necessary to protect myself. Who is the Elder here?" Angel called out, throwing his voice over the heads of those watching. He might not be a big man, but he knew how to project his voice with authority.

No one moved. Humans and vamps alike stared, and Angel tried to keep an eye on every corner of the bar, searching. For there to be this many vampires in one place there must be an Elder nearby, a vampire to control the lesser undead. He was hoping at least since he couldn't very well keep his two vamps as slaves and walk out of the bar without having every vamp in the city wanting to kill him.

"Necromancer," a whisper graced his ear, and the shiver that ran down his spine was involuntary.

Angel tensed, his body instinctively reacting to the presence of a predator. The vamps at his feet hissed and snarled, twisting like snakes in reaction to his nerves. It was all the reaction he let himself show, and he made himself relax and turn to face the vampire that suddenly materialized behind him.

"You the Elder here?" Angel asked, doing his best not to show the pain of his injuries or the strain of holding raw veil-sourced power and two angry vamps to his will. Casting such a dynamic combination of instinctual spells and handling this much power was going to leave him dangerously exhausted if he didn't end this and soon.

The new vampire was dressed in a black tux and white tie that made him look like a red-headed James Bond. More auburn than true red, but he was hot, and his green eyes arrested a good portion of Angel's attention. Full sexy lips and a strong jaw, he was absolutely Angel's type, and if he wasn't an undead monster Angel was tempted to ask him for his number. He then remembered where he was and what was happening, and frowned.

"I am, necromancer. How are you this evening?" At the smoothly accented words, Angel's cock made its interest known, twitching and thrumming. The red-head's lips were unsmiling, but the corners twitched, and his eyes narrowed slightly. He could smell Angel's blood, not to mention see it as it ran down his neck and shoulder and stained his shirt. The bastard could also smell just how aroused Angel was getting, and that pissed him off even more than the biting and attacking.

"Oh, ya know. Hate Halloween. People always end up acting like idiots," Angel replied, and for some reason Angel wanted to smile at the older vamp despite his temper, but he restrained himself. "Came to pick up my drunk brother and his bestie, got puked on, decided to wash my boots off in the bathroom, and got molested by the fangheads here." Angel pointed at his feet, and the Elder's eyes flickered down for a nanosecond before returning to Angel's. "I said stop and they didn't listen. I got ...um.... Upset."

"Ah, so I see. Upset." The Elder glanced around the room, noting the tables in disarray and the bruises forming on vamps and humans alike, and his lips twitched again. "I wonder what damage you could cause if you were truly angered?" he mused in a soft, low tone that purred within his accent.

It was rhetorical, but Angel answered anyway. "Things get nasty."

"I'm certain they do." The vampire looked around the room again, and straightened a cuff link that glittered from his sleeve. "It appears you have an apology due to you."

"That's nice of you," Angel said, and meant it. He was expecting to have to hand out some more threats, maybe blast a few more vamps, but if the old vamp wanted to play diplomat instead of entitled lord of the manor, that was good too.

The old vamp chuckled, but still no smile. Angel didn't know it was possible to laugh without smiling. "Nice. I haven't been called nice in centuries."

"Meh. Nice, smice. So, can I release my newest acquisitions without things getting nasty here?" Angel eyed the crowd, and saw some anger out there, eyes glittering. "After I get my apology of course, and not to mention a promise of no more violence against me or mine."

"Negotiations. How elegant. When you hold all the power here, necromancer. Two fledglings under your sway, and poisoned by your blood. By rights, you could leave them to die." The laughter was gone, but Angel saw something in the mossy depths of the master vamp's eyes. Respect, maybe? He sensed nothing reminiscent of anger. The vamp was as calm as a frozen lake in January.

"I get my apology, I release the two idiots licking my boots, and we all part ways, calm and alive," Angel loudly enough for everyone to hear. "Oh, and no violence against me or mine."

"And if I cannot guarantee any of what you are requesting?" The vamp leaned down slightly, his voice low, the sexy burr to his words making Angel's nerves dance with something other than fear.

"Then I level this building on my way out, with undead bonfires lighting my path." Angel may not be able to level this building before he was torn apart, but he could certainly end a few immortal lives before he died.

It wouldn't be the first time he decimated a swarm of undead.

The vamps at his feet hissed, twisting against his will, staring up at the Elder vamp. He stared back at them for a long moment and then nodded his head.

"I am Simeon, Elder of my Master's Bloodclan. You are?" Simeon was an ancient name and fell out of use over a hundred years ago. That just elevated this vampire's age in Angel's estimation.

Angel hesitated, thinking. It wouldn't be hard to track him down, he knew for a fact he was the only necromancer in the whole state, so withholding his name was pointless. If they wanted to track him down later, they could, especially since Isaac and Greg were in here for hours.

"Angel Salvatore." Simeon's eye twitched again, and Angel knew it was because of his name. Simeon recognized it, as did most supernats in the greater Boston area. In fact, most of the fangheads in the Northeast knew his name, and his reputation earned him a wide berth. "No violence or harm to me or mine. That includes the two men passed out in my car. My brother Isaac Salvatore and Gregory Doyle."

Simeon watched him for a breathless moment as if trying to see past Angel's name to the man underneath. Everyone who knew the history of how Boston's Blood Wars ended knew his name and that wasn't arrogance. Especially the vampires. Simeon gave a short nod, and then to Angel's surprise, gifted him with a brief but sincere bow at the waist, Simeon's glittering eyes briefly aglow from deep within with a flash of power.

"I offer my sincerest apologies, Necromancer Angel Salvatore, for the affronts made to your person and safety while under our roof.

May you leave in peace, and no violence or harm shall be offered by our hands, to you or those you claim as yours."

Angel searched his eyes as the vampire's words rang out through the bar. The subtle hissing stopped, and even without looking, Angel, sensed a lessening of tension in the room. Angel saw no sign of deceit in the emerald green eyes still holding his and nodded curtly in acceptance.

Angel looked away from Simeon and stepped back, the two vamps following him as if he held their leashes in truth. Angel saw hatred in their eyes, and fear. He had removed their freewill, and easily, and for an undead creature accustomed to being on top of the food chain, it must be a horrible thing to experience. Angel refused to feel bad, and steeled himself against any remorse.

Angel could still feel his blood in their bodies, saw the drying sheen of it on their lips. He closed his eyes and called to it. Sorcery required an absolute knowledge of one's body and a complete awareness of self. This extended to the living parts, so viable blood cells lining the throats of a vampire counted as well.

He pulled at the power still rushing through his body and called to the blood in the vampires. He needed to get it out of them anyway, as his blood was about to be making them very ill any minute now. Their eyes bulged as they suddenly started to gag, and Angel loosened the bindings on their bodies enough for them to vomit on the floor. Thankfully none landed on Angel, and the stink of blood and whatever liquid that passed as vampire bile filled the air.

"Back away," Angel warned quietly and took a step back himself. He sent a burst of kinetic magic out, pushing the two vamps away, causing them to skid on their knees across the tiled dance floor. Simeon moved with him, and Angel leveled his focus on the puddle of bloody vomit.

Angel took his hand away from his neck, and held bloody fingers over the floor. He could feel everyone's gaze on him, especially the searching regard of Elder Simeon. Angel let go of the power he was pulling through the veil, and the atmospheric pressure dropped in the room. As it left, he snapped his fingers.

The fire flared fast and hot, the puddle of vomited blood burning to ash in seconds. Red and orange light danced across the faces of humans and vampires, and Simeon hissed in surprise beside him.

Smoke lifted slowly into the air, and the black mark on the floor was all that remained of the blood. He was a sorcerer—leaving any usable traces of his blood behind was an invitation for another magic-user to exploit it. That was a risk he couldn't afford to take. Angel sighed, and stretched his neck, shoulders tight. He needed a fucking nap. And a shower. *And some stitches, dammit.*

The two vamps stood fast and snarled at Angel, eyes wild and promising death. They managed one step forward until a wave of cold, foreign power knocked them back. Their faces relaxed, and they dropped back to their knees. All the fight was gone from them, and it wasn't Angel's doing at all. The power was cool and sweet, with a hint of a spicy chocolate essence. Angel flicked his eyes over to Simeon, and there was shimmer in the air around him as he flexed whatever Elder vamp mojo he was packing.

Simeon turned his back on the cowed vamps, and the room's occupants slowly started to move as everyone made an obvious effort to go back to their business. Angel held his ground when Simeon came into his personal space, forcing him to look up. Simeon was over six feet tall, and his suit clung to him like a second skin, showcasing a chiseled physique that flowed over the floor with a supernatural grace. Not even the most talented ballet dancer could move with the elegance of an old master vampire.

Pale skin was normal for a vamp, and Angel could see small flashes of tattoos that peeked above his jacket collar. His hair was long, but not too long, swept back in thick waves that made Angel's fingers itch to touch. A chuckle, rich and smooth, brought him out of his musings. Angel flushed, realizing he had been staring, and for a while now. He looked back into Simeon's eyes, the green so vibrant and true that the shade colored his whole horizon.

Angel dropped his eyes and took a small half-step back. Staring into a master vamp's eyes was an invitation to lose your life. He knew better, but the old vamp's appeal was strong. There was not much a vampire could do to him that he couldn't get free of eventually, but he didn't want to take his chances. Not even the promise of no violence would keep him safe from seduction.

"I need to go," Angel said, looking back up but not making eye contact for longer than a second.

"Wait," the vampire said, one hand stretching out towards Angel as he backed away. There was desire in his eyes, and Angel found himself wanting to reach out and take the vampire's hand. That was such a bad idea. Angel shook his head, and turned around, pushing his way through the crowd. Once people saw who he was they parted before him in a rush, whispers and growls following him as he left the building.

Angel got in his car, and after checking on the two idiots passed out in the back seat, and he left before he could do anything else remarkably stupid, like burning down the building or kissing the Elder. It was a shame, really—Simeon was exactly Angel's type, and he wanted nothing more than to climb that supernat like an amped up eight-year-old attacking a jungle gym at the park.

There was a ton of reasons why it was a bad idea for the lone surviving Salvatore necromancer to get involved with a vampire—many of whom were dead, and their ashes scattered over the holy ground King's Chapel.

Angel Salvatore may be the only necromancer in the state, but ten years ago, the Salvatore Clan was the most powerful and distinguished magical family in the Northeast, right up until the end of the Blood Wars. Angel's family, all but for him and Isaac, died at the climax of a generations' long war between Clans, their throats ripped out by an army of vampiric assassins.

Angel and Isaac lived because Angel burned that army to ash and dust.

※

THE KISS WAS SOFT, sweet, and Angel was too tired to move away. That's what he told himself, but as Simeon's mouth slanted over his and the bigger male rolled until Angel was under his hefty weight, his whole thought process about how bad of an idea this was flew out the window. When Simeon's tongue slid between his lips and took a leisurely stroll through his mouth, Angel moaned in encouragement and lifted his hips, desperate for some friction on his achingly hard cock. Simeon slid between his thighs, and Angel moaned again, loving the way the big vamp's hips held his legs open, his weight pushing him down into the bed.

It was the iron-hard length pressing insistently to his own that snapped him out of his passion-dazed state. Angel pulled his mouth away, and his head pushed down on the mattress so he got enough distance to look the elder vamp in the eyes. "Up, now."

Simeon's mouth was wet, his lips red and swollen from their kiss. His eyes were dark with desire, and they settled on Angel's mouth, his luscious mouth begging for another taste. Angel fought back his hormones, refusing to press another kiss to the lips of the very dangerous predator holding him down on the bed...no matter how damn good it felt, this was a bad idea.

"You taste like sin," Simeon whispered over his mouth, and Angel's tongue darted out of its own volition and ran along Simeon's lower lip. A sharp white fang nipped the tip of his tongue before Simeon sucked him back in for another kiss. Angel arched his hips off the bed, kissing him back, heart racing. Why was this a bad idea again?

Somewhere in the apartment, a door crashed, and heavy footfalls stomped across his hardwood floors. Simeon tensed on top of him, and they both ended the kiss and turned to the bedroom door just in time for the wood panel to explode inwards, shards flying across the room. Simeon moved so fast Angel forgot how to breathe, rolling them both off the bed to the floor. Simeon landed beside him, fangs bared, eyes glowing. Angel flattened himself to the floor, watching underneath his bed as clawed feet crushed the remains of his door, gouging the floor and rugs as the intruder came into his room.

Chattering, like beetles scuttling over stones, filled his room, and

Angel's eyes widened in disbelief as a multitude of clipped voices quietly called his name.

"Angelus, Angelus...." The chattering increased, making his ears hurt. A rumble vibrated under his hand, and Angel turned to see Simeon snarling, his body taut as piano strings. Angel gripped a handful of Simeon's shirt and pulled until Simeon looked at him, his green eyes aglow. He shook his head, silently pleading Simeon to stay down.

A single vampire, even one as old as Simeon, was no match for a demon.

3

EVEN DEMONS NEED A BREAK

"Don't! Stay here," Angel breathed in Simeon's ear, and he yanked on the vampire's shirt when he tensed in reaction to the demon's shadow racing over the wall. "It will kill you."

The floor shook as the demon crushed the shattered pieces of the bedroom door underfoot, its shoulders scraping the sides of the doorway. He looked back at it through the empty space under his bed, and the sight of grey-scaled and yellow clawed feet attached to thick, heavily muscled legs made his stomach want to crawl out around his spine and hide. The air stank of damp earth and rotting flesh, and Angel swallowed back a dry heave as he struggled to breathe past the odor and his building fear.

"What is it?" Simeon hissed back, but Angel had no time to answer. He had seconds to stop the beast before they were both torn to strips of red meat.

Angel looked up at his nightstand, his alarm clock showing it was minutes 'til sunrise. He just had to last until then. A demon this big had to have been summoned nearby, since he hadn't heard screaming from civilians and the sounds of police sirens. If he could find the circle, he could stop the demon.

"Angelus..." The demon's voice was many, a teeming mass of fractured tongues weaving together to form words in a language not its own. A large, three-fingered hand rose over the bed, latching into the edge of the bedframe inches above their heads.

Angel let go of Simeon's shirt, bringing his hands together. He had no time to summon the ambient energy or pull from the veil—this was fast and dirty. Angel pulled on his dwindling reserves, still recovering from the last couple of days of doing major work and little sleep. It hurt, like he was setting fire to his insides—he pulled his palms apart, and the shimmering ball of fire and light that appeared between his hands crackled.

The demon roared, so loud Angel's ears throbbed with pain, and the bed was ripped away, the mattress going one way, the frame breaking apart. Angel yelled, tossing the ball of raw power straight at the demon's scaled and warped face. It screamed, rearing back, a twisted amalgamation of humanoid and reptilian characteristics. Simeon grabbed Angel around the waist and ran—as only a vampire could, blurring Angel's apartment as Simeon took them past the demon, out of his bedroom, and out past the living room. They ended up in the hall outside his front door just as the demon screamed in thwarted rage, tearing after them.

"Outside! Get us outside!" Angel yelled, and Simeon hesitated. It was nearly dawn, so Angel understood Simeon's reluctance, but the enraged beast charging at them gave them little in the way of options. Angel ran down the hall, heading for the stairs, but Simeon came up behind him and picked him up, speeding them down the three flights of stairs and out to the street in mere seconds.

The building he lived in was at the back end of the statehouse, at the three-way intersection of Hancock, Myrtle, and Derne, and at this time of morning should be busy with early traffic. Simeon stopped them in the middle of the street, and Angel staggered back, head swimming from the shock at the vampire elder's speed. His bare foot scraped over the pavement, and he looked down.

Angel backed away from the scorched and melted summoning circle charred into the surface of the intersection. It was the point of summoning, and Angel cursed himself mentally for being too tired to notice a fucking summoning in what amounted to his front yard. He would have noticed the surge of veil-drawn power when the sorcerer summoned the demon through dimensional boundaries if he wasn't running on empty.

The streets were quiet, the air still and heavy. Dawn was lightening the city, but it was minutes away. He had some time. The demon, depending on how powerful it was and the type of binding used to hold it here in this plane, would either disappear with the dawn's light, or run amok on the streets, the spell controlling its actions disintegrated with the sunlight. As long as the summoning circle was intact, the demon may be able to stay in this dimension after dawn.

Angel rapidly scanned all four directions, even checking the rooftops along the back of the statehouse, but there was nothing. No sign of the sorcerer who summoned the demon in a wanton display of reckless *artis praecantatio*. The street should have traffic, pedestrians and cars, yet nothing. It smelled of swamp and rotted meat, and Angel faced the townhouse that held his apartment just as a roar shook the windows and the shadowy silhouette of the demon filled the main entrance.

It stalked down the short stairs, claws sparking on the sidewalk. It swiped at a car parked at the curb, and metal screamed as rips in the metal body appeared beneath the beast's claws. Ten feet tall, with a hunched back and large, greyish-green scales that glittered in the pre-dawn light and streetlamps, the demon moved with a disjointed gait that invoked an instinctual reaction to back away from that which wasn't normal, wasn't part of this world. Its head was lizard-like, with a many-toothed mouth that held more tongues than necessary, a writhing red mass of wet flesh that resulted in the multi-toned voice from one mouth, all hissing Angel's birth-name.

"We need to leave!" Simeon shouted, grabbing Angel's hand, preparing to zip them away again. The demon advanced, crouching on all fours, its long, whipcord tail smacking the ground and cars as it joined them in the road.

"We leave, it'll start killing people as it tries to follow! I have to banish it!"

"Dawn is coming, Angel...." Simeon said, his cold hand around Angel's hand tightening, dragging him backward as the demon approached. It hissed, head down, tail lifting as it changed its balance, the demon becoming more animalistic, less humanoid, its nature warping again in its preparation to attack. Angel gathered another ball of raw energy, his insides aching as he pulled on his almost empty energy reserves.

He threw it, and the scales along its face scorched and the beast screamed, shaking its head as sparks fell. Red flesh showed through the worst of the burns on its snout, and it roared at Angel, scoring the pavement with its claws.

"I know! Distract it! Don't let it grab you!" Angel said, hoping Simeon would do as he asked and not disappear. The first rays of sunlight would soon start reflecting off the cloud cover, and depending on how old Simeon really was, he would either be able to withstand the early light or begin to burn.

Simeon snarled, frustrated, but Angel was thankful when Simeon blurred, and instead of running away from beast and dawn, charged the demon crouching in preparation for its leap. A splash of rancid blood flared out along its side as Simeon raked it with his own claws, and the beast spun to follow him. Angel ducked as its tail flew over his head, whistling through the air.

Angel let Simeon play bait and turned his attention to the circle burnt into the intersection. It was about twelve feet across, the runes and lines made of melted asphalt. Shoving aside his curiosity at what could burn that hot and be so precise, he searched amongst the designs for the markers that held both the demon here on this plane and sent it after Angel.

A vampiric screech made him flinch, but the swearing that soon followed in some form of ancient Gaelic reassured him Simeon was still in the fight. He spared a glance over his shoulder, to see Simeon darting and slashing, a housecat foolishly tangling with a larger, far meaner cougar. If the demon caught Simeon, he would be dead…again.

Returning his efforts to the symbols in the summoning circle, he sent his will out, the pain at reaching for the veil tearing at his spirit, his insides. Pain both physical and spiritual, that he pushed aside. He would sleep when he was dead, or hopefully after the demon was banished.

"Angel! Speed up your efforts, *mo ghra!*" Simeon shouted at him, grunting, his feet scraping over the road as a blow sent him past Angel where he knelt on the ground.

Angel found the rune that held the demon in thrall, and next to it was the marker, in a Latin-based jargon, of his name. There was a pile of ash inside the rune, and Angel caught a hint of burnt hair as he leaned down. There was an anchoring rune poorly drawn underneath the ashes.

Someone used his hair. Summoned a demon and sent it after him. Regardless of where he lived and the time of day, someone wanted him dead and cared not for collateral, didn't care at all that he lived in a busy section of Beacon Hill and that there were three families in his building with small children—someone wanted him dead, and were willing to do anything to make it happen. The anchoring rune meant that once Angel was dead, or the rune destroyed, the demon would depart, helped along by the emerging light of dawn.

Rage filled him, and Angel opened the veil and pulled. Power came pouring through the dimensional wall and into his body, his mind and spirit. Simeon screamed, just as Angel lifted his hand, standing tall, the power spindling around him.

He would destroy the diagram and anchoring rune the demon here, and with dawn arriving, the demon would have no choice but to retreat back to its home dimension, purpose unfulfilled. It could be summoned again, and the *geas* placed on it by the original summoner would kick back in, but Angel would be prepared.

"Angel!" Simeon cried, but Angel was centered on this one thing, destroying the summoning circle and runes, and he had to hope Simeon would last until he was done.

The demon tossed Simeon, the vampire limp with limbs flailing as he crashed into the iron-wrought fence that wrapped around the rear of the statehouse. Angel saw the first rays of dawn bloom above the city, and released the power downward, blasting the circle.

This was going to hurt.

And it did.

DETECTIVE GRANT COLLINS was Irish to the core, dark haired, late thirties, looked fantastic in a dove gray designer suit that clung to every slim, lean line of his toned body, and he hated Angel with every ounce of his considerable intellect.

"Let me get this straight," Detective Collins drawled, waving a slim hand in the direction of what was once an intersection in one of the busiest parts of Beacon Hill and was now a crater that exposed parts of the sewer system and the power lines, "A demon crashed into your place, tries to kill you, and then you run out here and blow up the street and banish it back to Hell?"

"Not Hell, actually. No such place." Angel corrected, leaning back on the front stoop of his apartment building, blinking his eyes to clear them from the glare put off by the countless cop cars and firetrucks filling all sides of the intersection. "It was a native sentient species of another dimension that got warped and manipulated by crossing the boundaries, and there was a *geas* placed on it by whoever summoned it, making it attack when it otherwise would have gone into hiding, seeing as how it was in a hostile dimension and foreign environment. Western magical practitioners incorrectly call such a creature a demon, when I would describe it as a kidnapped inter-dimensional alien."

Detective Collins opened and closed his mouth a few times, hand raised, finger pointed right at Angel. He sighed, and sent his eyes over the block, trying to see where Simeon went. He was vague on explaining exactly who he was with when the demon attacked, and he was worried about the elder vamp. He hadn't seen Simeon when he woke up at the bottom of the crater, soaking wet from a ruptured water line. It was dawn, the street lit by the golden glow reflecting off the heavy morning dew that descended over the street, everything wet and glistening. It was a beautiful morning, but the smell of ozone, car exhaust, and rotting flesh was overwhelming, and all Angel wanted was to shower, something to eat, and his bed. Not necessarily in that order, either.

"I should have you arrested for destruction of public property!" Collins found his voice, winding up for what looked like an impressive diatribe. Angel had no doubt he might end up in jail for his misadventure that morning, but he was too tired to care. He might actually get some sleep in jail.

Angel tuned out Collins as he went on and on, spouting some of his anti-Salvatore rhetoric and his opinion of Angel, which wasn't very high. Angel knew why to some degree Collins didn't like him, but Angel barely saw the man more than a couple times a year, so this animosity was exasperating as much as it was annoying. Angel would occasionally consult with Boston PD when it came to magical matters their own specialists weren't equipped to handle. He didn't make a practice of it, though, since Angel preferred to keep to himself and getting involved in police matters was a fast way to get the wrong kind of attention.

Not to mention that the Collins clan hated his guts with an animosity that was legendary.

Angel was a teacher. Not in public schools—he lacked the patience—but one on one with gifted students, who were looking for higher level instruction in the art of practicing magic. That meant newly advanced sorcery-level students, who had the potential ability, but not the skillset, and they came to Angel for what they couldn't get from their private schools or families. Angel was the only necromancer in the state, but he wasn't the only sorcerer, but because of what happened ten years ago in the Blood Wars, he was the most well-known, the most notorious, and the youngsters started appearing on his doorstep a couple of years after the Wars ended.

Which ended, coincidentally enough, with another leveled street, quite similar to this one.

He was no master burdened with an apprentice, though, he avoided such dependency in his students. A sorcerer needed to learn how to survive on their own, as they were the only ones who could summon and control veil-drawn magical energy, and too many people tried to cozen their way into a sorcerer's good graces and take advantage. Self-reliance was a big deal to Angel, and he tried to impart that sentiment in his students. Some listened and took his advice to heart, and others didn't.

He was thankful none of his students were here at the moment, since he didn't want a frightened twenty-something blowing up more things than necessary in fear and overreaction at the sight of a demon. He snorted, amused at himself. There really was no way to overreact to the sight of a demon. Angel smirked at that thought, looking at the ruin of the street and the leaking water lines creating a pond, not twenty feet from where he sat.

Angel scooted over on the step, letting a few uniformed cops and crime scene techs exit his apartment building. They were presumably upstairs in his place, and he hoped they didn't make more of a mess than there already was—at this rate he wouldn't be sleeping anytime soon. He needed a new front door, not to mention a bedroom door. And his bed was a pile of kindling and exposed box springs, too. Rubbing his hands through his short hair, Angel heaved a deep breath and stood, startling Detective Collins mid-tirade.

"Am I being arrested, or not?" Angel asked, his list of things to do and people to track down growing by the minute. He had to find Isaac and make sure he was alive, find Simeon and make sure he wasn't a pile of dust somewhere, and his place was a mess, and for that matter so was he.

For fuck's sake, I'm in nothing but my pajama pants.... still.

"No, you're not," said a rough voice, one scourged by years of whiskey and cigarettes. Angel smiled at Detective Collins' partner, a heavy-set man who wore a rumpled suit and a permanent scowl.

Detective James O'Malley was a throwback to the old days of cops and robbers and was always one bad case away from retirement.

Detective Collins made to protest, but O'Malley cut him off with a sharp motion of his hand and a deep frown. "He's not responsible for what happened. Security cameras across the way on top the state building caught the whole thing. Some pissant rolled up in a limo an hour before dawn and burns up the street, but it's clear enough to see the crazy ass summon a demon. Can't see much on the footage after that as whatever he did messed with the recording, but it wasn't Salvatore, Collins, so shove it."

"He blew up the street!" Collins yelled, flinging an arm out at the destruction. "There's a fucking crater ten feet deep in the intersection!"

"In self-defense!" Angel yelled back, thoroughly fed up. "Next time I outta just let the damn demon rampage through Beacon Hill then, since it's so fucking important to ya that no one blows up the fucking street!"

He wasn't going to mention that the spell might have lifted with the dawn, but it was a minuscule chance, and he was certain his course of action was the only one he could have taken. Simeon wouldn't have lasted much longer. Seeing Simeon die was on the long list of things Angel never wanted to see, ever.

For a second, Angel was certain Collins was going to hit him. He stood on the front steps, panting with exertion from his outburst, thinking he was about to get his ass kicked and then thrown in jail. Collins took a step in his direction, a murderous expression on his face, and Angel found himself pushed back up the steps away from the irate detective. O'Malley dropped his arm and then got between him and Collins.

"We got plates and a clear picture of the man's face, Angel. I'll get an officer by here later with the picture, see if you recognize the man. If we're lucky, we can get him on felony charges of illegal casting, public endangerment, and attempted murder. You might wanna think about laying low, seeing as how someone just sent a demon after you," O'Malley said, and Angel snorted back a laugh. "Think about people who'd wanna see you turned into demon food."

"There's more than a few who've probably thought about it," Collins sneered, and Angel, at the end of his tether, flipped off the detective with both hands.

Collins lunged for him, but O'Malley was there again, holding back his partner as he started to swear at Angel in a rough, slang-riddled version of Latin. Broken spells from a second rate caster and Angel brushed them off with a bare twinge of effort, sneering at Collins. "Angel, how about you go back to your place? I'll send a uniform around later with that pic," O'Malley said, impressively calm for a man physically restraining his enraged partner who was still trying to toss spells Angel's way.

Angel left, not taking any chances on O'Malley restraining Collins. The enraged detective may suck at casting, but he still could throw a punch. He took the stairs, his whole body complaining at the effort, and he could still hear O'Malley and Collins shouting at each other down on the street. Angel closed what was left of his front door, and headed for his bathroom.

He paused in the center of his living room and ignored the sounds coming from the street. He breathed in, centered himself, and sent out a small tendril of awareness. His inner vision bloomed, and Angel spent a few minutes reassuring himself that Simeon was not in his apartment or the building, as either a pile of dust or a sunburned vamp. Wherever Simeon was, it wasn't here. He pulled his awareness back in, and wavered, dizzy and exhausted.

Shower first, then sleep. He was of no use to anyone exhausted and dead on his feet. Cracking a rough smile at that thought, Angel stumbled to the bathroom, glad he could shut out the sounds of Collins and O'Malley still going at each other on the street.

Putting Collins out of his mind took a few minutes, and he wondered at the man's increasing hostility. It wasn't like Angel had sent an army of vampiric assassins after his family at the pinnacle of a multi-clan magical war that spanned generations, killing almost everyone he loved.

Angel turned on the shower, and got in, not bothering to wait for the water to run hot. He yanked off his dirty pajama bottoms and threw the soggy clothing into the trash-bin by the toilet.

Angel stood under the spray, thinking about the past, wishing the water would wash away the memories just like the dirt.

Ten years ago, at the height of the Blood Wars, an alliance of three clans combined their collective abilities and coerced vampires into attacking the Salvatore Clan. Angel's entire family, with the exception of himself and the then thirteen-year-old Isaac, died in the attack.

One of those clans was the Macavoy family, and Detective Grant Collins was a distant cousin of the founding family. If anyone should hate anyone, it should be Angel hating Collins. He didn't though—all he wanted was to live what was left of his life in peace, and forget the past.

And leave the dead buried with it, too.

4

FAMILY OF CHOICE

W*hoever's cell is ringing is gonna get hexed....* oh, wait. Angel smacked his cell on the coffee table, prying one eye open to see who was calling him. He groaned, and clumsily accepted the call, hitting the speaker button.

"What?" Angel whined, feeling wretched and not at all rested. He eyed the clock on his wall, and the damn thing had to be lying. It didn't feel like eight hours had passed.

"Are you fucking insane?" Screeched his partner, and Angel flinched. Dame Mildred Fontaine was a beautiful, gracious, and refined lady of unmentionable years who had a long tradition of decorum and exquisite manners—right up until someone pissed her off.

"Milly..."

"Don't 'Milly' me, young man! I had to hear it from that rude cunt of a detective that you were attacked by a demon!!! A demon! Instead of my teaching partner and dearest friend telling me he was attacked and God forbid he tells me that he's okay! And then I had to sit there and answer questions about what exactly we teach here at the studio, as if teaching youngsters how to responsibly wield their gifts is a crime—and he has the audacity to imply that you had something to do with summoning it! Explain yourself, now."

"Rude cunt.... Oh, you mean Collins," Angel said, yawning and slowly sitting up. His brain was catching up to Milly's questions, but it would go a lot swifter if he was actually awake and not aching all over. He wasn't as drained as he was before, but he was by no means recovered. Sleeping on his couch stopped being comfortable after the first hour, and he was feeling it now. "What was he doing there again?"

'There' being their studio on the fourth floor above the University Bookstore, a small collection of rooms that were heavily shielded and warded, and a short walk away that was greatly appreciated at the end of a long day teaching stubborn teenagers and know-it-all twenty-somethings.

Was it even the same day? He pulled back and checked the date on his cell, and it was indeed still the same day, well evening now, of the demon's pre-breakfast attack.

"Are you listening to me, Angelus Salvatore?" Milly was near panting, sounding as if she was speed-walking down the sidewalk. Which she probably was.... time to get up.

"Nope," Angel replied, standing and stretching, muscles complaining and joints popping. He walked to the windows overlooking the street, and peered down Hancock. In the street lamps he could just make out Milly's diminutive silhouette marching down the sidewalk. He was in trouble.

"I'll have tea on," Angel said, tapping the cell and ending the call before Milly could tear into him again.

He went to the bathroom and then got dressed, tossing on a pair of clean jeans and a dark blue polo that clung enough to show he had some muscle mass, and walked barefoot into the kitchen just as the sound of high heels on the hardwood flooring of the hall met his ears. He set a kettle to boil on the stove and went to his fridge, pulling out a partially cut cheesecake. It was plain, with a thick graham cracker layer, and just the right kind of sweet to temper a certain sorceress's ire.

Dame Mildred Fontaine swept into his kitchen, tossing down her Luis Vuitton purse and scarf onto the kitchen island in a flurry of fabric and swirling coat. She was older than he, anywhere from her early forties to sixties, but Angel had yet to narrow it down and lacked the balls to inquire as to her actual age. Her porcelain skin and upswept dark gray hair and unlined face, couple with a trim and tiny physique, all lent to the lady-like and immaculate image she portrayed to the world.

Right up until....

"Your lily-fresh ass is mine unless you tell me what exactly..." Milly stormed up to him, and somehow managed to invade his space in her tiny heels that put her at maybe five-foot-four, and held a finger up, long wicked nail under his nose, "You tell me what the fuck is going on!"

Angel resisted the urge to roll his eyes, and gave her instead a charming grin and a look from what she usually called his 'evil puppy eyes'. She glared back at him, narrowing her eyes, and she flicked the tip of his nose with her finger.

"Ow!" He winced, rubbing his nose. "I made you tea."

"And cheesecake, so I see," she said, making a disapproving harrumph before spinning on one very expensive high heel and heading for the now whistling kettle on the stove.

"Is it true?" She asked, her back to him as she turned off the burner and lifted the kettle, bringing it to the island. She kept herself in profile, but he could see the worry underneath the anger. He sighed, and walked around the small island, setting up the tea cups and bags.

"Well, since I don't know what the ...what did you call him? The 'rude cunt'?" She made a very unladylike snort at that, and he continued, "Since I don't know what Collins told you, I'll just start at the beginning."

Angel recounted the whole night, from getting back to his apartment the night before after work, to going to bed, then being awakened by the Master's slaves and taken to vamp HQ. She sipped her tea and nibbled on her cheesecake, her clear, almost colorless blue eyes locked on his face the whole time, observing and withholding her opinion until he was done.

"So to recap," Milly began, putting down her fork and delicately wiping her mouth with a napkin, "Gregory Doyle was compelled to break into the Master's clan house yet do nothing once inside. You were then summoned to deal with him once his identity was revealed, due to your very ingeniously wrought oath from a clan elder that he cannot be harmed. After releasing him from the spell, you pass out in a room full of vampires—I'll yell at you for that bit of foolishness later—and then you wake to a demon crashing in your front door. At which point the supernatural man you were sleeping with—another topic for discussion later—fought off the demon until you could destroy the summoning circle and send the partially bound demon back to its home realm. Did I miss anything?"

Angel took a bite of his cheesecake and thought about it. Swallowing, he said, "Nope, sounds about right."

"You're fucking lucky, Angel."

He thought about the last twenty-four hours and had to disagree. "How so?"

"Someone is after you."

"I noticed that," Angel said, pushing off from the island and picking up their plates. He went to the sink, feeling her eyes on him the whole time. "So how is that lucky?"

"You're lucky you're not dead, young man."

Angel rolled his eyes, and got a crumpled napkin tossed at him for his trouble. It bounced from his shoulder to land at his feet, and he scooped it up and threw it in the nearby trashcan.

"Finding out if the events around Mr. Doyle are connected to the demon's summoning might narrow down any list of potential enemies you may have." He turned to watch Milly as she poured herself another cup of tea, dunking the bag as she ruminated over her thoughts. She sipped her tea, and her eyes were unfocused, deep in thought. "There are plenty of people, be they human, supernatural, or magical that would like to see you dead, even after all these years. Have you pissed off anyone in particular in the last few weeks?"

Angel thought about it, but other than Detective Collins and his frequent dislike, there wasn't much to draw on for possible subjects. Most of his enemies were lessened by time, distance, or death.

"I turned away that one potential student a few months ago. You remember, the necromancer groupie who was far too interested in my history than in learning higher magic?" Angel asked, and she nodded. "I sent him packing, and I know he cast some threats out as he left. I don't remember his name, though."

"Yes, I recall. The young man was rather rude. He had made an appointment so he's in the book somewhere, I'll check in the morning. Are you coming in, my dear? We have two students scheduled for shielding work tomorrow, and it will require both of us there."

"I'll be there. Sorry I slept through the day, it wasn't my intent. I meant to show up for the afternoon sessions, but…"

"Yes, dear, I know. It's fine. Sleep tonight? Eat something healthy, and go back to bed. I'll see you tomorrow, bright and early." Milly gathered up her coat and purse, and came around to give him a kiss on the cheek. He smiled and gave her a hug, which she tolerated with a chuckle before stepping back. "Ward your doors, Angelus."

"Yes, mum." Angel teased with a grin, following her to the front door. At some point the building super left a large plank of plywood in the hall outside his door, and he sighed, already regretting waking up. He would need to fix his door if he was going to be leaving anytime soon.

Milly put on her coat in the hall, the dark blue and gray fabric accentuating her pale skin and dark gray hair. She always reminded him of an old-fashioned Hollywood icon, impeccable, enigmatic and striking. She put her purse on her shoulder and frowned.

"Angel, my dear."

"Yes, Mildred?"

"You just destroyed the circle, yes? At dawn's first light?" She asked, and he nodded. Already ahead of her.

"Yes, I did. The dawn and the breaking of the circle and the anchoring rune chased it back to its home dimension, but may not have released the *geas* on the demon itself."

"If the sorcerer who summoned it calls back the same creature..."

"The *geas* will snap back into place, and it will come for me again. I'm aware."

She glared at him, probably because of his too calm tone of voice. He was on guard now, when he should have been before. Ten years of peace made him soft in some ways.

"If he had the hair to cast it once, he may have more. He can summon not just that one demon, but another, and send them after you."

"And I can get hit by a bus full of tourists on my way to the Aquarium. Worrying will do nothing but keep me awake at night. I'll be careful. I got a good look at the runes used in the circle. I'll check the books we have at the studio, see if I can't narrow down the technique of the caster, get a better idea of who this is. I can handle this, Milly."

"Yes, my dear, I think everyone knows just how much you can handle. My next point is that you don't have to do this alone."

Angel gave her a rueful smile, and nodded. "I'm sorry. I know I'm not alone. Thank you, Milly."

"Forgiven, as always. Now don't fuck this up. I'll see you at the studio."

"Goodnight, Mildred," Angel said as his teaching partner nodded graciously and swept off down the hall, majestic as always. He watched until she was out of sight, and then went to go back inside.

"Ward your doors, dammit!" She hollered up the stairs, and he chuckled.

※

ANGEL ARRANGED the last nail and hit it once with his finger, knocking it home. He couldn't recall where he put his hammer, so he was hitting nails in place with a bit of kinetic magic, the tap of his fingertip enough to set the nails deep in the wood. The plywood sheet was now nailed to what remained of his door, and the doorknob and lock still functioned, so he would be able to close it and leave if he wanted.

He walked back into his apartment and shut the door. It wasn't perfect but would do until the super found a replacement. They lived in a historical landmark building, and the new door would need to match the aesthetic of the rest of the doors. He wasn't too picky; it would make do. Especially after he reactivated his wards.

After the Wars ended ten years' prior, Angel and Isaac had moved out of the family estate and taken an apartment here. There were too many nightmarish memories to remain in the house where they both grew up, so leaving was what was best. In the early years after the final battle, Angel had laid the foundations for an impressive and exhaustive series of shields and wards around the apartment and the building itself. Unwilling to take the chance that his presence would place the mundane human occupants of the apartment building in danger, Angel layered protections between his place and the apartments above, below, and the other apartment that shared the same floor as his.

Most shields created by magic-users were put in place to protect the conjurer from magical attacks. Stronger, more gifted practitioners were able to generate shields that could block physical attacks, but those were incredibly hard to maintain for longer than a few minutes, or the sorcerer who cast it would be drained near to death and would collapse. Fueling a shield with veil energy was possible, but doing so left the caster splitting their attention between the veil and the shield. A shield was generally put in place at the moment of need, and would then be unmade after the threat passed.

Wards were best described as magical alarm systems. They were varied in type and purpose, yet the ones Angel had in place were of the kind used in hostile situations. A lifetime of growing up in what amounted to a warzone left Angel proficient in hostile wards. A ward could be used to alert, notify, even identify and mark trespassers. Stronger, higher level wards could even entrap and snare one type of supernatural being, while leaving other species unaffected. Runes, the physical representation of spells, could be inscribed permanently into wood or stone, and placed in areas that needed warding, and then were charged by the creator, or if the spells were designed correctly, anyone with the ability to do so. Wards could be created and sold, and it was a major part of the magic-driven economy in the last decade.

Angel's wards and shields were his design, and not even Milly or Isaac knew how he engineered them or how they were placed. A particularly gifted and skilled sorcerer, if given the time, could eventually examine and discern how he built them, but they would need more time than any casual observer could take, and any in-depth examinations would use enough energy that Angel would be able to sense it if he were home, and leave traces of the nosy magic-user behind.

Angel went and changed. He put on warmer clothes, a heavy wool sweater warded against bad weather to replace a jacket, and thick socks and boots. It was raining, the downpour a mix of thick drizzle and fat raindrops. The wind was blowing, driving the rain harder, and was plastering leaves everywhere. Usually, it was the type of evening to stay in, but he had to find Isaac and see if Simeon was unharmed. Isaac wasn't answering his cell, and Angel was past annoyed and into a familiar mix of anger and concern. Angel was certain Simeon was alive and well, but the vamp did stick around until dawn and help him by holding off the demon long enough for him to destroy the circle, so he felt an annoying wiggle of obligation to make sure he was unharmed.

He kept his mind off the breath-stealing kisses and how his body remembered Simeon's weight and hard strength. Last thing he needed was to fuel a disastrous infatuation with the vampire elder.

He returned to his front door, and stepped into the hall, and instead of trying to set the lock, put his hand on the wall beside the door. He leaned into his hand, pressing on the wall, and called to his wards. The shields would lay quiet for now; they weren't needed if he wasn't home, as there was nothing worth spending that amount of power on in the apartment to begin with. The wards woke, near-sentient spells that slept in the very bones of the building, in the floor and walls and ceilings. The windows were covered in invisible marks and runes, the thresholds of doors painted in his will. He set the wards for ill-intent and aggression, and powered up the set for tracers. If anyone did manage to get inside his apartment while he was gone, the tracers would place a small energy signature upon the trespasser and allow Angel to follow that signature to the perpetrator. These dots of energy were so small that unless someone was intimately involved in their engineering they would be dismissed as ambient magic.

To his mind's eye his apartment and the surrounding walls glowed with a vibrant green fire the color of new spring leaves, interspersed with undertones of emerald and moss. A part of him always found it ironic that a sorcerer with an affinity for Death would have a magical signature usually seen in those whose element was for life and growing things. Angel always thought it was a gift from his mother's side of the family, as she had in her family line dozens of elemental witches with an affinity for the earth and plants. His father's bloodline won out in the end though, gifting Angel with sorcery-level abilities and the death affinity.

A hum reverberated up his arm through his hand when the wards awoke. He took one last look, made sure they were properly set, and then withdrew his mind. Angel blinked, eyes blurry, but they cleared after a moment or two. He headed down the hall to the stairs, the windows in the stairwell revealing a dark evening lit only by streetlamps and the reflective shine of falling rain.

VAMPIRE HQ HAD AN ACTUAL NAME, not that Angel or anyone else in town bothered to recall it. It was a tall stone building in downtown Boston and had the distinction of being one of the oldest buildings in the whole of New England, not just the city. The oldest parts of HQ were the areas the public had access to, and the rear of the building abutted a ten-story luxury condominium and casino complex. The Master's rooms were rumored to be in the penthouse though Angel thought that unwise, considering the penthouse's exposure to sunlight, and the unreliable nature of anti-UV spells and treated glass. Gossiping blood slaves and vampire groupies weren't really the best sources of information, never mind they spent a better part of their days and nights with a vampire attached to various pulse points. His personal guess was somewhere in the sublevels of the tower, safe from light and curious eyes. Hiding where the oldest and most powerful vamp in Boston slept was a wise precaution, one not unexpected in a vampire as old as the Master purported to be.

The front façade was three stories tall, with a vaulted front entranceway that oozed elitism and wealth, and was kept a chilly forty-five Fahrenheit year round. Vampires didn't need much in the way of heating though the humans who attached themselves as donors and slaves had heated quarters.

Angel gripped the brass bar of the heavy wood and glass front door, and pulled it open, stepping into the lobby. His cab pulled away when he went inside, as if he had been expecting Angel to return to his senses and come back before it was too late. The cabbie's haste showed how prevalent the fear and superstition was surrounding the vampires' clan house in the city.

The reception desk was a heavy monstrosity of white and gray marble carved from a single block of stone, and curved in a half-moon around the lone occupant, a young, nondescript man in a gray suit to match the stone. It stood against the left hand wall, while a pair of brass-doored elevators were on the right hand side. A set of wide, red-carpet covered stairs disappeared upwards, and to either side of the staircase hallways and doors led deeper into the building. Somewhere back there was the entrance to the residence tower and private casino and the vamp's club.

It was quiet, the faintest scuffle of a shoe on the floor echoing, and the rustle of paper and keystrokes loud enough to be right in his ear instead of halfway across the room. Angel was glad he wasn't the poor man at the desk, as he would likely go insane due to the oppressive atmosphere.

"Mr. Salvatore?" Angel turned to the speaker, the young man now standing behind the desk, hands folded in front of him, gazing at Angel with a blank expression. He wasn't surprised the receptionist knew who he was. While most days he spent at his studio instructing youngsters on how to channel veil-drawn magic, in the last two years he'd unfortunately spent a few evenings here in vamp HQ, dealing with cursed and hexed vamps and humans too stupid to leave the local magic practitioner populace alone.

It was an oddity that after the Halloween confrontation two years before between Angel and the vampire clan at the club, that instead of giving him a wide berth or trying to have him killed, the Master, and his Elders, routinely sought him out for assistance in magical problems. He'd lost track of how many young vamps he'd cured of magic poisoning, the fools drinking from humans with a smidgen of magic in their family tree. Anything within two generations was enough to make a vamp ill, and a full-blood's veins ran with enough magical poisoning to kill a vamp. Boston was not a healthy place to be a vampire, since the city was a stronghold for hereditary practitioners. Why there was a Master and Clan here in town Angel had no idea. Though most Clans used screened donors and blood banks for food sources, so they must have enough to sustain them in Boston.

"Yes, Angel Salvatore, here to see Elder Simeon," Angel finally replied to the receptionist, who gave him a slight nod and reached for the phone behind the desk. Angel turned his attention to the windows, watching the rain fall in the light cast from the iron wrought torches outside the building.

The rain had yet to let up, and Angel could feel the shifting in the atmosphere, the scent of frost and snow on the wind. Soon it would be cold enough that the rain would become snow, and everything would ice over.

A subtle but powerful thrum went through his boots, and Angel tensed as the building's wards were activated. He waited, cautiously eyeing the street and the bowels of the building, waiting for the building's alarms to sound next. The receptionist was still on the phone, and not paying Angel any attention whatsoever.

He waited, but nothing further happened. The building's wards were old, as old as the structure, and were sunk deeply into the foundation and the earth. He sent out a tendril of awareness, investigating what could have triggered them, but all he got from the wards was a wary watchfulness and a sense of expectancy. They weren't responding to anything specific, not that he could sense. Perhaps they were merely set to come awake at this time of night, though it was odd for wards in a vampire clan house to come on at night when they were most vulnerable during the day and needed more protection.

There was another jump in the wards, almost as if someone was casting too close to the boundaries. It was sporadic, and didn't feel intentional, but the ambient magic moved in waves that said whoever it was must be a sorcerer, since the veil was tapped. It cut off a moment later, and Angel went back to listening to the wards. If he didn't know any better, he would think an apprentice was botching an attempt at casting with the veil, but there were no sorcery students in the Tower. They hummed, at a higher pitch, then settled back down, still aware and watching, but no longer reacting. If there was a sorcerer in vamp HQ or the Tower, as the condominiums were nicknamed, then the only way he or she could be there was by invitation, and Angel put the incident out of his mind.

He relaxed, though he kept his mind open to the wards in case something changed. He didn't want to repeat the demon attack in vamp HQ—though it would be nice to not deal with the mess afterwards.

"Mr. Salvatore?"

Angel looked to the receptionist, who was wearing an apologetic expression on his otherwise bland face.

"Yes?"

"Elder Simeon is unavailable at the moment; may I take a message?" The receptionist must be used to violent reactions to denials if he was going to cringe while telling Angel Simeon was not up to talking. Or maybe his confrontation with the demon that morning had already made the rounds, and the poor thing was afraid of Angel. He bit back a smile at that odd thought. Being smaller than average and slim left most humans underestimating him.

"Unavailable? So he's here?" Angel asked, making sure. If Simeon was dead or injured surely the response wouldn't be for him to leave a message. Relief swamped him when the receptionist gave a hesitant nod. "No, no message. Just tell him I was here, I guess. Thank you."

Trying not to show how relieved he was that Simeon was still alive and presumably well, Angel put his hands in his pockets and walked to the door. The wards under his feet hummed and writhed as he pushed the door open with his shoulder, and Angel stepped out onto the front steps. The overhang kept him dry, and Angel looked up and down the street, looking for a cab. He really didn't want to call for one, since the cabbies usually put up a fuss about picking people up at Vamp HQ, and Angel had to give them a bigger tip to encourage them out this way.

He walked down the steps, pulling the thick collar of his warded sweater higher around his neck. It kept the rain from his skin, and blocked most of the wind. He felt the outer wards around Vamp HQ cling to him as he passed through them, and heard an almost audible pop as he left them behind. The wards hummed behind him while he walked down the street, and he marveled at the complexity and strength in the old magical constructs. Several sorcerers of adept ranking must have spent years crafting the wards in concert for them to be so vibrant decades later.

He looked back once at HQ, the Tower glowing above it, and saw a figure in the foyer where no one had been before. It moved with a lithe grace no human could come close to obtaining, but the vampire was too slim, and hair a dark brown instead of auburn, so it wasn't Simeon, and Angel turned away, walking down the sidewalk.

Isaac's apartment wasn't too far away, and he could walk it in about thirty minutes. He was reluctant to be exposed for so long though—whoever sent the demon after him could easily do so again, and he didn't want to be out in public if that happened. Too easy for innocent people to get killed in the fallout.

Angel frowned, something bothering him, but there was nothing he could sense, even with his second sight, that gave him that odd feeling. He pulled in the ambient magic around him, and used it as a spider would a web, and charged the gathered magic, sending it back out, tendrils out at his sides, front and back, even above. He would know for at least a block out in all directions if anything was coming his way, be it undead, demon, or human.

The street was empty. Not even a random pedestrian, foolhardy enough to brave the weather. Angel grumbled to himself but kept walking, keeping his eyes open and senses alert. He didn't want to be caught unawares again, whether it was a mugger or a demon.

✤

Isaac, at the incredibly wise age of twenty-three, decided he wanted to get his own place. That was a problem for Angel and for Isaac, not that his little brother would ever admit he wasn't suited to live alone. Money wasn't a problem, considering they were the sole two remaining heirs for the Salvatore fortune, but the problem lay in Isaac himself and his remarkable lack of maturity. And for Angel, it was an issue because keeping Isaac out of trouble was far easier when they shared a roof.

Angel skirted the dirty laundry on the floor next to the door, and he pocketed his keys. The wards he put in place to protect his brother were quiescent and thin, as if they hadn't been used or charged since Angel laid them in place months earlier.

Which appeared to be the case.

He peered into the shadows of the unlit rooms, and tried to see if anyone was present. The smell of bong water, weed, and stale beer was heavy, and he curled his lip at the half-eaten pizza left to go bad on the coffee table. He should be more upset than he was already, but Isaac was never one for cleaning, and at twenty-three, didn't care all that much about doing the dishes or laundry. It was over ten years since either of them had the benefit of servants, and Isaac was still acting like someone would come along and clean up after him. This bad habit of his carried over into the rest of his life, too. Angel lost track of how many times he'd rescued Isaac over the years, and Greg Doyle by extension, since that man was never far from Isaac's side.

Except when he was cruising through gay bars and getting compelled by lowlife wizards.

Just thinking about last night's excursion and Greg Doyle's idiocy made Angel simmer. He walked down the hall, flipping switches as he went, but the lights stayed off. Isaac probably forgot to pay the utilities again. Isaac received a hefty quarterly stipend from his trust fund, so Isaac didn't need to work to support himself. He needed to be reminded that he had to pay bills and actually eat something other than beer and pizza on a regular basis, and Angel was afraid to look in the refrigerator after the last time.

"Isaac! Are you home? Don't tell me you forgot to pay the light bill again, you know they charge a bigger deposit each time to get the power back on..." Angel called out as he headed through the dark for Isaac's room. He heard moaning, and what sounded like whispering, and braced himself for what he might see when he opened the door. Knocking and waiting would just mean he would spend the rest of his life in this hallway waiting on Isaac to open the door.

"You better be getting attacked by vampires, I don't need to see..." Angel pushed open the door to his brother's room, and blinked as his eyes adjusted to the shadows and the light streaming in from the windows that faced the street. "For fuck's sake, didn't you hear me knocking and yelling your name?"

Greg Doyle pulled his mouth off Isaac's cock, lips wet and red. Isaac grabbed at his head and tried to pull him back down, but Angel's glare made Greg squirm free of Isaac's grip and get to his feet from where he was kneeling beside the bed. Angel looked away from his naked brother and his excited state, glaring at the ceiling.

"Dammit, Angie, what the hell? Don't you know how to fucking knock?" Isaac swore as he grabbed a pillow and covered his lap with it, and Angel looked down to see Greg hurriedly pulling on a pair of jeans. Isaac's long dark hair was highlighted in deep red and long enough to brush his shoulders, and messy from what Angel's nose was telling him was a marathon day of bedroom antics. Nose itching, Angel tried the light switch but the lights stayed dark.

"I did knock, and I yelled, and I waited, but I guess you were occupied. Why are the lights out?" Angel said, leaning in the doorway and crossing his arms. "And why the hell haven't you been answering your cell?"

"You haven't called! And why should I answer you anyway?" Isaac was a champion pouter, a hold-over from his teenage years, and Angel again wondered for the millionth time where he went wrong raising Isaac after their parents died. Though it was problematic for a twenty-year-old man to suddenly be responsible for the well-being of a thirteen-year-old boy, even if they were brothers. Angel had spent his own teenage years studying sorcery and the higher level magics, leaving little time for quality time with Isaac. He never regretted that more than he did now as an adult, looking at Isaac's angry and unrepentant face.

"You should answer me because I was worried, you little shit. I had to go clean out your fuck buddy's brains last night after he got compelled to break into Vamp HQ, and this morning I got attacked by a demon and had to blow up the street to banish it. And you fucking wouldn't answer your phone!"

"Demons don't attack in daylight," Isaac said, rooting about the bed, and pulling out a pair of boxer-briefs. Angel was thankful his brother decided to put on some clothing, and he noted the addition of another set of tattoos on his arms and torso. Isaac pulled a wrinkled tee over his chest before Angel could get a better look in the shadows.

"How would you know? You don't practice," Angel snarked back, "and I banished it with dawn's light and destruction of the circle. Don't distract me. Why the hell are the lights out? Is your cell down too?" Angel kept his eyes on Isaac, and saw the minuscule flinch as Angel's words hit home. "Great. You get paid a ridiculous amount of money to live like a prince and you can't even bother to pay your bills? You're twenty-three, Isaac, not a damn kid."

"You're right! I'm not a kid! So why don't you leave me alone?" Isaac snarled, and Angel tensed. That was a common refrain from Isaac, that Angel leave him be, but the second Isaac got drunk and ended up lost in the city without his wallet or cash, or thrown in jail and needed bail, it was Angel he called to come save his ass. Every time.

"I would leave you alone," Angel gritted out, barely restraining himself. Greg was watching them both, shirt forgotten in his hands, eyes darting back and forth between them. "I would leave you be if I wasn't so damn sure you'd end up either dead or in jail if I didn't keep an eye on you. The wards aren't even powered up! Have you done anything with them since I put them in place? And did you not hear me say that your cock-sucking buddy over there got compelled to invade Vamp HQ, or that a demon went after me this morning?"

"Dead or in jail I wouldn't have to listen to you bitch all the damn time," Isaac snapped back, and Angel tamped down on his anger. This was how it always went between them now, ending in arguments and fights. Where the hell did the quiet, bookish boy go who used to follow him around all day asking questions?

"And yeah, Greg told me about the hex. Probably just a prank went wrong. And you're such an ass, Angel, I'm not surprised someone sent a demon after you. You probably have a whole list of people wanting you dead."

"No one pays five-thousand dollars and drops a hex on someone to break into the Master of Boston's headquarters and not steal something all for a damn prank, Isaac. That shit just doesn't happen. No wizard-ranked practitioner is going to risk himself like that for a joke. Someone is circling us, I know it, and if you aren't careful they could come for you next. So that means you pay your electric bill, power your wards up, turn your cell back on, and make smarter choices about who you fuck."

He knew, from the second the words left his mouth, that all he was doing was making it worse. Yet he couldn't stop himself; there was no reason that he knew of for Isaac to live like a slob and be so irresponsible, and his choice of lover and friend in Greg Doyle would forever confound him. Isaac's face twisted with fury, and he threw his pillow at Angel. He batted it away, and Isaac sprang to his feet, pointing at him, whole body shaking with anger.

"You're a fucking stuck-up hypocrite, Angie. I'm not the one sleeping with vampires and teaching kids how to blow shit up and bend the veil. What you're doing is an insult to our family's memory," Isaac was so mad his eyes were wild and his finger shook as he stabbed Angel in the chest with the tip. Isaac was taller than him now, over six feet, and was long, lanky muscles over slim bones. Isaac was a handsome man, when he wasn't hungover and needing a shower.

Angel was so struck by the difference in Isaac from the boy he raised that it took Isaac poking him hard enough to make him stumble that he thought about what his brother said. "I'm not sleeping with any vampires, dammit. And our family has taught high sorcery for hundreds of years, so how is that a disgrace to their memory?"

"So you aren't fucking the Celt? That's not what I heard," Isaac tossed his hair back out of his eyes, glaring, and Angel slapped Isaac's finger away from his chest. Typically, Isaac ignored anything he didn't want to acknowledge, and he disregarded the fact that the Salvatore family history was full of teachers. Greg Doyle seemed to find something interesting in the corner to stare at, and Angel scowled at him before glaring back at Isaac. "Detective Collins says the Celt spent the night in your bed."

"How the fuck...." Angel started, but he bit it off. The cameras across the street would have shown Simeon carrying Angel up into his apartment after the vamp took him home. "The statehouse cameras. Goddammit. Did Collins give you trouble? That rude ass tried to curse me this morning after I banished the demon."

"I told that ass I had no idea what was going on and to shove his questions, right before I slammed the door in his face," Isaac snapped back, which Angel could easily see since that's what Isaac did to him every time they spoke. "So you are sleeping with him? And you dare complain about Greg?"

"I am not sleeping with Elder Simeon. And if I was," Angel stressed his next words, "It would be none of your business. The Master and his Elders are not part of the clan who killed our family, your animosity does nothing but piss off the wrong people."

"A fanghead is a fanghead," Isaac said, brushing past Angel into the hall. Angel followed him down the hallway to the kitchen, where Isaac opened the fridge and then slammed it shut again, the light inside staying dark. "Fuck! I guess the power is out."

"That is what happens when you don't pay the bills," Angel muttered, kicking aside a few pairs of dirty socks. Who took off their socks in the kitchen? "And why go to vamp bars all the time if you bear them such a grudge?"

"They have the best booze."

Personally, Angel thought it was because of all the places Isaac could go to party, he always went to a vampire bar, both courting danger and being protected by it—he was a sorcerer, so he wasn't food; he was a Salvatore, so he was hated and reviled; he was safe in the clan bars as he would not be in human establishments—Angel's vow from Simeon meant Isaac was untouchable in all the places run by the vampire clan in Boston and surrounding areas.

Angel could see the destructive behavior, but had no answer for it. He didn't know what drove Isaac to ignore him and yet when he was in trouble, Angel was always the person Isaac called first—in fact, he was the only person Isaac called. It both broke his heart and left him frustrated.

Angel rolled his eyes and sat in the lone chair at the tiny, cluttered table in the kitchen. He refused to guess what any of the items were that littered the table top. "Why haven't you activated the wards I put in place? You know how to power them, I taught you myself."

Isaac was facing the sink, probably trying to find a clean glass amongst the dirty dishes covering the counter top and filling the basin. Angel looked around, and it seemed like every piece of cutlery was dirty, and there was a fine layer of dust on the appliances. Isaac was never this bad when he lived with Angel. Isaac didn't answer him, and Angel took in his stiff shoulders and his lowered head. Isaac was stubborn and reckless with his safety, and Angel had no idea why. Ever since Isaac turned eighteen, his attitude and behavior grew steadily worse. They may never have been close as children, with Angel being seven years the elder, but Isaac had been somewhat responsible as a teenager after Angel took custody. This belligerence and casual disregard for his own safety, and lack of concern for his own brother, was troubling.

"Isaac? The wards?" Angel reiterated, trying to get a response.

"I forgot about them! Fuck! Why is it so damn important to you that I activate the fucking wards?" Isaac snapped, and a glass broke in the sink with a racket, shards bouncing off the steel. Energy pooled in a scarlet glow around Isaac's tense frame, and Angel waited, hoping Isaac found his control.

"Because, as I was just reminded by you a few moments ago, vampires killed our whole family, and not many people like me, so that means they can get to me through you. Because someone tried to get your lover killed by sending him into Vamp HQ under compulsion. Because, Isaac, *a demon destroyed my apartment and tried to kill me.*" Angel stressed, one hand gripping the table as Isaac's power tumbled through the room. "History has proven that when one Salvatore is in danger, so are we all. There is no coincidence in the very small world of those who practice. You know this. Please use the damn wards."

"I don't practice. I don't use magic," Isaac all but growled at him, and Angel sighed, fed up. That glass broke because Isaac wasn't exerting enough control over his abilities.

"Your aura is out of control, Isaac, and you're spilling energy into the kitchen. Use your magic and what I've taught you, or your magic will use you."

Silence greeted his last statement, and Angel waited. The scent of heating metal rose from the sink, and the edge of the steel basin glowed beneath his brother's hands. Angel stilled, ready to intercede if Isaac lost control and set fire to his kitchen. He waited, but Isaac pulled most of it back, and Angel relaxed. Isaac pushed away from the sink and walked past Angel without looking at him. "Get out, Angie. Leave me alone."

Isaac left the kitchen, red aura spilling and twisting in flashy trails of light behind him. He slammed the door to his room, leaving Angel at the table. Angel slouched in the chair, alone in the smelly, dusty, disgusting excuse for a kitchen, and broke a long-standing promise to himself to never hire someone to do something for Isaac or himself that they could do on their own.

He pulled out his cell, and started searching for cleaning services. His brother was not going to live in squalor in an apartment that cost in a year as much as the average household's car.

Angel got up from the table, and walked out to the living room, taking in the sad state of the expensive apartment his brother treated like a crash pad. Less than a year on his own and Isaac was living like a squatter in his own home.

Angel sent one last look down the hall to where he could hear Isaac and Greg talking, their words indistinct. Leaving Isaac unprotected was not an option. He saved a link to a high-rated cleaning service, and tucked his cell away.

Closing his eyes, Angel sent his awareness out, and activated the wards. They were barely awake, lacking in power, and it was more than obvious that Isaac hadn't even spared them a single line of energy since Angel put them in place the day Isaac moved in. Angel opened up his connection to the veil, a thin line that was more than enough to charge the wards to full power. He let the power build, activating all of them, and then laid down a new layer, one that would prevent Isaac from turning them off. His brother was powerful enough to do it, but Angel was certain Isaac was too lazy to bother spending the effort required to bring them down. Better safe than sorry, though, so he locked Isaac out of the wards.

Angel withdrew from his connection to the veil and pulled his mind away from the wards. They glowed to his inner eye, vibrant and active. Angel left Isaac's apartment, making sure the door was locked behind him. He dialed the cleaners' number as he walked back out to the street.

***

THE SNOW WAS MELTING AS SOON as it touched the ground. The faintest of hissing sounds made by the tiny flakes falling and his breathing were the only sounds in the quiet cemetery, Angel the only living soul present. Angel gripped the iron spikes of the fence that surrounded King's Chapel Burying Grounds, the shadows deep, seamless. The closest rows of headstones were visible, the dates and names wore down by time and weather. Coastal winds were unkind to the markings of man, scouring them to nothing and toppling even the strongest of stones.

His family, all of them but for Isaac, were dead. Their bodies burned to prevent their enemies from using their remains in spells and stealing their magic, and the ashes were scattered on the holy ground of King's Chapel. His parents, grandparents, uncles and aunts. His few cousins, too. All of them dead in an attack that left the Salvatore Mansion a ruin and then spilled out into the streets, leaving bodies of vampires and sorcerers alike littering the ground like leaves. Over a hundred undead had been sent for the Salvatore Clan, and he and his family had cut them all down...but not before the greatest of losses.

Only Angel and Isaac survived.

Angel's body seized up, and curled in on itself, as if covering a mortal wound. He clung to the fence, the only thing keeping him upright as memories clamored to be heard, and garish visions of loved ones torn to pieces of bloody meat danced across the inside of his eyelids.

He let one sob escape before he bit his lip, tasting blood, staying conscious against the incipient panic attack that threatened to sweep him under. He breathed through the pain and regret, the terror and the horrible, devastating grief that haunted him every time he was weak and let it under his guard. Angel went through his days as if the past was only that, gone forever and forgettable. If he dwelled on the agony of his loss, he would never get back up.

If not for Isaac needing him, depending on him, Angel may well have joined his family after that horrific night. Angel might have ended the Blood Wars in a terrifying display of death magic, but his efforts came too late. No wonder Isaac wanted nothing to do with him. Who would want to be around the person who let his whole family die? Now that he was grown and on his own, maybe dealing with Angel was too much for Isaac to stomach.

He let go of the fence, dropping to his knees. The wet pavement instantly chilled him, but he was beyond caring. Angel stared through the iron, the ground covered with a thin layer of fresh snow. It covered the markers of people long dead, no one left to remember them or mourn.

5

MOURNING SICKNESS

The half-finished arcs made by the youngsters' shields meshed for a heartbeat before cracking and falling apart in a burst of light and smoke, ozone filling the heavily warded workroom.

Angel hit a switch on the wall next to him, and fans circulated in fresh air from the vents in the ceiling. Milly sent him a look that on the surface that was calm and controlled, but Angel saw the frustration under the mask. Two weeks now they'd been teaching defensive shield theory to the Serfano kids, and today's practical lesson was a failure. Not unusual, but it was with these two—both bright, strong academic backgrounds, and quick studies, Samuel and Mark Serfano were twenty and twenty-one respectively, and had both graduated from the Hollingsbrook Academy with high marks. They shouldn't be having such trouble in melding magics. It was common curriculum for students to meld magic with each other and instructors, and happened routinely in courses throughout a student's time in the practitioner's academies. And as brothers, their magic was similar and should meld easily.

Should—but it wasn't happening.

Angel pushed off from the wall he was leaning on and walked

into the center of the room, knocking down the reforming fledgling shields with a negligent wave of his hand and a minor expenditure of power. The eldest brother, Mark, glared at him from beneath heavy brows, and Angel thought for an inappropriate second that a face like his was the same as every bully Angel faced growing up. While Mark was intelligent, he was also spoiled and self-centered, and any lack of success on his part was a result of bad teaching instead of his inability to bend his pride and say he needed help learning.

Samuel, the younger brother by a year, was quiet, and reminded Angel of Isaac as a teenager. Before the attitude and simmering resentment, at least. Where Mark led, Samuel followed, and Angel had a feeling that Samuel understood the basics but refused to show his brother up, and let his half of the shield work collapse when he saw his brother struggling.

"This isn't working," Mark complained, dark eyes and wrinkled brow teeming with what Angel imagined was embarrassment behind bruised pride. "Why should a sorcerer learn to meld shields with another anyway? I thought the higher ranks didn't need to combine magics like this—this is witch-ranked stuff for weaker practitioners."

"Mark, come on..." Samuel started, but his brother shot him a glance and Samuel snapped his mouth shut.

Milly sighed, and pushed away from her position on the far wall opposite Angel. The floor between them, where Samuel and Mark stood, was heavily warded, and overlapping concentric circles of varying sizes were burned into the wood floor, shimmering in the overhead lights and the sun pouring in through the skylight.

"Mr. Serfano, every sorcerer learns how to meld magic, whether it be with blood relations like your brother, or a perfect stranger they've just met," Milly stated as she daintily picked her way over the black and iridescent lines that hummed with energy, even powered down. "While blending magic is indeed a common practice among the lower ranks of practitioners when they need to increase their power base, the joining of shields is a crucial skill that can one day save your life. Not all dangers in this world are seen from afar, and not all confrontations with magic are handled on a field of honor between single combatants."

"And joining shields is the most basic of skills, and the one most likely to save your life. Instead of having to tap into the veil and drawing attention to yourself, you can meld magics and shield yourself and your companion faster if you know how to meld your magics with another sorcerer. If an enemy is as powerful as you are, or even more so, tapping into the veil can create a surge that he or she can detect, giving away your position." Angel spoke without much hope of Mark truly grasping the necessity of learning the defensive spells of shield work. He was temperamental and aggressive, only putting his best efforts into the offensive arts. One day that lack of study could be his undoing.

"Enemy? Giving away my position? The Blood Wars are over, Salvatore. No one's fighting anymore, everyone is dead. This is stupid," Mark blurted, crossing his arms over his beefy chest and almost pouting. "And speaking of the Wars, I'd rather learn how to beat someone in a battle, but that's never gonna happen here. Fucking waste of time. I bet you won on a fucking fluke. Stroke of luck."

Angel tensed at the mention to the Wars, and Milly and Samuel both sent Mark a nasty glare. Angel mentally brushed off the young man's attempt to rile him, instead keeping his face a blank slate. Mark glowered when his remark fell flat, and Angel turned away before his lips could quirk up in a small smile. Milly saw though, and he could see her relief that Mark's barb missed its mark.

Long practice teaching told him when things started to get nasty, end the lesson and pick it up after a break. He needed to step back, for his sake and theirs. Years of teaching together gave Milly the impeccable ability to read him, and she nodded when he tilted his head at the door.

"Let's pick this up next week," Milly said as Angel went to the door, opening it. Fresh air rolled in from the rest of the suite, taking away the scent of ozone and attitude. Samuel looked like he wanted to argue, but Mark wasted no time in escaping the workroom and heading for the closet where their gear was stored. Milly escorted Samuel past Angel, and Angel gave the younger man a sincere goodbye before Milly walked the boys out.

Angel left behind the workroom, heading for the office he and Milly shared that overlooked the street below. It was late afternoon now, and Angel wanted to head home. He heard the door shut behind the brothers, and Milly's heels on the hardwood as she headed his direction. Angel had time to find his chair and kick back before Millicent sweep in majestically, radiating tension and aggravation.

"Maybe we need to let Mark go as a student," she said, working around to take a seat at her desk, his and hers facing each other from either side of the room, their backs to the walls and a wide space between them covered by a thick rug and several chairs for guests and prospective students. "At this point in his development, he won't change his thoughts or attitude unless something drastic happens. Samuel is leaps and bounds ahead of his brother, and is handicapping his own progress so as not to show up Mark. That isn't good, for either of them."

"You read my mind, Millicent," Angel said, dropping his head back and staring at the ceiling. He was so tired. "Samuel would do better without Mark's influence, but that won't happen unless he wants it enough."

"Perhaps we can call them in for different sessions? Alone, so Samuel can grow into his full potential and Mark can try and pull his head out of his ass?"

Angel cracked out a surprised laugh, looking at his friend, Millicent's guileless expression enough to make him shake his head. He felt a bit better, though he was still tired as hell. He thought longingly of his bed and soft pillows, though sleeping in his bed would have to wait. He needed a new one after the demon's attack, and the couch was slowly killing him.

"Give it a few days and call Samuel, see if he'll go for it," Angel said, and Milly nodded in agreement. "Their parents are paying an obscene amount of money for lessons, it won't matter really if the boys are taught together or separately."

Angel reached for his keys and cell, the device left on his desk so the magical energies in the workroom didn't fry it. He checked his messages, but there was nothing. Isaac only contacted him for bail or a ride home, and it seemed a certain Elder was deciding it was prudent to avoid him. He might get to enjoy his undead existence longer if he stayed away from Angel. He rubbed a hand over his heart as a soft pang of regret echoed at that thought.

"Has anything happened since the demon's attack?" Milly asked suddenly, and she fiddled with the immaculate surface of her desk, adjusting a neat row of pens with slim, manicured fingertips.

"Not a blessed thing," Angel said, "Did you see if I suddenly had an arch enemy sprout from the list of the rejected students?"

"You are so funny," Milly retorted, and Angel smiled, standing. It was time to go home. He wanted something to eat, and a pillow under his head. The couch would do for another night. "I couldn't find the name from that one young man who you turned away months ago. Do you recall anything about him in particular?"

"He was rude and arrogant," Angel said, pocketing his stuff and walking for the door, Milly standing and following him out. "Not unattractive, but nothing that makes him stick out in my mind. Young, twenty or so, blond, and swore at me when I ordered him out of the office after he got too nosy about...well, you know."

The young man had asked after the night Angel's family died, and the spell Angel cast to strike down the undead that killed his loved ones. Though it was years since someone asked him point blank to his face about what happened that night, the avid and callous nature of the curious still left him bitter and angry. Of course, with the way Mark Serfano was acting lately, that idiot was probably gearing up to ask about it as well. Nothing appealed more to belligerent people than spells of mass destruction. If Mark asked, Angel would cut him loose as a student and hope Samuel stayed.

"That's almost every student we've had the last few years," Milly stated, and Angel would have to agree. Milly thankfully, and with more kindness than most people credited her with, didn't touch on the topic of his family. She knew enough of what happened that night to leave it all well enough alone. "Most of the magical families have ill-behavior and arrogance bred into their bones."

"No argument from me," Angel agreed, thinking briefly of his own heritage. The older and more powerful the family, the more arrogant and insufferable they became. Though his had redeemable members.... before they all died.

"Did you do as I asked? You got some sleep?" Milly said as they walked to the front of the suite, collecting their coats from the closet. Milly hit the light switches, darkening the space as Angel got his keys.

"Eventually," Angel said, opening the door and holding it for Milly, the small landing right outside their door barely large enough for the both of them to stand. He locked the door, and was about to make up a spectacular lie about going to sleep and not gallivanting about town when Milly let lose a shrill scream.

Angel grabbed at Milly, yanking her behind him so she stood between him and the wall. A shield rose in front of him, his instincts coming to the fore, a shimmering wall of glass-like energy that coursed with thin green rivers. He slammed it forward, making space between where they stood and figure on the stairs.

The stairs were shadowed and quiet; no breathing, no words, just his pounding heart and Milly's startled gasps.

And the sound of blood dripping.

He knew that sound; hard not to, even a decade later. Blood splat with a particular cadence, a lazy roll of patters and drops that crept into his nightmares.

Angel eyed the figure in the dark stairwell, and there was no movement. "Angel?" Milly whispered, clutching at the back of his coat with one hand, trying to peer around him.

"Milly, call 911," Angel ordered, straightening from the protective stance he'd fallen into when he pulled Milly behind him. He poured more power into his shield, and green hellfire illuminated the walls and steps. "And an ambulance, but I think it's too late for that."

The body leaning against the wall on the lower landing a dozen steps down was covered in blood, which made sense since it was torn to shreds. Angel would guess it was a man, going by the remains of the clothing and the size of the body, but he couldn't tell much beyond that. Blood, fresh and dripping in small waterfalls, pooled and eddied on the landing, running in a cascade down the turn on the landing to the next set of stairs. Angel couldn't see past the ninety-degree turn in the stairs, and whoever left the body there could be right around the corner.

Milly had her cell out, and she was talking to the dispatcher, giving their address and describing the situation. Angel was about to suggest they go back inside to wait for the police when he heard what sounded like movement on the stairs. If he were alone Angel would have run down the stairs and confronted whoever was leaving freshly killed corpses on his stairs, but Milly's presence reined him in.

His shield snapped and thrummed with power as Angel tapped into the veil, augmenting his own reserves, and he kept his eyes on the stairs and the body as he walked backwards, herding Milly back inside the suite. The sound came again, and Angel held a hand up, silencing Milly.

A sigh, a sliding susurration of hissing air....and Angel knew that sound. Like blood dripping from a body, Angel would never forget the sound of a hunting vampire. It was the kind of sound that made prey break cover and run, only to get caught in the open and eaten. Another hiss and a mocking chuckle drifted up the stairs, and Angel could hear the taunting challenge in the rasping laugh.

"Do you dare, Angelus?" Words spun out from the hiss, barely decipherable, and Angel tensed as understanding flooded him.

He was being taunted. A person was dead and laid out like a tossed gauntlet, and the monster on his stairs was laughing. It was still daylight, though the light was waning, but it was dark in the staircase, no sunlight whatsoever. It must have snuck in through the back alley, a narrow strip of cement that never got any sunlight, the shadows deep enough to provide cover. A car parked at the mouth of the alley would be under cover of deep shade as well.

Vowing to have skylights put into the stairwell ceiling as soon as possible, Angel held his ground as the monster's words finally sank in.

"Do you dare? Come face me, necromancer."

Rage unlike anything he'd ever felt before swelled up from his center, and Angel took a step forward before caution could pull him back from the edge of recklessness. He wasn't alone—Milly was here, and while she was formidable and skilled, she had never been in combat with a vampire before, and her last duel was over twenty years ago. Milly caught him by the arm, and he would have shrugged her off, but the steely determination on her face and the fear behind it cooled his fury. Angel swore under his breath, and took a step back, leaving his shield active, barring the unknown predator out in the hall. Milly dragged him backwards, and she grabbed his keys from his hand and unlocked the door, and yanked him into the suite, slamming the door and clicking the lock.

It was hard to hold onto his patience, but Milly's arm around his waist kept Angel from tearing into the uniform police officer taking their statements. Angel knew it was routine procedure to separate witnesses, but he must be pouring off more energy than he was aware, since everyone was giving him a wide berth and he was getting wide-eyed stares and was hearing cautious whispers from the milling crowd.

They were on the street in front of the University Bookstore, and their offices were on the top floor of the building. It was a redo of the other morning, cop cars and ambulance and forensic techs running around, plainclothes detectives drinking coffee and directing the uniformed personnel. Except it was evening now, and twilight was slipping away into the dark of night. Angel was exhausted again, but his collared rage was fueling him enough to keep his senses on high alert and his magic writhing like a caged beast under his skin. Traffic was blocked at either end of the street, yellow crime scene tape and the coroner's van in Angel's line of sight. A gurney was being wheeled down off the curb, frame squeaking as it headed to the transport, a black body bag weighing it down.

Angel shifted, and Milly tightened her grip on him, as if she was afraid he would spontaneously combust and destroy the whole street. He was barely holding on to his temper, and the snide attitude of the sergeant taking their statements wasn't helping.

"So what did the voice say again?" The sergeant asked, brows raised as he stood with arms crossed, hip cocked out, pompous attitude rolling off him in waves. Angel narrowed his eyes, and drew in a breath, preparing to verbally flay the jackass when Milly answered for him.

"The vampire said, 'Do you dare'," she stated calmly, "it used his birth-name, and that's all it said before we went back inside and locked the door. The lot of you showed up two minutes later."

"Uh-huh. And how do you know what a vampire sounds like? How do you know it was a vamp? Did you use a spell or something?" The cop was making it clear he didn't believe a word coming from Milly's mouth, and Angel clenched his free hand, holding back the urge to toss a hex at the man's face.

"It was a vampire," Angel stated firmly, voice flat and crisp. "That was the hissing sound they make while hunting. It typically frightens prey into running. I know that sound better than I know my own voice. I didn't need a spell. There is no doubt to me that the killer is a vampire."

"But you didn't see the other person on the stairs. You just said you didn't cast a spell to learn who it was on the stairs. You said whoever spoke was around the corner from the landing. So how do you know?"

"Because I've heard vampires hunting before," Angel snarled, and the air snapped, small bright green sparks flashing to brief life around them. Milly pinched his side, and Angel pulled his magic back in, struggling not to show it on his face that he was losing control. "I heard it the night a bewitched army of vampires swarmed my family home and tore my kin to pieces of meat. Like the poor man on the stairs! That's how I know!"

The green sparks finally registered with the sergeant, who took a cautious step back, arms coming down, one hand hovering near his firearm on his hip. "Your name is Salvatore, you said?"

"As if you don't fucking know already," Angel snapped, seeing the epiphany in the sergeant's eyes. "I am Angelus Salvatore. And whoever that vampire was on the stairs killed and left that man's body is coming after me because of who I am. He knew my name."

"Heard you killed a hundred vampires with a thought back in the day," the sergeant said, suspicion clouding his words. "Why wouldn't you take on one? Sorcerer like you should be able to handle it."

"Fuck. You," Angel gritted out, and the sergeant put a hand on top of his firearm.

"Doesn't make sense that a bad-ass sorcerer with your reputation wouldn't have taken out one vampire in that situation. You sure someone was there? Maybe you were just hearing things. Maybe there wasn't anyone else there at all, and you put the body there."

"Angel!" Milly said, yanking him backward when he raised his right hand, green fire snaking between his fingers. "He's just an asshole. He wants you to attack him. Look at his name tag!"

Angel tore his eyes from the smirking bastard's face and looked at the silver tag resting over his right breast pocket. Sergeant Collins, BPD.

"A fucking Collins. What they hell, do the lot of you go around planning on how you're going to harass me every time something happens? Is there a secret 'We hate Salvatore' club I'm not aware of?"

"I've half a mind to throw a set of iron cuffs on you," Sergeant Collins started, patting the leather case on his other hip that presumably held his cuffs. Iron was used to incapacitate most magic-users, as it dampened the internal energy a caster carried.

"Half a mind is too generous," Angel retorted, and the sergeant mottled red with anger.

Angel could probably burn through iron cuffs with enough veil power, but he wouldn't do such a thing unless the need were dire and his life was in danger, and escaping police custody and being hunted as a fugitive was not a viable option compared to calling his lawyer.

A couple of plainclothes detectives were walking over, apparently deciding that they didn't want the sergeant flattened on the pavement. They stepped up next to Milly and Angel just as Milly took up his defense.

"Angel didn't kill the victim," Milly snapped at the sergeant, "We don't even know who he is."

Angel dragged in a breath, trying to cool his temper. Grief battled anger, merging to become rage in his heart. He wanted to leave and track down the monster who decided to one of the kill the last remaining links to his past. "Actually, Milly, I know who that dead guy is. I saw his face before the cops pulled him off the wall."

"What?" Milly gasped out, turning to look up at him. "Who is it?"

"My old mentor and my father's best friend, a sorcerer named August Remington."

6

DEARLY DEPARTED

Angel trudged up the stairs to his place, rounding the last landing before getting to his floor. If he never saw another staircase again it would be too soon. It had to be around three or so in the morning, and he was exhausted. Running on fumes and anger, and then a dose of grief and painful memories left Angel cursing his decision to wake up that morning. Or yesterday morning, now.

He dug out his keys, so tired he was tripping over his own feet. He stopped in front of his door, but the sight of two feet clad in black leather shoes, topped by long, muscular legs in dark navy slacks and then a lean waist and broad shoulders under a perfectly tailored tuxedo jacket short-circuited his brain and left him gaping.

Resplendent in a dark blue tux with a crisp white shirt and shiny blue silk tie, Simeon leaned against the wall next to Angel's apartment, hands in his pockets, a charming smile on his lips. Angel caught a tiny flash of fang as Simeon smiled wider, chuckling. Angel flashed back to the first time he ever saw Simeon and felt the same wrenching need to reach out and touch.

"Not often that I see you speechless, *mo ghra*," Simeon purred, seductive lilt on full force. By all that was unholy, he had an undead

Irish James Bond in his hallway. "What has you so tired, and out so late?"

"Dead guy," Angel whispered, coughing before trying again. Simeon in a tux was the last thing he expected at three in the morning. His heart was jumping all over the place. "A vamp left a dead man outside my office. I just spent the whole night at the police station."

Simeon went still, a motionless state of being that no human could achieve, and his green eyes lit over Angel with a swift examination. Suddenly, so fast Angel couldn't see when Simeon went from the wall into his personal space, Simeon was leaning over him, sniffing deep, stone-cold hands gripping Angel's biceps and holding him still.

"I cannot scent another vampire on you, Angel. He or she did not touch you. Which is good for them, for they would not live another night if they had." Simeon pulled Angel in, roping thick arms around his back, and Angel found himself cradled in a deep embrace, cheek resting over the silent place where a heartbeat should be heard. "Tell me what happened?"

"Why are you here?" Angel asked instead, too tired to listen to the tiny voice in his head saying that snuggling with a vampire Elder when another vampire was depositing dead people at his feet like an evil cat was a bad idea. He squashed that voice, and did something he rarely ever contemplated—took the comfort offered.

"I am here because I thought perhaps it was time," Simeon whispered, his cool lips gliding over Angel's hair, strong hands rubbing his back. "And I arrive to see I am more needed than I expected. Tell me what happened, *mo ghra*, so that I may help."

"What do you mean, you think it's time for what? And are you okay?" Angel asked, pulling back enough to look up into Simeon's face. "The demon tossed you so hard, and then dawn broke..."

"Nothing but a few bruises and a mild sunburn, Angel. My limo was a block away and I made it just in time for you to blow up the street. Now stop changing the subject. Will you tell me what's going on?"

"You're one to talk about changing the subject. I'll tell you, but not in the hall," Angel gave in, sighing. If anyone could help him find out who killed his old teacher it was Simeon. He was Elder of the only vampire Bloodclan in the city. He lifted his keys, but Simeon took them from his hand and opened Angel's battered front door, stepping inside and flicking on the lights. Angel humphed, and followed Simeon in, closing and locking the door.

Simeon stepped gracefully into Angel's living room, the blanket and pillow he'd used still on the floor, and Angel was about to go around Simeon and pick them up when he halted, in shock.

He stared at Simeon, who was the epitome of masculine elegance and sophistication, every fangbanger's wet dream come to undead life. "How...how did you get in here? I've never invited you in. And my wards let you through. They're still active, and they aren't reacting at all. In fact, you were in my bed the other night, too!"

Simeon unbuttoned his tuxedo jacket, and sat on the couch, patting the cushion next to him. Angel narrowed his eyes, and somehow found the strength left to summon a bit of green hellfire about his fingers, spitting, and hissing. "What the fuck, Simeon."

"Peace, Angel. Your vulgarity is charming, has anyone told you that? Come sit beside me." Simeon patted the cushions again, and Angel snapped his fingers, a tiny dart of hellfire slinging past Simeon's face to spatter and smoke out on the hardwood floor behind the couch. Simeon didn't even flinch, his smile in place and his green eyes glowing with what Angel uneasily identified as appreciation and...affection?

Angel stood, unyielding, and Simeon chuckled, a deep rumble that made Angel's cock twitch despite his best efforts to keep himself under control.

"Fine then, my love. The other night when I brought you home, you were so exhausted you barely had the cohesive thought to invite me in, but your invitation was explicit enough that the *geas* which prevents the undead from entering the dwellings of the living was lifted, and as such, it translates to your wards as well, whether or not they were active at the time. My invitation into your home means I am allowed to be here, and so your wards have no effect on me whatsoever."

"Holy shit, an invitation makes you impervious to wards," Angel breathed out, incredulous, letting the hellfire die. "Why doesn't everyone know that?"

He mentally smacked himself, thinking it would be a foolish move to disclose such an advantage, especially since the rest of the world believed a vampire could be kept out by wards, even with a standing invitation into someone's home. "Is that just you, or all vampires?"

Simeon sent him a wry glance, and Angel shrugged. "Had to ask. So you can now come and go, and no matter what wards I have in place, you can still pass through them?"

"Yes. Until you decide I am no longer welcome in your home, and you revoke my invitation. You do that, the wards will be effective once again and I will be forced to leave." Simeon gave him an answer so easily that Angel had to doubt the veracity of his revelation, but he was too damn exhausted to do anything other than mentally file it under Things He Would Freak Out Over Later. Yet Simeon had never lied to him, or offered him anything but the truth, so maybe, this time, his inclination to distrust was not warranted. "Come sit with me, Angel. Tell me what's going on. Is it to do with the demon attacking us, this dead man?"

Angel mentally said fuck it and stumbled over to the couch. He sat down heavily, and Simeon gave him a mild look of exasperation before he reached out and with one long arm, pulled Angel to his side and held him close. Snuggling was a foreign experience, and Angel held himself stiffly until Simeon made no further moves, just held him.

"Always so prickly, so wary." Simeon cradled Angel to his side, the vamp smug yet also tender. Angel spied him with suspicion, but he was willing to be held as long as Simeon kept his hands in PG-13 areas of his body. While his cock would disagree, Angel didn't want a repeat of the other morning in his bed...he didn't think he did, at least. Every time he saw Simeon these days, he ended up allowing one more little thing, from a touch to this...this snuggling. Angel was used to quick, hard fucks that scratched an itch with no names exchanged and no numbers, not this quiet intimacy. "*Mo ghra*, you are a delight."

"I am not your love, Simeon," Angel groused, peeved. He was tired and cranky, and bothering a cranky sorcerer was a recipe for disaster. Simeon merely responded by manhandling Angel, ignoring his growls and complaints, until Angel straddled Simeon's lap, hands on his chest, palms cushioned by the soft and decadent fabric of Simeon's tuxedo jacket. "I'm not some twink you can play with, either."

"Twink. I hate that word, reminds me of a snack." Simeon flashed his fangs, and Angel humphed again, unimpressed. "This modern age leaves me despondent some days," Simeon said, putting a hand on Angel's back and pressing him forward, leaving no space between them. Angel was small enough compared to Simeon that he still had to look up to see Simeon's face, even sitting on the vamp's lap. "A man has the freedom to love another though any hope of intelligent conversation needs to be abandoned at the door. Not so with you, Angel. Never a disappointment."

"I thought you wanted to know about the dead man?" Angel asked, arching a brow, yet settling in comfortably. Simeon may be cool to the touch, but he was warming where their bodies met, and Angel was so tired that for once being held wasn't something to be borne but enjoyed. In fact, he could not recall at all the last time he was just...held.

"Yes, tell me of this dead man. He meant something to you?"

"How do you know?" Angel asked, rubbing his cheek against the soft fabric covering Simeon's chest.

"I can smell your sadness."

"What? Can you really?" Angel tried to lift his head, curious, but Simeon shushed him and put his head back down. Angel growled, but all Simeon did was chuckle. "I knew vamps can smell certain things, like anger and, um, arousal."

A hand slid down to the base of his spine, fingertips dipping briefly under his waistband. Angel tensed, but the hand went no further, and he relaxed.

"So I can, *mo ghra*." Simeon was all but purring, and Angel had the insane image of a fat Cheshire cat licking its lips, sharp teeth gleaming in the shadows. Oddly enough, that thought made him smile, and he relaxed even more. The words came before he even realized he was talking.

"Augustus Remington was my last teacher, and my father's best friend," Angel said. "He was out of town at a wedding when the.... when...." Angel's whole body shook once, hard, and Simeon soothed him, rubbing his back and shoulders. "Well, you know. When my family died."

"I do, Angelus. I know the tale. No need to explain."

"Yes, well.... I saw him at the funeral services afterward. He was broken, destroyed. He loved my father a great deal. August and my father were inseparable as children and young men at university. He was a natural choice, according to my father, to teach me the finer points of high sorcery once I left school."

"Why did your father not teach you? It's my understanding that Raine Salvatore was the premier instructor of high sorcery in all of the Northeast."

"And he was." Angel coughed, his chest tightening at the thought of his father, but he kept going. "My father and I were too much alike. The teacher/student dynamic was too much on top of father/son."

Simeon chuckled, and Angel thrilled internally that he could hear the sound at its genesis, his ear pressed tightly over Simeon's chest. "I imagine that was difficult."

"That's one word for it. I would have chosen apocalyptic, but whatever works."

Simeon laughed, and Angel smiled despite the grief-tainted memories.

"So, anyway...he wasn't there that night when my family died. He came back as soon as he heard, but obviously, it was too late. August just...broke. I'd already passed my trials, so technically he wasn't my instructor anymore, but the relationship was still there. I thought of him as an uncle of sorts, I grew up with him in my father's shadow."

"When was the last time you saw him?" Simeon asked, quiet, almost gentle. A vampire with a heart was an oddity, and Angel was charmed despite his reservations. It helped he was sprawled across the supernat's lap like a lazy stripper or a housecat.

"It was just after he released me from my student status, and confirmed I passed my trials. He told me that even if I hadn't already completed them, that ...that night would have earned me sorcerer rank anyway. It was a cruel thought, that I...never mind. I saw him again a week or so later, after the funerals, and then that afternoon at the police station when they finally dragged me in for questioning. Apparently humans had an issue with an army of undead spontaneously combusting and then setting a whole street on fire."

"The police arrested you for stopping the undead legion that killed your family?" Simeon sounded aghast, grievously peeved in fact, and Angel laughed this time. It was harsh and bitter, but a laugh all the same.

"There were enough neighbors from the surrounding estates as witnesses, and the wizards on the police forensic squad were able to piece together what happened after the fires were put out. I wasn't charged with anything, cleared by self-defense. It was just bullshit from the Collins family since most of them are in the BPD. The Collins are related to the Macavoys, the family that led our enemies in the Blood Wars."

"From what I understand, the Macavoys are no longer a power player in the city." Simeon would know since the Master probably knew everything about all the magical families in the state, let alone the city. It stood the reason that Simeon, as an Elder, knew just as much as his Master. Simeon's clan had only been here a few years, arriving not long before they met for the first time.

"No, not anymore. After that night, the humans were able to intervene, since the undead that came for us tore through anyone in their way, and that meant the human guards and staff in the house and on the grounds that night. Thirty humans died. So the cops came in, the state authorities finally had enough to use against the Macavoys, and most of those responsible for the attack on my home were sent to prison."

"Most of them?"

"I'm not sure the cops got all the people responsible. I have no proof, but the people who went to jail weren't the ones in real positions of power. The head of the family is Leicaster Macavoy, and nothing happened to him, and his son Daniel was only ten or so at the time. All he got was a slap on the wrist for not controlling his people better."

"Didn't you just say that the Collins in the BPD are related to the Macavoys? Makes sense they would cover up his involvement as best they could," Simeon said, a growl under his words.

"Yeah, I would agree. But no proof. I was twenty and a mess, and everyone was either afraid of me or treating me like glass. I was in no place to really push for more answers. There wasn't anyone left from the Bloodclan that got enthralled, either, so none of them could come forward to place blame on the particular sorcerer who destroyed their clan. They all died."

Angel was lost to memory, the sound of ripping flesh and hissing, screams of terror and pain ricocheting behind his eyes and filling his ears. He squeezed his eyes tight, and clung tightly to Simeon, willing the horrors to retreat.

"Even the Master and his Elders? We knew of the history when our Master moved us here, but there are many pieces still missing to the tale. We absorbed the few lone vampires here in the city, but they knew nothing about what happened. What do you know?"

Angel thought about it, but his mind was stumbling, images of August propped up against the wall, interspersed with memories of his family strung out across the floor and in the front yard of his childhood home too much to handle. Here was comfort, and support, and all he could do was cling, and hope Simeon knew what to do after that. Tomorrow was soon enough to be strong. All he could do right now was try and hold himself together.

"It was a clan from Rhode Island? Maybe Providence? I can't

remember ever asking, I wasn't in a place to get answers. I don't know if the Master and his Elders fell with the rest of their clan. When they attacked, they were as rapid and unthinking as zombies, and a helluva lot faster. None of them were capable of rational thought, even when my family cut them down in droves before being overrun." Too late to stop it, a sob broke free, and Angel buried his face in the soft silk of Simeon's tie. He was going to end up ruining the silk with his tears, but Simeon held him tighter and Angel let them come.

For years, he'd been alone. Even when Isaac was living with him, Angel was alone. Being a parent and big brother left little time for mourning, and there had been no one to turn to after his family died. August had bailed, too overcome by his own grief, and the foolish belief that if he'd been with Raine Salvatore the night of the attack that he might have been able to save them. Angel had been home that night, and all he could do was get Isaac to safety in the mansion's panic room and then run back into the fray, expecting fully to die.

"Haven't seen August for years," Angel said, muffled by Simeon's tie. "I thought he left town. I heard at one point he moved to Hartford. Why was he here? Why didn't he come see me if he was in town? I might have saved him from…Maybe."

"Perhaps, *mo ghra*, you were a reminder of his grief. Seeing you would have been too much. Not fair, but only too human." Simeon had stopped rubbing, merely cradling Angel in a protective embrace, and Angel's lids drooped, and he was moments from sleep, even as he struggled to think. Simeon kept talking, lips brushing over the top shell of his ear, and Angel let some more tears slip free. "Don't put his death on yourself. Only the one who killed him is responsible."

"I know," Angel replied, but he had yet to believe it. What he wouldn't give for a quiet life, free from his past. "I don't know why he's dead, other than it's to do with me. That means someone out there wants me and is willing to do anything to get to me, including summoning demons and killing innocent people to do it. And I don't think the cops will be doing anything to stop it."

Simeon was gone again when he woke in the morning, and it was sometime before noon by the angle of the sun. Angel was tucked in on the couch, his boots off, stripped down to his underwear, under the ratty afghan that he'd taken from his old home years before. For a foolish second, he thought to check for bite marks, but Simeon wasn't an idiot. It was a guaranteed second death for a vampire to drink from someone like Angel unless Angel felt like saving him or he could get to another magic-user in time.

"Dammit, he never told me why he was in a tux. Fuck, was he fine," Angel grumbled, sitting up, afghan pooling in his lap.

"I was dressed in a tux, Angelus because there was a welcoming party for a foreign dignitary. I'm glad you appreciated the sight, my love," Simeon said from behind him, and Angel squawked, falling from the couch and standing in a mad scramble of limbs. "I left when it became too onerous. Which I'm glad for, incidentally, as you needed me last night."

"Holy shit! Don't do that!" Angel shouted, confused. "It's daytime!"

It was indeed, the sun streaming in from the street-side windows, alighting across the couch and most of the living room. Simeon was standing in the kitchen, covered by shadows and holding still.

"Why the fuck are you here, Simeon? Do you have a second death wish?" Angel was freaking out. If Simeon took even a single step forward, he would be a pile of ash. "Why didn't you go home?"

"A vampire came into your place of business, your territory, and killed a man you knew and cared about. This is after a demon was sent here to kill you. Did you truly think I would leave you alone, Angelus?" Simeon asked, tiny flashes of fang showing Angel just how displeased he was.

"That's sweet and all, but I've been taking care of myself for years now, I don't need a sitter."

"I beg to differ."

Angel gaped at Simeon, who did nothing but smirk at him and cross his arms over his wide chest and wait while Angel figured out how to reply. "People actually say that?" Angel whispered, and

Simeon snorted, an inelegant sound that contrasted with the silk dress shirt he still wore.

The tuxedo jacket was draped over the back of the couch, and Angel found himself reaching for it, caressing the smooth cloth, enjoying the heavy yet fine feel to the fabric. "How long have you been trapped in the kitchen?"

Simeon appeared to think about it, but he answered quick enough. "Since dawn. The sun should make it into the kitchen in an hour or so. I would have been safer in your bedroom, but I was most reluctant to have you out of my sight."

He rolled his eyes at the overprotective statement but made no comment. Angel couldn't hear the worry in his voice, but Simeon would indeed be trapped and then exposed as the day waxed on. Angel didn't have blinds sufficient to block the sun and keep Simeon from burning.

"Hold on a few minutes. Stay in there, okay?"

"Nowhere else to go, *mo ghra*."

Angel chuckled at the sardonic reply, and carefully put the jacket back down.

He wasn't as tired as he should be, for some reason. Maybe there was some magical benefit to sleeping on a vampire's lap though he doubted it. He remembered feeling safe, and relaxed, even with his painful memories. Sleeping with Simeon left him refreshed, and he didn't know what to do about that.

Angel faced the windows, pale gold light streaming in. The sky was clear, a few random fluffy white clouds coming into view before the wind chased them away. It was a day shiny and bright, a rarity this late in the season. It wouldn't last, though, the evening bringing more rain and some snow. Angel stepped closer to the windows and closed his eyes.

He called his second sight to the fore, and the sigils and runes written on the windows shone like liquid gold. They were part of his wards, to keep them from being broken and forcibly opened. Glass was highly receptive to spells and magic, and these windows already knew his magic. Angel reached for the veil, and with a thin tendril of thought, opened it to a trickle. Even with so small an opening in the veil, the energy that poured out from the fissure into Angel was enough to make him mentally stagger. He absorbed it, made it his own, and kept a part of his mind on monitoring the energy flow. He welcomed the filling of his mental reserves, and exhaled, relaxing as best he could.

As best as anyone knew, vampires were of a magical origin to which sunlight was inimical, the radiant energies put off by the UV and the extreme magical energies of the solar system's yellow star of a sufficient strength to tear apart the mysterious force that animated the undead. Angel recognized it as a type of death magic, the force that animated the sentient undead, a primordial magic that was ancient and enigmatic and impossible to fully understand. The actual *how* of a vampire's existence left him stumped, along with millennia of necromancers. What he knew for certain was that if Simeon was exposed to direct sunlight, he would die a second death, reduced to ash.

Angel's wards hummed and vibrated when he made contact, the near-sentient magical constructs responding to him as would a trained pet. He spoke to them all, wordless murmurs of affection and reinforcement. He searched among them for the runes that identified Angel as their master and creator, and saw how they reflected his will —and there, as Simeon had said, was their recognition of the vampire's permission to be there in Angel's space. Where Angel's magical signature varied from emerald green to new spring verdant, Simeon's Invitation was a sapphire and silver cord, cool and sweet to the touch. Angel tasted chocolate and spices on his tongue in a sensory overlap, his body creating an echo in response to Simeon's presence in the wards.

The sigils on the windows were the ones he needed to change. He spoke to the runes and sigils, the designs responding quickly, and when he pulled at them, twisting their shapes, they almost resisted, until he showed them what they were to become—the magical equivalent of a mirror. Able to distinguish between those welcome, and uninvited. The sigils latched onto the Invitation, and Angel fed them power, guiding and tweaking as the sigils rewrote themselves to match the mental diagrams he worked out as he went along.

When it was done, when it was successful, a single tone resonated through Angel and the wards. It rocked Angel to his very center, and he laughed in response, awed and overjoyed. Magic done right, a magic that created, even for a necromancer, was joy and celebration and brought with it a euphoric high. Angel rode out the wave, and slowly withdrew from his wards.

"What have you wrought, necromancer?" Simeon's shocked whisper brought him all the way back, to see Simeon staring at him. The sunlight had moved closer to Simeon while Angel was occupied, and a tiny sliver was touching Simeon's shoe, creeping up his lower legs.

"I...," he coughed and tried again. Angel opened the connection to the veil and let more energy fill him up, making it his own. The hours of restful sleep and channeling the veil into his reserves directly was restoring him faster than days off from casting could ever manage. "I made UV and radiant magic reflective runes. Radiant magic is the rare type of magic that is inherent in raw sunlight, and is partially responsible for why vamps burn. Though I'm sure you know that. Instead of spells that maintain grayish-translucent panes of glass and allow heavily filtered light to pass through, which is done with commercially treated glass, I'm letting the light through, the visible radiation that our eyes translate as sunlight—but the radiant magic and the UV rays that burn vampires, is reflected back out. So, sunlight can come in, but the parts of it that would kill you stay outside."

Angel smirked at the absolutely bemused and confounded expression on Simeon's face. The Elder vampire finally looked away from him to the sunlight climbing his legs, and Angel chuckled when Simeon hesitated. "Seriously, Simeon, cleaning ash outta the floorboards would be a pain in the ass. It's safe. I used your vampiric magical Enter At Will Card, your Invitation, as the basis for the spell. The wards won't let you burn."

Simeon growled, but he bravely took a step forward, fully into the light. Angel held his breath, a tiny part of him afraid he messed up somewhere, but when Simeon stood for a whole minute in direct sunlight without a single whiff of smoke or flame, Angel grinned. "Awesome. And, man, you need a tan."

Simeon's pale complexion was obvious and stark in the golden fall of light. Angel smiled at the fiery highlights in the vampire's dark auburn hair, and his green eyes reflected the light like shards of glass. Simeon lifted his hands, gazing at the shadows his fingers made, still lost to wonder. Angel laughed again, then noticed he was damn near naked. He was wearing just his underwear and been standing around almost naked, casting in front of Simeon the whole time.

Coffee, food, and clothes. A shower and a toothbrush would be nice, too. "Gods, I'm gross. I'm gonna go take a shower. Don't step outside or you're going to fry."

Walking into his bathroom and turning on the water, Angel waited for the hot water to kick in. He just managed to strip off his underwear and get under the spray when he found himself crowded back against the shower stall, six plus feet of naked, horny vampire looming over him.

Tongues melding, hands grabbing and holding, and steam rising. Angel gasped, Simeon taking his opening and kissing Angel as if he were starving and a kiss was his only sustenance. A rapidly warming hand tilted his head back, another gripped his hip and yanked him forward, lifting him off the slippery tiles. Angel grabbed Simeon's shoulders and wrapped his legs around the vampire's lean waist. Simeon chuckled, and Angel growled back, too turned on to do anything but buck impatiently with his hips, nails scoring Simeon's white flesh.

He gasped when Simeon pulled his lips away, the vampire kissing down the side of his neck, his big hands reaching down to cup Angel's ass, fingertips dipping into the crease of his ass. Simeon sucked hard on his neck, working up a mark, and Angel arched into it, feeling a dangerous hint of fangs. No punctures, but near enough that Angel moaned, his cock so hard he could feel his heart beating in the throbbing length. "Simeon!"

Simeon lifted his head, green eyes taking up Angel's entire field of vision, and the vampire snarled, "You are a treasure, and you give me such a marvelous gift as the light. Will you be mine, *mo ghra*? No one else's, only mine. Be mine, mine to treasure forever."

A hand worked its ways down between them and wrapped tight around their cocks. Simeon stroked, hard and slow, squeezing almost to the point of pain, jerking them off as one. One stroke, then two, and Angel broke. Angel came with a scream, writhing, and he answered without thinking. "Yes!"

The next few minutes were a strange mix of languid kisses and sleepy sighs, wandering, exploring hands and shivers. Angel rode a high greater than any magical one before it, his brain futilely trying to catch up to what just happened. If it wasn't for the fact the water was starting to run cold, he would think he was still asleep.

Simeon carried him out of the shower, drying him with a towel and setting him on his feet. Angel shook his head, trying to find his brain to form a coherent thought, but it took him a few minutes.

"What was that?" he asked, rubbing his face as Simeon knelt naked at his feet, drying his toes. "And oh god, that's an image."

Simeon grinned up at him through wet bangs, and Angel found his fingers threading through the strands. "Seriously, what just happened and why do I feel like I got hit by a demon train?"

"That, my Angel, was an orgasm. Surely you've had one of those before?"

"Not like that." His whole body was quivering. His fingers were buzzing and his head swam, and he moaned as his cock valiantly tried to rise to the sight of Simeon kneeling naked and wet at his feet.

"Then it's good I'm here now, isn't it?" Simeon said, smug only as a naked man can be as he rose to his feet, tossing aside the towel. Angel got his first good look at the vampire since the whirlwind jerkoff in the shower. "I plan to give you more of those."

Simeon was a mix between a marble statue carved by an old master, and one of those naked veteran pictures on social media. Covered in ancient tattoo designs and scars cut in place while he was alive, Simeon was all warrior. The sophisticated undead James Bond from the night before was gone, and in his place was a wild and untamed man, regardless of his lack of heartbeat. Angel swallowed, and his cock went right back to interested. Simeon noticed, but he made no move to touch. Simeon's own cock rose thick and hard from a neatly trimmed patch of dark red hair, uncut and flushed with the faintest of rosy hues, large balls nestled tight under the base of the shaft, showing Angel just how aroused Simeon was. Angel wanted to touch, and badly, and he was having trouble remembering why he shouldn't. Why was he fighting this so hard?

"*Leannán anam*, you tempt me. But somehow I think your mind has yet to catch up to what just occurred. You give me the gift of sunlight, unasked for and generously beautiful, and I mob you in the shower like an untried fledgling fresh from the grave. Forgive me," Simeon held out his hand, and Angel took it. He felt like he was sleepwalking, and Simeon was right. His mind had yet to catch up. Fingers meshing, Simeon gently tugged, not demanding, but asking now.

Angel went, and Simeon gathered him close, arms rising to hold him secure and tight. Angel exhaled, a ragged breath, but let his head fall to rest on Simeon's hard chest, and his own arms came up to return the embrace. "I don't know what's going on."

"I know, *mo ghra*," Simeon whispered back. "I'm certain it'll kick in soon enough."

IT WAS NOW EVENING, the sun down by a few minutes, and vampire-safe outside his walls. Angel had spent the whole day cleaning his place, taking the rubble of the destroyed bed to the trash chute a few feet down the hall from his apartment door. Angel had fun flipping the torn mattress down the stairs and out to the curb, thankful that big item pickup was the next morning as he dragged it down the street half a block and left it at the designated spot.

Simeon offered commentary from his spot on the couch, like a housecat that learned to talk. Angel ended up giving the Elder his laptop and the passwords to his video streaming service and let the undead man binge watch TV all day, sitting in the sun. Angel got a kick out of Simeon watching a teen television show about vampires, the vampire sighing or shaking his head the whole time.

Angel tugged on his coat, pocketing his keys and cell. His bag was slung over his shoulder, packed with supplies he would need on his errand tonight. Simeon was behind him, patiently waiting, and Angel seethed. Simeon had been right, and when Angel's brain kicked in, he was plenty mad. Not at Simeon, not entirely. He could have set the vamp on fire and kicked his ass outta his shower, but he didn't and now he kept hearing the words 'will you be mine', over and over in his head. And his own needy agreement. The joy and satisfaction he'd experienced telling Simeon yes still left him dazed.

"So it's not a spell?" Angel asked again, turning on his heel and skewering Simeon where he stood in his rumpled tux, still looking hot enough to melt Angel's resolve. "I'm not magically your mate or something? I didn't promise away my soul or something equally ridiculous?"

"Where do you get your ideas? Were you watching that dreadful TV show over my shoulder?" Simeon cracked a smile, shaking his head side to side, and Angel glared at him some more. "No, *mo ghra*, you're not magically my mate. We vampires are not wolves, to take mates in bouts of passion and with no thought. I asked because I've wanted you for years now, and you left me overwhelmed by your generosity. You gave me the sun, and it only took you a thought's time and some ingenious tinkering. My restraint is now non-existent where it comes to you. So I asked, as any man would, for you to give me your heart, as you've always had mine."

"Give you my heart? I haven't said anything about my heart."

"No you did not, but I see the way you look at me, and the desire your body holds for me. You are not indifferent to me, and one day I hope to earn your love."

"Oh, okay then," Angel refused to admit he was blushing. He could blow up a street with a demon trying to rip him apart, but have a centuries-old vampire admit to wanting him and he lost it. He turned back to the door, and yanked it open, making the board nailed to it rattle. He glared at the door, and walked out into the hall, letting Simeon follow. Simeon shut the door and Angel locked it, powering up his wards with a quick thought before having a small epiphany. "Wait, are you saying you're in love…"

Angel was interrupted by a kiss, cool lips molded to his own, and a hand holding his chin. The kiss was chaste and brief, but Angel got the message. Grumbling, he pulled away and strode off down the hall. Declarations of love were not what he was expecting, not like this, and never from a vampire. His relationship with the local Bloodclan was an aberration; his name and affinity was anathema to all vampires past the borders of Boston and its surrounding towns. He never knew why Simeon and his Master hadn't fought to get out of Angel's non-aggression agreement, or even why they sought him out as often as they did for magical assistance that any other sorcerer-level practitioner could provide. Simeon, from the night they met, had always set his attentions on Angel, and only in the last week had Simeon moved from polite but intense appreciation to open affection and endearments. Angel didn't know what prompted the change in Simeon, but it left him confused, horny, and his heart hurt.

He wanted what Simeon was offering him. Yet the wary side of his nature, the one scarred by War and death, told him not to believe and keep himself safe. He was tired of listening to that side of himself, yet he couldn't stop. And to love a vampire? When Simeon's kind hated him, and with good reason? How would that work in the long run, if at all?

"What are your plans for this evening? Someone, or several people, want you dead," Simeon called after him. "Leaving your apartment and its wards is not wise."

"I'm aware!" Angel called back over his shoulder as he took the stairs down, Simeon following on his heels. "But I'm not going to wait around for this asshole to make another move. He took someone from me. Sure, August hasn't been around for the last decade, but he was still part of my family, or what's left of it, anyway. I refuse to let this go any further. Milly or Isaac could be next—hell, even you, and I will not let that happen. This fucker is going down."

Angel hit the street, and he did take a look both ways down the darkened street before heading south towards the Commons. Thankful that the sidewalks were still intact, Angel walked past the crater at the three-way intersection, the hole covered in metal sheets and surrounded by a forest of orange warning cones. Through traffic was nonexistent now, and Angel grinned for a moment, thinking about the piece in the paper that morning about how he managed to get the statehouse employees a day off from work due to "magical disturbances" near the building.

Simeon followed him and walked beside him once there was room. It was cold, and damp, and the tiniest of flakes fell around them. The snowfall might pick up, but the days' worth of rain was slicking, turning to ice, and the wind blew in from the ocean. Brine, smoke, and fish assaulted Angel's nose, but he was used to it.

Angel pulled out his cell, and after checking his messages, sent one of his own.

You okay?- AS

A minute passed, but he got a reply. Milly wasn't a texter, but she knew enough to respond.

I am. What are you doing? You NEVER text me. -MF

Have you heard from anyone at BPD? Are they looking into anyone from the old families who may be after me? -AS

My contact says no. There's been next to no casework done on August's murder or who sent the demon after you. The videotape of the summoner outside your townhouse hasn't been processed either. Someone high up has stalled things. -MF

Not surprised. They probably know who it is or want the killer to succeed in getting me. -AS

What are you doing? -MF

Asking an old friend who killed him.-AS

NO. DON'T YOU DARE!-MF

Angel smiled at her use of CAPS, and replied.

You know what to say if the fools in blue come by?-AS

I won't have to say anything if you don't do it!-MF

True. But I'm going to anyway. -AS

You tell me just so I freak out, don't even act nonchalant. Don't get caught. Goddamit. Erase your texts. -MF

Angel chuckled and erased his texts before sending one last message.

Isaac—August Remington was murdered yesterday and his body dumped at my office. BE CAREFUL. -AS

As usual, he got no reply. He knew Isaac's cell was back on as he paid the bill himself yesterday morning, so his brother got his message. Whether he heeded Angel's warning or not was another thing entirely.

"What do you mean, you're going to ask a friend who killed him?" Simeon asked from next to him as they crossed the street, the Commons rising out of the fog as they moved down another block. The lamps were lit, the shadows through the trees ominous and spooky, but Angel wasn't concerned. He was recognizable enough that muggers stayed clear, and most vampires stayed out of Beacon Hill, due to the heavy practitioner population. No one to snack on. The other supernats in the city were more likely to avoid trouble than humans, and wolves, as a rule, avoided cities. Too many chances for trouble, and none of it ending well for the supernat in question. Boston had a very high population of practitioners and mundane humans, which kept the supernatural numbers down. Most large cities could boast several bloodclans, but Boston had only the one.

And the big vampire walking at his side was a deterrent for trouble. "Were you reading my texts over my shoulder?"

"Yes. Do explain, I hope you don't mean what I think you do."

At least, he wasn't hiding it. Angel could appreciate the honesty. "I meant it. I'm going to ask August Remington who killed him. The morgue conducts all autopsies on murdered sorcerers in the first twenty-four hours, and then the body is burned once COD is confirmed. I checked the news, and no COD has been released yet. His body should still be there. Which is kind of odd, since he was torn to shreds, but the BPD is notorious for messing up so they may have put a hold on the cremation. I also don't see BPD rushing this investigation. Most of them would be glad to see me dead."

"I thought raising the dead was banned. It's considered a sacrilege by many in the magic community, I believe." Angel sent Simeon a sideways look, the vampire gazing back at him. He didn't see any condemnation, just curiosity, and some wariness.

"It is banned, by the High Court of Sorcery and blah-blah-blah. In fact, life-long imprisonment and castration of gifts are a common punishment. Though if I want to stop this asshole, I'm going to break some rules. No one else is dying."

"Walking around at night is not the best way to stay alive, Angelus," Simeon retorted, though Angel could see a soft glow in Simeon's green eyes. "And then raising the dead."

"You don't have to come with me if you're afraid, Elder," Angel snapped.

"I'm afraid of what will happen to you, *mo ghra*, if I leave you alone," Simeon replied, voice smooth and rumbling and making his heart skip.

Afraid to think about what that meant, Angel snarked back, "Are you going to follow me around all night? Don't you have some blood slaves to drain and nefarious evil vampire things to do?"

"I ate last night, thank you. I could make some trite generalization about necromancers, but as we are apparently going to be raising the dead, I find myself withholding comment."

Angel laughed, delighted despite the danger inherent in his errand. Simeon smiled at him, that same soft look in his eyes, and Angel briefly smiled back before minding the sidewalk in front of them.

※

ANGEL STARED at the chain-link fence from half a block away, the coiled barb wire on top giving him some doubts about his plan. The coroner's office and the city morgue was a fairly large building, not too far from the hospital, surrounded by scattered parking lots, narrow streets, and a marvelous view of downtown and the harbor that was wasted on the occupants. The building was a few stories tall, with an attached multi-bay garage around the back that vehicles could pull up to, discharging and picking up the deceased.

Near the front, the lobby was lit by flickering fluorescent lights and glass walls, the sterile colors and tiled floors giving a cold impression. Angel knew it well, unfortunately. He'd been here the first time many years before, identifying his family and their slain mundane human retainers. Several times since then for the BPD and private citizens for after-death investigations and consultations.

"What is your plan, *mo ghra*?" Simeon whispered over his shoulder, and Angel flicked at his nose to get him to back off. Simeon chuckled and pressed closer to his back, and Angel sighed. The vampire felt good back there, reassuring.

"The place never closes down. City is too big—people are rudely dying all the time, so it stays open. The staff isn't as heavy at night as it is during the day, but there're at least six people in there right now. Living ones, I should say. Plenty of dead." Angel kept surveying the exterior of the building, noting the lack of foot traffic. The overnight shift was just that—the shift change was around six am, so he had several hours before there was movement. Unless a body showed up, and it was only suspicious deaths or murders with police priority that typically spurred the night-shift coroner on duty to leave his office.

"And just how do you know that, my love?"

"Not the first time I've been here, actually. I've gotten calls before, from the cops or family members requesting I check to see if someone was killed by sacrificial magic or died from hexes. I'm the only necromancer in the state, so it happens a few times a month. Haven't found a lot of those cases were actually malevolent acts, but sometimes people can't accept a loved one's death, so they go looking for answers that aren't there. And the DA has put the screws to BPD hard enough that they call me, even if they'd rather not. Most of them aren't very willing to reach out to me for help." Angel leaned forward a bit, peeking around the corner, checking the traffic out by the main road. A few random cars, but nothing coming down the morgue's access road. Simeon put a hand on his hip as if afraid Angel were either going to bolt or tip over. Angel couldn't help the hot flush on his cheeks or the flutter in his belly, but he kept his mind on his task. He leaned back, and bit his lip, thinking. Simeon's hand stayed on his hip, the vampire's fingers rubbing his skin where his shirt rode up a bit. "You sure you want to come? As an Elder, you can probably get out of being arrested or shot if we're caught, but I don't want you to think you need to do this."

"Stop stalling, and tell me your plan," Simeon teased with a growl, and Angel poked his gut with an elbow.

"The night receptionist is someone I know. Same guy the last dozen times I've been here. He's going to know I haven't been called in, and there're no police cars in the lot, so there aren't any cops in the building waiting for me to come in and offer an opinion."

"Security?"

"Cameras at the garage doors, all regular doors and fire access. Keycard swipes and access pins. Cameras feed into the screens at the reception desk. One security guard. He stays in his tiny little office until his rounds, which aren't for another two hours."

"And your plan is what, exactly?"

"Get in there and not get caught," Angel quipped and went back to watching the open space between their hiding spot and the rear of the morgue.

The lights from the high-rises in downtown glittered over the water in the harbor, and while it was some distance away, the scent of brine and exhaust overwhelmed each breath he took. The wind carried the damp sea air over the shore, up through the parking lots and low warehouses before swirling around the morgue and then on to where Angel and Simeon hid in the shadows. The air was chilly and damp and sank into his bones. Angel shivered and pulled the weather-proof collar of his heavy sweater up higher around his neck.

Angel pulled his bag around and dug inside. He'd brought what he need for the raising and an assortment of spellcasting odds-and-ends for any contingency. Angel searched until he found a small silver and glass jar of powdered sea salt, topped with a cork and bound in twine. The jar and its contents were older than the city they stood in, and he had to be careful with it. He closed his bag and slung it back over his shoulder, and kept an eye on the morgue and the access road.

"Don't interrupt me," Angel warned quietly and leaned back on the building, thankful Simeon didn't ask what he was doing.

Angel knew elemental magic, as all higher-ranked casters did, but his affinity was for death and came easiest for him. He could use elemental magic, but it took more focus, and more preparation though he had the power base for it. He couldn't use the veil—the coroner was a wizard, and while the coroner couldn't access the veil, he might be able to sense Angel accessing it since he was so close. Accessing the veil created a surge in ambient magic fields, and the higher ranked practitioners could sense it when a sorcerer made contact if they were close enough.

Angel carefully unwound the twine, pulling the cork free and letting it dangle from the cord. The sea salt inside was ground to a fine powder, and the strong, clean odor rose and filled his nose. His mouth watered, and he cupped his hands tighter around the jar.

"*Ventus et mare, spiritus et aqua,*" Angel whispered, staring hard at the shiny contents, and pulled power from his center and fed it through the jar. This was an old spell, ancient as the shores of far-off Greece that was the home of the salt, and it was used once upon a time by the seafaring battle-mages of that island-rich country.

The fine particles moved, rolling like tiny waves as they danced. A thin stream rose from the jar and hung in front of his face as he continued to whisper. He sent his awareness out, and the salt followed. His second sight kicked in, and the harbor glowed with a powerful green-blue light, the elemental energies moving in a near constant exchange between the air and the water.

The weather report for that night gave a high chance of rain and snow, but the sky was clear right now, and so if anyone was watching at the moment, the sudden increase of fog in the harbor might raise some brows. The fog roiled and swelled, and crept toward the shore. The wind blowing over the water picked it up and pulled it inland.

With half his mind on the spell, Angel carefully closed the jar, making sure the cork was seated and the twine tied off. He put the jar back in his bag and gave the spell his full attention.

Feeding it his own energy, Angel whispered the incantation over and over, the words now meaningless, all they were now just a means to focus. The fog rolled over the shore in heavy waves, and quickly filled the lots and streets, thicker than pea soup and salty and tangy on his tongue as he breathed it in. Angel relaxed, and weaned the spell from his consciousness, letting the words fade away. The spell was still being fed by his personal energy, but he could hold it long enough to finish his task. Once he was done, the fog would remain, though not as thick and cloying. It would stay like this for the next few hours, the majority of it burned away by the dawn.

"C'mon," Angel whispered, and pushed away from the building he was leaning against. Simeon stayed at his heels, the fog thick enough that they would lose sight of each other in seconds if they separated.

Sounds were muffled, even their footsteps, and light absorbed after a few feet. The world took a dim gray hue, bright enough to see, but nothing more than a stride away. Angel kept moving straight, counting on the curb and the chain link fence to lead him to the lowered bar that kept all but emergency and mortuary vehicles from entering the garage area of the morgue.

Angel hurried, not wanting to be on the road if a vehicle decided to drive through, and found the curb, turning left toward the gate. He concentrated on watching his step since he could barely see the ground beneath his feet. They made the gate, and Angel looked up, unable to see the camera that covered the gate. If he couldn't see the camera, the camera couldn't see them.

Angel ducked under the bar, the fog eddying around their legs as they ran across the rear lot, heading for the garage bay doors. There were several, and Angel knew from past visits that he wanted the one on the near side, so he could take the short hall that led to the storage room where the bodies were kept post-autopsy.

It took him a few minutes in the fog, but Angel managed to find the right door, the gray concrete and steel building looming above them. He pulled a pair of thin leather gloves from his bag, and tugged them on, not wanting to leave behind prints. Getting away with casting a prohibited spell would be ruined by being hauled in for felony B&E.

The steel corrugated doors were all closed, and Angel blew out a breath, thinking through his repertoire of spells for something that would trigger the garage door opener on the inside. He went for his bag, but the large shadow at his side chuckled, and Simeon leaned over, listening through the door.

"No heartbeats—no one alive in the garage bay," Simeon said quietly, and Angel felt his jaw drop open when Simeon slipped his fingertips under the garage door and lifted. There was a faint screech, and Simeon paused, listening, holding still for long moments before lifting again. Without any evidence of strain, Simeon forced the heavy steel door to open, exposing the unlit bay beyond. Simeon gave Angel a slow wink and a salacious grin, and Angel snapped his mouth closed and fought back a blush at being caught staring.

The door was open a few feet, enough for Angel to hoist himself up, and crouch in the darkness on the cold floor as Simeon joined him. "Don't move," Angel whispered, and lifted a hand, summoning the fog inside. It rolled in past their feet, a thin sheet that separated into tendrils, gray snakes that coiled and waited for his commands. "There's cameras on the doors and access points."

Simeon looked as if he were about to ask, but Angel waved his hand once in a short motion, and the fog snakes leapt into action. The garage bay quickly became as murky as the outside, but it was nearly pitch black, so anyone watching on the cameras wouldn't, hopefully, notice. The tiny red light of a camera above the inner door was blinking, and the fog hugged the camera, obscuring its view. Not completely, but enough to make it impossible for their identity to be discerned, no matter how good the digital technician in any police lab.

"We need to be fast," Angel said, quickly standing and moving for the door. Simeon beat him to it, and listened again, nodding once.

Angel stepped up, and rubbed his fingertips together, the fine leather gloves not impeding the surge of static energy he pulled from the friction. He tapped the access panel, and with a small blue spark, the door beeped and the panel flashed green. Angel opened the door, and the fog snakes slithered through, entering the hallway.

Angel gave them a moment, and then followed, Simeon right behind. The hall was dark too, only lit by overhead lighting at the far end, the cameras covered by the fog, the door to the main areas of the morgue shut. Angel sprinted down the hall, stopping halfway at a door on the left. Simeon repeated his listening trick, and when Angel got his nod, his zapped the panel again, opening the door to the large storage area. There were no cameras in here, as all the occupants were dead, after all, the claimed waiting to be sent to any number of mortuaries and crematoriums in the state and beyond.

Heavy with the scent of death, the air in the room was filled with chemicals and the stench of decomposing flesh impossible to miss. Angel sneezed, rubbing his nose with his sleeve as he headed for a nearby desk. He flipped the pages of the inventory sheet, heading for the R's.

Remington, August. Locker 33.

Angel turned to see Simeon carefully shutting the door, the vampire watching him with open curiosity. What Angel was about to do was illegal in every country in the world—raising the dead outlawed over a century ago, prohibited with the sternest of penalties attached. It was still practiced in third-world countries in the depths of rural communities out of the law's reach though no recorded resurrection had happened in the USA in the last sixty years. Life imprisonment and the castration of his gifts was one outcome if they were caught—if he wasn't killed in prison. The sacrilegious viewpoints that came with the public's opinions of necromancy would garner him no favors if caught.

"I'm about to break about a dozen laws. Last chance to leave."

"My love, we've committed to our endeavor. I'll not leave you," Simeon admonished, coming towards him, looking down from his glittering green eyes in a way that made Angel almost forget why they were there in the first place. "Besides, I've not seen a raising before—this should be interesting."

"You're over four hundred years old, and you've never seen someone raised from the dead? What the hell have you been doing with eternity?" Angel asked as he grabbed a gurney from the wall, rolling it behind him as he searched the numbered doors set into the wall. He found Number 33, and put his hand on the steel door, head down, listening. Not as Simeon had before, but with his other senses—and got an echo back.

His heart clenched, and his jaw ached from how hard he bit down. It hurt, what he was about to do—that he would talk to a man he loved as an uncle and mentor again only after he was dead. There was no longer any time for them to reconnect in this life, to repair whatever broke when the Salvatore's were murdered. Angel would find out what happened, and he would have his revenge. There was no justice left in this city for those carrying the Salvatore name and their allies—the Macavoys may have been reduced to a handful, but the lesser branch of the family, the Collins, were everywhere, choking the foundations of BPD like ivy, cracking and separating the individual blocks into those who weren't to be trusted, and those who could do nothing.

"Did you guess at my age, *mo ghra*, or has someone in the clan been talking?" Simeon asked, going to the other side of the gurney and holding it in place as Angel grabbed the handle to the storage locker, the cold metal chilling his hand through his glove. He opened the locker, the door releasing with a hiss and flood of cold air.

"So I'm right then? Early 1600's, late 1500's?" he said, and while looking at Simeon's face instead of into the black, square void that held his friend's body. He was inches away from doing something horrible and necessary and all he could do was focus on Simeon, and keep his voice from cracking. "And your clan ignores me unless I need to save a fledgling from a bad case of I-ate-a-witch. They don't talk to me."

"Yes, you are right," Simeon agreed, his gaze cautious as he watched Angel though his lips quirked at Angel's exercise of wit.

Simeon wisely refrained from speaking about his clanmates. "Though I'm not certain exactly what year I was turned. Around then is a good estimation."

"Tattoos give you away," Angel gestured vaguely with his right hand as he gripped the ice cold steel of the bottom of the positive temperature unit. He pulled, and the mechanism smoothly slid forward in a well-oiled motion. A beige sheet covering the body did little to disguise the form underneath it, and Angel held his breath as he hit the latch that would bring the slab down to waist height. It gave a soft jerk, then quietly lowered, resting atop the gurney with a moan. Best to keep everything at this point, as they might need to get away fast if interrupted.

He sent a glance at the door, the fog swirling patiently as it waited for his next command. No motion came through the glass window, so they were alone for now. He needed to hurry, and he was, torn between the need to freeze up in personal horror and his desire for answers.

The body of August Remington was as torn and destroyed as it had been when Angel first saw it, moments after August's life bled out down his stairs. The sheet was damp, even in the cold, the sundered flesh seeping bodily fluids even after death, giving a macabre outline to the mortal wounds below. No heartbeat to push blood through vein and artery; no, it was the flesh itself that wept, too many gashes to close, never mind the cuts made by the autopsy.

Angel gripped the top of the sheet, fingers curling around the edge, bunching it in his palm. He pulled it back, an unforgiving and unrelenting decision that stole the air from his lungs.

August Remington was a man no more. Just a body, the echo Angel sensed through the steel door even bigger, louder. Recently departed and glaringly vacant, the corpse before him was both better and worse than many he had seen in the past. His eyes picked out the telltale slash patterns of a vampire attack, the retractable claws on each finger lethally sharp and a few inches long depending on the vamp's age. Across the arteries on both sides of his neck, his abdomen disemboweled, and one of his femoral arteries sliced to the bone, all done in the leanest of seconds. He was slain not as food, but as a vampire would attack with the intent to only murder. August was spared being a food source, only to die in a great rush of blood and pain.

Angel looked up at his companion as Simeon growled, a feral sound that should have Angel worried. He was alone in a room of dead people with an undead creature that killed in much the same way as the killer did to August—yet Angel was not afraid. Not of Simeon. He'd never been afraid of Simeon, he realized—insanely attracted, and emotionally engaged for the first time in his adult life.

"He died fast, *mo ghra*," Simeon whispered, meeting his gaze. "He had no time to suffer."

"I know," Angel whispered. "He's still dead, though."

"I have the scent of the one who killed him. I will be able to identify the killer if we meet in person, and he will die for what he has done to your friend. Have no fear that justice will not find the killer."

"Whether by your hand or my magic, I have no fear of the killer getting away with this," Angel vowed.

He was afraid, though. Fear raced through his heart and mind as he came face-to-face with his purpose here.

Angel was afraid of himself, and the inexorable way he came to the conclusion that he would be raising the dead. Where was the man who lived a quiet life, teaching because he couldn't see himself doing anything else, and who bemusedly mourned the loss of his brother while he yet lived? Where was the cranky and prickly sorcerer who looked for random hookups and never slept in the same bed with another soul? Where was the man who neatly exorcised himself from the remnants of the Blood War, refusing to live as if he were still trapped in battle every day?

All he was now, in this moment, was a man again ravaged by grief and frustration, powerful beyond his peers, and no notion of restraint or caution as he ran towards a legion of killers, be-damned the consequences.

"Fuck it."

7

FELONIOUS CONVERSATIONS

Angel pulled his bag off his shoulder, dropping it at his feet and crouching next to it. He pulled out a foot-long black-and-green malachite-gripped athame and braided black leather rope, and a small red pot, the clay soaked in ocher and sealed with red wax.

Angel moved his bag out of the way and stood, and he handed the jar to Simeon, who took it with a raised brow and no questions. Angel tossed the ropes on the body in front of him, and yanked the sheet away totally, letting it flutter to the floor.

"He hasn't been autopsied yet," Angel said, aghast. It was over the twenty-four-hour time limit placed on deceased practitioners—August should be sewn up and prepared for the crematorium by now. Fresh anger coiled in his core, and Angel let out a soft snarl that made Simeon blink at him in surprise. "I think it's obvious the police couldn't give a shit about August now that they know who he is. A Salvatore ally, no matter how far removed, gets no consideration in this town. Add this to the fact that the police never came by with the picture of the summoner's face they supposedly got from the statehouse cameras. Someone is trying really hard to set me up to die."

Angel was so mad his fingers ached where they held the stone and metal grip of his athame, the hard ridges digging into his palm and the underside of his fingers. The long, wavy watered steel blade shimmered in the pale light, its latent power responding to his emotions. He set the blade down carefully on the metal slab, making sure not to touch the corpse before closing his eyes and breathing in deep, trying to find his calm, his center. This was not combative magic, fueled by emotions—this was pure high sorcery, and while he had the strength to do this spell without the artifacts and rites, to do so he would need to open the veil, and alert any practitioner within a block to his presence. To do magic at this high level without veil-sourced power meant Angel needed the artifacts to both give him supplemental energy for the working and provide anchors for the spell. He would be providing most of the power for the resurrection, along with maintaining the fog spell. He would be useless once done.

It was a good thing Simeon came along after all. Angel grinned, somehow the thought of the vampire carting his limp and exhausted ass home after draining himself to passing out making him want to laugh. Angel opened his eyes, and held his hands out in front of him, over the body.

Angel called to his hellfire, the green flames snapping and writhing to life around his hands, up to his wrists, his gloves remaining untouched and whole. Angel kept his breathing slow and measured, and picked up the coiled leather rope, the black leather supple and smooth. The leather resisted the hellfire, treated by spells to remain intact just as his gloves were until a major working was completed and Angel let it burn. Hands aflame, Angel snaked the rope across the corpse's legs at the ankles and tied them down. He then moved the rope up, and tied down the hands and the waist of the corpse, looping the long rope under the slab and gurney, keeping the entire length intact.

There was just enough rope left to lash across the corpse's throat, though not too tight.

August would need room to speak.

Angel then picked up the athame, the blade leaping to life with hellfire of its own, matching Angel's. He held out his hand for the jar his silent and watchful companion still held, and Simeon cautiously dropped the tiny red jar into Angel's fiery palm.

"What is so potent you open it with hellfire and blade, *mo ghra*?" Simeon asked him quietly as Angel used the athame to pry the cork free from the red jar, flakes of wax evaporating in soft hisses as it melted in his hellfire.

"The venom of a thousand pit vipers, from a massive nest, found beneath an Egyptian pharaoh's tomb," Angel said casually, the cork popping free and landing on the slab. "Concentrated liquid death, kinda. It carries the essence of passage between this world and the next. I'm not sure what effect it'll have on the undead, so don't touch the cork." Simeon eyed the cork with suspicion and put his hands behind his back, his disarrayed tux giving him a dashing mien, even surrounded by death and the scent of loosening flesh.

Angel dipped the tip of the athame in the contents of the jar, a clear, viscous fluid dripping thickly from the sharp steel. The flames lit the fluid, and it burned even as it pooled and dripped back into the jar. He waited for the excess to fall away, then put the jar down, and with great care, put the cork back in place. Angel took a moment, then began.

A cut. Less than an inch, just above the groin, the burning venom lining the flesh. Angel moved the blade, feeling the energy create a line, anchored by the venom, and it pulled on his hand as he moved the athame up the body to hover over the sternum. Another cut, deep enough to separate flesh, the venom locking in, a burning line of hellfire connecting the two cuts. Angel moved the blade, now with both hands, fighting the pull of the two anchors. He dragged the blade down, slicing first one wrist, and moving slowly, his boots almost losing traction with the force pulling against him, Angel awkwardly went around the slab and gurney to cut the other wrist. Each deposit of venom, each new line of hellfire connected in a macabre constellation, Angel felt a lessening of his reserves. It was draining him and fast.

Angel was sweating, arms shaking, breathing in ragged gasps as he fought against the horrendous pull on the athame. His hellfire now snapped and hissed on the nearly complete design, and he had two cuts left. Over the head, Angel cut the space midway on the corpse's forehead, the flame darker, more static, and Angel felt his shoulders twitch, muscles ready to give out. His whole body was battling, moving the athame as if it weighed hundreds of pounds, and he knew if he made it through this, he would be beyond sore in the morning.

Simeon hovered next to him, hands up as if to help, but a short jerk of Angel's head stopped him. Angel fought and strained, the line of hellfire dripping from the athame's point, sizzling and snapping, fighting him in return. He was warping the very fabric of the natural world—the design he was cutting in place was both map and target for the spirit he was calling on the Other Side. It had to be complete, and perfect this first time, because he would not have the strength to try again, not before August's body was burned.

With a strangled cry of triumph, Angel made a tiny cut on the corpse's bottom lip, and he fell backward as all tension left the blade, the constellation of venom and fire snapping into place, reverberating through the room with a deep, almost inaudible roll of sound.

Arms numb, fingers tingling, Angel stood, sweat pouring down his temples and back. He sucked in some air, and coughed, feeling as if all the strength in his body was draining out of his pores into the cold air. In a way, it was.

"August Remington. Friend, brother, son, lover, teacher. I call to you. Find your way back to life's remains. Hear me, and obey." His words were ragged but as clear as he could make them. He gripped the athame tighter, and pointed it at the body, the constellation writhing, smokeless and yet the air was thick with sulfur. The venom made the air bitter, and Angel stepped back to the body, holding the athame's point over the ravaged flesh where beneath a quiet heart lay. "August! Hear me, and obey! Return to life's remains!"

He called to the echo, the vast emptiness he sensed within the body. He sent his words towards the place of nothing, the place all souls passed through when the body failed. The body was merely one place from which to access the nothingness beyond, but it was the surest way to recall the departed.

The soul already knew the way.

"*Angelus...*" A thin whisper, nothing more. It echoed about the room, as sharp as ice and far colder. The burning lines froze, then simmered, the flames dying down, becoming green embers that roiled and spit. The body was now more than connective tissue and flesh—it was no longer empty.

A jerky and short inhale, muscles trying to function after hours of starvation and the flaccid state of decomposition. Enough air made it through a ravaged throat into lungs left silent, and the corpse that was once a living man named August opened its eyes.

There are moments in Angel's life where he has perfect clarity, where the world is crystalline and bright, and every atom of existence can be recalled in exact form years later. And it was with a flash of deep regret that this became one of those moments. Heart heavy, Angel took a hand from the athame and cupped the bone-white cheek of the man he once called uncle and mentor.

"Hey, man. Been a while," he said softly, holding back his tears. The smile was strained, but Angel managed it. Dull, flat eyes swiveled and spun before locking on his own, the once brilliant blue reminiscent of dirty water. Where living eyes held a glimmer of emotion, these were truly dead, void of anything but a slim awareness. "Do you know who I am?"

"*Angelus Salvatore......Necromancer. My best friend's son....my student...*" August's spirit whispered past dry, cracked lips, the venom-burnt lower lip splitting with a twisted mockery of a smile. "*Angel....no, what...have you done?*"

"I've done what you once warned me not to do," Angel said, his whisper full of the tears he refused to shed. A cool hand came to rest on the middle of his back, and Angel drew some small measure of strength from Simeon's offer of comfort. "I'll risk it to avenge you, Uncle Auggie."

The old nickname slipped free before he could stop it, but it came naturally. A decade may have passed, but old emotions were still strong.

"*Avenge me?*" Split lips cracked further, hellfire embers hissing. Hollow eyes that held the tiniest of awareness glimmered like a flame in the far distance, and Angel dug deeper, pouring more power into the dark constellation that kept August's spirit in this place and time. "*Vengeance for what? Where am I?*"

"City Morgue in Boston, Auggie. I've called you back. You got murdered, my old friend. Right in front of me, I might add. Can you tell me who killed you?"

"*Vampire.*" August's spirit stirred, the distant flame sparking brighter as if experiencing remembered terror from the moments before his last living breath were coming back, revisited on this side of the veil. Angel bit his tongue, hating himself in that second. The longer he held August's spirit here the more the spirit would recall, and surely none of it was good.

"Yes, I know," Angel assured his old friend, holding August's face, imparting what comfort he could. "Do you know the bastard's name? Can you tell me what happened?"

"*Came for me at home,*" August replied, Angel leaning closer, dry lips brushing his ear. "*Took me from the street. Vampires, one old. Very old. Old World vampire, he had an accent, still strong.*"

August would know, too. He had been a canny sorcerer, observant and intuitive. If he claimed one of his attackers to be an old vampire, then he was right. The average age of most vampires in the United States was around the two hundred mark or younger, and any vampire older than that would be one of the rarer ones. The older generation of vampires escaped Europe during the Napoleonic Wars in the early 1800s, and they came to America with the intent to claim territory and raise new clans. The strongest of them were rumored to be over a thousand years old, like Boston's new Master. The older the vampire, the more known they were, each year on this earth spreading their influence through fledglings and the human species' capacity for propagating urban legends down generations.

"Why? Do you know who they were?"

"Yes....."

"Who was it, August? Was it the new Master of Boston?" It only made sense for Angel to ask, though if August had lived in Hartford for the last ten years he may not know who the new Master was here in town. Even Angel had only seen him once, and never in person, a distant glimpse at vamp HQ when he had gone to cure the newest crop of fledglings sick from magic poisoning.

A door creaked down the hall, taking Angel's attention from his questioning, head turning to the door. Simeon moved so fast he was impossible to see, the door to the room they were in swaying shut as the Elder went out into the hall. Trusting Simeon to handle whoever may be coming, Angel looked back to August, the hand holding the athame over August's heart shaking once with strain. He needed to hurry.

"Who killed you, August?"

"*Deimos*," August answered, the flickering flame in his dull eyes sporadically flaring before dimming. Angel wavered on his feet, beginning to feel the effects of severe power drain. "*His name was Deimos.*"

Angel had no idea who that was, but he could find out.

The door slammed open, Simeon appearing in a violent rush of fog, a man wearing a security guard uniform hanging limply from one hand. Simeon dropped him to the floor, where the man gave a disheartened groan and passed out, obviously in no fit state to do his job. Angel quirked a brow at the Elder vamp, but Simeon was staring at the revenant, his face stricken.

"Simeon? What—"

"We are out of time, *mo ghra*," Simeon said, breaking free of whatever state he'd been in and coming to Angel's side. "The fog was noticed. The receptionist will be raising the alarm once he realizes the guard won't be back."

"Fuck, the coroner will be back here next." The coroner was a wizard and was capable of giving Angel more than enough trouble, not to mention he would be able to ID him to authorities. Angel's face was well known here.

"*Angel...*"

"Hey, Auggie," his lack of time and choices careened around in his head and heart, and the tears came even as he moved the athame closer to the corpse's chest. It was time to say goodbye.

The revenant's eyes blazed, August's spirit clawing its way closer, more of the man he once was present in his lifeless eyes. "*Forgive me for abandoning you. My guilt was too much. After Raine.... he was my everything. Seeing you was like seeing him.*"

The love between August Remington and Raine Salvatore had always been part of Angel's life. He grew up in their shadow, the two men inseparable, even after Raine married and had kids. Angel closely resembled his father and seeing him every day must have been too much for August to bear. Getting away from the surviving Salvatore boys was probably the only way August could function. Angel couldn't completely understand it, but he could forgive it.

"It's okay, Auggie. I get it. I'm not mad at you, I never was," Angel whispered, pressing the athame's tip to the corpse's chest, separating flesh. "I swear I'll avenge you."

"*He wants you dead because of that night, Angel. He fears you,*" the revenant whispered, the spirit retreating, the dark constellation dying down to ash. Angel let his hellfire die with it. He had seconds left. "*Deimos fears your power. Deimos wanted to know what I taught you, how you killed so many vampires at once that night. I refused to tell him how you did it, even when threatened with my death. I left him no choice but to kill me.*"

"His mistake," Angel replied with a harsh whisper, thrusting blade through bone and muscle into the heart below. "Rest, August. I'll see you again one day."

The blade sliced through the heart, thrust to the hilt, and the dark constellation went out with a soft sigh and flicker of smoke. The lifeless eyes were empty, the spirit returned to its proper place, the body once again a collection of dead flesh and bone.

Angel yanked the athame free, falling back against the wall of lockers, gasping for air. The drain on his reserves was cut, and his power rebounded back into him, and Angel battled for control. Fog writhed and twisted, and Angel heard voices yelling near the front of the building.

"Angel?" Simeon said his name, and he could hear a touch of worry under the accent. Angel pushed off from the wall and grabbed the black leather rope, his hellfire surging along its length. Angel broke the fire resistant spells in the woven thongs, and the leather burst into flame, falling to gray ashes in seconds. He needed to erase their presence and fast. At least enough that identifying who had been in here would be impossible. The venom and the dark constellation's remains might be traceable back to Angel, considering the rarity of the spell and ingredients. He had erroneously assumed that August would be autopsied by now, and ready to be sent to the crematorium, and any evidence of his tampering would remain undiscovered and burnt with the body.

"Simeon, grab the body!"

Angel fed power to the fog, creating a white wall in the hallway that obscured all sight. He carefully repacked his bag, making sure the jars and athame were secure before yanking open a line to the veil. They were already discovered—now he had one last task to complete and no time for subtlety.

He knew the second the coroner sensed his presence, as the alarms in the morgue went off, red lights flickering.

Thankful Simeon did as he asked, and the vampire hefted the corpse over his shoulder in a fireman's carry without any hint of squeamishness. Angel led the way to the hall, trusting in luck they wouldn't run into anyone standing in the mist. Voices, muffled by the fog, rose behind them as they jogged for the garage bay. It took them longer than he liked, but they made the parking lot. Sirens wailed in the distance, evidence someone called the police.

He had to get at least a block, even two, away before his presence would be undetectable to the coroner.

Angel ran, Simeon at his side, pulling a thick wall of fog around them as they regained the streets adjacent to the morgue, the sound of their passage swallowed by the mist. Angel led Simeon down side streets for almost twenty minutes, needing to look up at a corner to see the street signs to know for certain where they were. They were most certainly out of range, and he opened the veil further, channeling more power into his core and making it his own. Rarely did he open himself so fully to the wild energy past the veil, but he needed to be at his best right now—getting caught so soon hadn't been ideal, and he had no time to crash after that major spellcasting.

Angel sighed in relief. They weren't that far from Beacon Hill and the Commons. Another ten minutes, the city around them empty of all signs of life, human or otherwise. Trees rose from the fog, and Angel ran faster, Simeon and his cargo silent at his side. Even in the dark of night and the wall of fog that cushioned them, Angel recognized the Commons, and they ran into the park.

"Central Burying Grounds, hurry," Angel gasped out, deciding he would need to get back into swimming, his lungs burning from their rapid escape. Simeon, of course, showed zero signs of strain, even with the burden he carried. They took the winding paths towards the old cemetery, the dormant trees popping up out of the fog like specters.

All practitioners were to be burned, ostensibly to keep the body safe from desecration by other magic-users attempting to steal latent powers from the deceased, but it was also tradition, long-standing and ancient, dating back to the days when men cast spells with the bones of mammoths and wore cloaks made of dire wolf pelts. Casting the ashes on holy ground was another layer of protection preventing abuse of a deceased's remains.

It was what Angel did with his family.

Not soon enough for Angel, they made the cemetery, the short iron fence no match as Angel gripped the top and jumped over, his bag banging on his hip. Simeon was over before Angel even landed in the dead grass, and Angel pointed to a spot nearby, a few feet from the slim headstones. Simeon carefully put the body down in the wet, dead grass, and Angel took the Elder's arm and pulled him away.

One last thing to do.

Angel turned his mind inward, and raw, wild and unfettered, veil power surged up from his core, and he let it free, giving it one focus, one command. Death magic in its truest form, the consumption of life and matter, thought and desire—the mourning pyre was how all of Angel's kind used to depart this world, and never more true than for a necromancer. It was a bittersweet and heavy irony that Angel would be the one to light the pyre for his mentor, the man who taught him the spell in the first place. It was no longer common practice for the spell to be taught, with the onset of laws and government facilities taking over the disposal of human remains.

"Ignis luctus pyra," Angel cast, and with a sub-audible *woomfph*, the body burst into flame. Grass burned to a crisp in a short radius around the body, flames rising several feet in the air. It was an ancient spell, and once given a target, the mourning fire consumed it entirely until nothing remained but ashes, feeding on the death magic.

8
MAKING ALIBIS

"Angel?"

"Hmm?" Angel stared at the makeshift pyre, mind lost to memory and flame. The grass was wet beneath his ass, his pants soaked in a few places, but he'd been too close to his limit and sitting down and catching his breath, not to mention settling his careening emotions, had been the wisest thing he'd decided in ages.

"Why did I steal his body?" Simeon sat beside him, cross-legged and looking more than rumpled. His tux was stained, from the body and the grass and their swift escape from the morgue. The vampire was still visually arresting and beyond appealing, his hair falling in a dashing manner over his brow, his green eyes catching the light from the failing fire, glittering like tiny shards of glass.

"August deserved a proper send-off," Angel muttered, eyes locked on the lowering flames. The fire, veil-fed, had quickly consumed August's remains, and all traces of Angel's casting gone with him. All that was left was a few stubborn pieces of blackened bone, but the mourning fire was steadily eating away at it. "And he wasn't going to get it from the authorities. Least I could do for the man who taught me most of what I know. And I figured we'd already broken a dozen laws resurrecting him, so what was a little body theft added on top?"

Simeon huffed a laugh as if surprised Angel could find any humor in their situation, and Angel could see Simeon smiling at him out of the corner of his eye. "Every day I see some new layer to you, *a ghra*, and I find myself drawn in deeper each time."

Simeon came closer until they sat hip to hip. Angel sighed, weary. While he was not tired in a magical sense, his connection to the veil still buzzing in the back of his mind and keeping him topped off, he was tired emotionally and mentally. His quiet life, while not exciting or full of affirming moments, had been all he knew for the last ten years. Now a vampire he'd never met before, and never heard of, was coming for him. His quiet and boring life was unraveling, revealing a new pattern in the thread that he wasn't too pleased with—but there was no changing it.

He was raised during the pinnacle of the Blood Wars—he was incapable of backing down from a mortal threat. Old, old habits were battling with his desire to keep his life quiet and uncomplicated.

Angel dropped his head, resting it on Simeon's shoulder. The Elder froze for a moment as if afraid Angel would change his mind and pull away, but the longer Angel stayed there, the more the vampire relaxed. Angel's body heat seeped into Simeon, the vampire warming, sharing the heat between them.

The bones grayed to ash and crumpled apart, and the meager light cast off by the dying flames fell to darkness. Death magic consumed, the mourning pyre went out. Human bodies, even sorcerers', had little in the way of death magic in their remains, and the mourning fire always went out when the body was consumed, keeping collateral damage to a minimum.

Unlike the undead. Angel cut off that dangerous thought before it could throw memories back in his face.

Overhead the moon and stars were obscured by gathering clouds and the growing fog, this time of nature's making. Darkness in the Commons was extreme, even amidst the scattered iron lamps and the reflected glares from the high rises.

"Who is Deimos, Simeon?" Angel asked after long minutes of quiet contemplation. The vampire's face when the revenant spoke the name was bothering him, and Angel could tell Simeon knew something.

Simeon was silent, and Angel could almost feel him thinking about whether or not to tell him anything. After a few minutes, Angel still leaning against the vampire, waiting patiently, Simeon spoke.

"My Master heard about what happened here when we moved the Bloodclan to Boston. About you and your family, I mean. Not many details to go on with the vampires slain, since supposedly none survived, but rumors abound. One rumor is that the clan destroyed was betrayed by one of the clan's legates—you know this term?" Simeon asked, interrupting himself.

"I do—it's the third rank in a Bloodclan hierarchy. Master, elder, legate, unranked masters and then the clan soldiers, and then the average bloodsucker."

"The only name we heard aside from the families directly involved in the feud was Deimos—who betrayed his clan in exchange for wealth and magical powers gifted by the Macavoys. My master sent inquiries to Blackguard Prison where the members of the Macavoy clan guilty of the attack on your family are serving out their sentences. The one name they got back was Deimos, and that he had been a legate in a smaller Providence Bloodclan. He disappeared just before the attack on your family. The assumption was that the Macavoys or one of the other families killed him to prevent him from disclosing details of the attack before it could be enacted. No one knows if anyone else survived, and that name was the only one we got."

Angel absorbed that bit of news, his body tensing for a moment before he consciously relaxed.

"Forgive me, *a ghra*, for not telling you," Simeon whispered, head down, face in shadow. "I did not wish to pain you more in regards to your past. All we had was a name, nothing more."

Angel stared ahead into the darkness, eyes unseeing, thinking. He should probably be mad. Angry that Simeon never told him any of this, but then common sense kicked in. Why get mad when he made it so no one was willing to discuss with him the events surrounding his family and their murders? Not that he would react that badly, but he never volunteered to speak of it, and never encouraged people to speak to him if they did broach the subject. He shut down, emotionally and behaviorally, and really, what would he have done if Simeon told him? Angel never went after the Macavoys after what they did, nor any of the other families. Knowing the name of a presumed dead traitor would have done nothing to change the fact his family was dead. And this traitor hadn't betrayed the Salvatore's, but his own kind and Bloodclan and any retribution that was owed him would come from the vampires, not Angel.

Simeon was quiet as if waiting for Angel to blow up at him. Angel turned his head a bit and looked up at Simeon. "I'm not mad you didn't tell me. What would I have done with the knowledge? Not a thing, not then. But now I do know, and he is alive, this traitor, and coming for me for some reason. But why now, why me, and why is he afraid of me? August said it was for what I did that night. Deimos wants to know what spell I used to destroy the army of undead. Everyone with half a brain and no manners has wanted to know for the last decade."

"It makes sense for Deimos to want to know how you managed it that night. Such a spell would give the wielder great power. I suspect that is in part why no one has come after you. Fear of what you can do has kept enemies from your door." Simeon stated proudly, and Angel smiled, surprising himself. "Even my master is most curious, *a ghra*, though I have ignored his polite requests for me to ask you. He understands loss, and grief, and was merely curious. Since they were requests, I did not need to press for answers."

"You're a big softie, aren't you?" Angel asked, chuckling. "I wondered why no one from the clan was asking me about it. I figured the Master either didn't want me to demonstrate it, or wanted to be on my good side in case I felt the urge to do it again. You were protecting me all along, weren't you?"

"Yes, Angel, of course, I was," Simeon said, simple and direct as if there was no other option. "I will always protect you."

"I believe you," Angel said, and he reached up with a gloved hand, fingers carding through thick auburn hair and tugging Simeon's head down. Their lips met, cold and wet, but the kiss quickly warmed. Angel kissed Simeon, doing his best to communicate how he was feeling—he was anything but mad.

Need, want, desire—it was all one welling emotion, one instinct that kept telling him to take what Simeon was offering him. Love, affection, care. Not once in two years had Simeon been anything but gentle with him—even when he was maintaining a polite distance, Simeon was looking out for him.

Tongues touched briefly before Angel pulled back, and Simeon let him. He wanted to crawl back into Simeon's lap and stay there, sheltered from the world. He couldn't, but the desire to do so was strong. "Why now? Why this, right now, and not then?"

"You mean Deimos?" Simeon whispered back, licking his lips, hands cradling Angel's face.

"No—why us, this between us. Why now, and not the last two years? I know you wanted me when we first met. Hell, you had to notice I wanted you, too."

"Ahhh, yes. I was wondering when you would ask me," Simeon said, arms going around Angel to pull him up and over his legs. Angel sighed, but let Simeon hold him in his lap. The vamp had to be able to read minds, or maybe he just knew Angel well enough by now that Simeon could understand what he wanted.

"So?"

"You came that other night, for Greg Doyle. You came in the middle of the night, nearly naked and exhausted, ready to commit murder you were so mad, but you came anyway. For him and the love your brother has for him, yes, but also for us. It was at my behest you came that night, and you were there instantly. The last two years, at my urging, my master has let you come and go freely from our headquarters, tending to our foolish young and helping them. You never asked for anything in return, even when my master offered to pay you for your skill and time. You came because they were sick, and needed help. You saved Mr. Doyle and exhausted yourself for us. Then you leaned on me and trusted me to keep you safe. I knew then that whatever hesitancy you had towards me, be it my nature or me personally, had worn down enough for me to show you how I truly felt without you withdrawing further."

Angel blinked up at Simeon, whose features were hidden in the dark, eyes catching the slim light that filtered through clouds and mist to where they sat.

"I have lived four hundred years, my love. Two years to earn your trust was a price I was more than willing to pay."

Angel grinned, and his cheeks grew warm. "Oh."

Simeon laughed. It was a smooth rumble of delight that slid through Angel's body and settled in his bones. Angel chuckled with him, and he put his arms around Simeon's neck and hugged him. Simeon hugged him back, and they held each other in the darkness.

"Are we going to need an alibi for tonight?" Simeon asked after a long silence.

"Oh hell yeah, we are. Me at least, for sure. They won't know you were there unless that guard can ID you?"

"No, he did not see my face. He may have heard you use my name, but it's doubtful. He most likely has a severe concussion."

"Any ideas then? I was just going to head home and bluff my way through this, but I don't think BPD will buy it. I wasn't planning on adding body theft to my list of felonies tonight. I erroneously assumed that August would have been prepped for cremation already or at least autopsied, and no one would notice my spell-work. Stealing August's remains will lead them right back to my doorstep. I was the one to ID him."

"I have an idea then, my love," Simeon said, kissing Angel on the lips, a hint of fang making him shiver. "We need an alibi, and I can provide one. Shall we go?"

"What?" Angel asked, suspicious. His place would be safer, considering his wards and the sunlight runes on the windows, but the cops would probably come armed with a warrant and break down his door. Depending who they had on their practitioner payroll they may or may not be able to get through his wards. He would know if the wards fell, but he didn't want to be there if the cops showed up. They wouldn't find anything in his place that could be used in a resurrection, but that didn't mean the cops wouldn't look everywhere, destroying his things and making a fucking mess.

"Where's your courage?" Simeon asked with a grin that Angel could feel against his lips, and he growled in reply. Simeon held Angel tight about the waist, and stood up, smooth and sexy and without a stagger. Angel gave a short laugh, appreciating the solid strength in the Elder's frame. He never enjoyed being manhandled, but with Simeon, it wasn't annoying as it could be. In fact, it wasn't annoying at all, not that he would ever say so. He gave Simeon a sneer, fighting back a smile, and winked. Simeon saw it and growled, teeth clenched, fangs glinting in the low light.

"Fine, let's go. I'll show you courage."

"You have already, my love."

THE WALK to the edge of the park was done in silence, Angel's hand in Simeon's. The Elder made a call, and they waited in the shadow of a bare-limbed oak for ten minutes until a sleek black limousine pulled up to the curb. The street was empty, dark, and the rain forecasted finally began to fall in heavy sheets as Angel got in the back, Simeon sliding in behind him and shutting the door.

The muffled sound of the rain falling on the roof of the limo and the sluicing of tires through puddles lulled Angel into a detached calm. Simeon went back to holding his hand, and Angel, in one part of his mind, was amused by how rapidly the vampire's hand warmed in his own. It was as if the vampire was aluminum, absorbing heat rapidly, then losing it just as fast once removed from the source of heat.

"Why were you in the tux, again?" Angel asked, eyeing the rumpled and stained ensemble Simeon still wore. He would have given Simeon something clean to wear before they left his place, but Simeon was a foot taller than he was and outweighed him by a lot, and none of his clothes would have fit the Elder.

"There was a welcome dinner for a visiting dignitary from the Atlanta Bloodclan. An older master, without rank but many fledglings and substantial wealth, wishes to join our clan. The other night was merely an informal function, where the foreign master presented his tithes and his request to join our clan. There will be a gala tomorrow night when my master either accepts or declines his request to join." Simeon looked down at Angel and shook his head as Angel opened his mouth to question him. "That was my thought as well—the vampire Deimos is, according to your departed comrade, an older vampire—what are the odds two old vampires come into Boston in the same week? Yet William Bridgerton is known to my Master, and has been a member of Atlanta's bloodclan for the last 100 years."

"Shit," Angel cursed. "That would have been too easy." Though that really didn't discount Bridgerton from being Deimos—the older the vamp, the more names they had. He kicked back and slouched on the butter-smooth leather seat, and his head found Simeon's shoulder on its own, and he thought about it. "Maybe one of his fledglings? Or entourage? Old masters travel with those, yeah?"

"Yes, Bridgerton has an honor guard and blood donors, along with his eldest fledglings. One of them may be the one we seek. I can discreetly inquire." Simeon was quiet for a moment, then seemed to make a decision to continue, his tone cautious. "They are all staying at Bloodclan Headquarters, my love. They will also be present at the gala. I was going to invite you if you took to my courtship favorably. Do you wish to go somewhere else, in case the one hunting you is there?"

"I grew up in the middle of a war," Angel scoffed, chuckling. "I've never run from a fight or a vampire. A party, though. I hate parties, but I'll not run. I'm not about to do it now. Bring it on, and if Deimos is there, then I'll offer my apologies to your Master after I've made a mess."

Angel must have dozed off, as he came to when the limo entered the underground parking garage used by the vampires who lived in the Tower. Simeon lifted his arm from Angel's shoulders, and Angel hid a smile. *What a difference a few days and a life-threatening situation make...*

It was Angel's first time in the Tower, as the high-rise attached to Vamp HQ was nicknamed. The elevator from the underground garage had its own guards, in the car and outside the doors at each floor. Angel recognized the guards as vampires right away, which was logical since it was still night, and the daytime guards were probably human. Dressed in nondescript black suits and earbuds, and an intimidating bulge under their arms from weapons, they made an impressive sight. Angel was watching the guard in the elevator from the corner of his eye, and saw the vamp tense when he got a good look at who exactly his Elder was with. Most vamps in Simeon's bloodclan now knew Angel on sight after the last two years. Simeon put a hand on Angel's shoulder possessively in a clear sign for the guard, and the vamp relaxed with an abrupt nod, moving away from the floor panel.

Simeon keyed his floor in by pressing his free hand flat on a sensor pad, and that lit up the numbered floor buttons on the panel, and Simeon then hit the button for the 9th floor. Not the penthouse, but the next level down. The penthouse was for the Master then, and as Simeon was an Elder, it made sense his room would be on the floor below.

Or suite, as it turned out.

Angel lost his brows in his hairline when Simeon escorted him into the foyer of an impressive suite, marble walls with gray veins snaking through them and brass lines cut through shiny black tiles gave a cool yet oddly welcoming impression, and the walls were covered in oil paintings, many of which Angel could guesstimate to be worth an absurd amount of money.

The foyer opened up into a wide living space, the rug a deep red, the furniture a soft buttercream that balanced out the dark hue of the carpet. A spacious seating area was strewn with chaise lounges and low, wide couches, and deep recliners big enough to hold more than one person. It was obvious that space was meant for entertaining, and from the faint depressions on the cushions, it was occupied often. Simeon was an Elder and over four centuries old; he probably had fledglings of his own, and numerous blood donors, unless he drank from bagged blood units, but somehow Angel had trouble seeing Simeon doing that.

Angel gave Simeon a weak smile, realizing that while the Elder knew almost everything about him, he knew so little about Simeon. The disparity was jarring and made him feel selfish. He banished it as best he could—if had a feeling where the night was heading, and feeling guilty was not the best way to make a decision.

"Pardon me, *a ghra*, I must change. The bar is there along the wall, please help yourself. I will be back shortly," Simeon murmured with a short bow of his shoulders, before slinking out of the room.

Angel followed Simeon deeper into the living space, before stopping next to a long, low couch. He examined it suspiciously before sitting, and was surprised by how comfortable it was. Considering the overt wealth of his surroundings, he could well imagine all the seating was much the same. He would bet the beds were even more luxurious.

Just thinking about the bed somewhere in the suite sent his eyes searching for Simeon. The Elder had vanished into the depths of the rooms, and Angel closed his hands, fists tight, his thighs tensing. He was alone with Simeon, in the Elder's space, in the depths of vamp HQ. He may be safe from being bitten, but not against physical violence or human blood slaves. He was trusting Simeon now more than he had ever done before. If he was forced to defend himself, Angel had doubts he would be able to get out without casualties and collateral damage. Simeon was an Elder, but that meant nothing if the Master, whom Angel had never dealt with directly, objected to a necromancer's presence in his domain. Simeon was honor bound to obey the Master; if Simeon was ordered to act against Angel in any way, Angel worried which side the Elder might choose. Simeon could speak of love, and call him all the endearments he wished, but Angel was too wary to not, at least, think about the worst outcomes of his sleepover.

The other part of him, the quiet and reserved man who spent his nights alone and his heart guarded behind precision sarcasm and snark, kept finding his focus sliding from exit strategies to a mental image of himself naked on satin sheets, fingers clawing at Simeon's pale shoulders as the vampire drove into his body over and over, pinning him to the mattress with his cock and hands.

Ages since he last got off without involving his right hand, Angel cursed under his breath when his cock hardened, painfully pushing up against his zipper, and his heart began to beat with an eager tempo. Mentally castigating himself for winging his plans and ending up in a position where he would be forced to make a decision—whether a relationship with another man, let alone a powerful vampire, was something he could do. He didn't do relationships—they were outside his experience. Simeon's regard—if sincere, and he had no reason to doubt it wasn't—left him with the very clear impression that the vampire cared for him deeply, maybe even to the point of love—surely that meant a relationship, something more permanent than the meager exchange of first names and a decision on who was bottoming for the night.

Angel needed to decide if that was something he could give Simeon—if he could give himself to such a depth. His body was an easy answer—but giving his heart to another left him as terrified as it did needy. A keen sense of want ran through his chest, making his eyes sting. He wanted, despite his best efforts, to lean his head, heart and troubles on the broad and strong shoulders of the Elder vampire, and just let himself simply exist.

A fine layer of sweat gathered on his brow, and his pulse danced merrily as his thoughts went increasingly haywire with lust. His fingertips were buzzing, and Angel breathed in slow and even, eyes locked on the floor, trying to control himself. Making a decision in his current state was such a bad idea.

"I hear your heart racing, Angel. Such a furious pace and your scent set my nerves aflame." Simeon spoke quietly from nearby. "Will you look at me, my love?"

Angel looked up at Simeon and nearly swallowed his tongue.

The Elder wore a simple black tee that hugged every ridge and bulge of carved muscle, and the pajama pants he wore were dark gray and silky, clinging to his lean hips and powerful thighs, perfectly outlining the bulge at his groin. Barefoot and sexy, the vampire padded across the thick carpet, coming to stand just out of reach of where Angel sat.

"I..." Angel lost whatever words he was going to speak, his tongue refusing to cooperate. His body knew what it wanted. His heart did, too. It was his mind that left him struggling.

"Yes?" Simeon asked softly, hands resting at his sides, green eyes bright, a patient smile on his lips.

"Did you mean it? What you said, about your heart being mine? Did you mean it, Simeon?" Angel asked, and winced. Tears came, stinging his eyes, yet he clung to what control he had left, despite his tongue blurting out the question his heart wanted to hear the answer to.

"Angelus Salvatore, I lost my heart to you the moment you threatened my life. So brave, so capable and enticing." Simeon replied, a smile lifting a corner of his mouth, a shiny fang glinting. "I meant what I said earlier, as well. I have lived a very long time, and two years were nothing to wait when the prize was your heart in return."

Angel pressed a hand to his mouth, breathing hard through his nose. His own heart was screaming at him to get up, to take what was offered and never let go.

"What holds you back, my love? You're so torn, it pains me. Tell me what holds you back when you so clearly want the same as I do. Is it because I'm a vampire?"

"YES!" Angel shouted, face burning, hands coming away from his mouth as if searching for something to hold. Simeon took a step back, shocked by his outburst.

"Do you hate my kind so much? For what was done to your family?" Simeon whispered, handsome visage torn by pain and regret.

Simeon's pain spurred his own, and Angel couldn't stop himself from speaking.

"No! No, Simeon." Angel stood, at last, hand outstretched to Simeon, hoping the Elder would take it. "I don't hate your kind. Those that came for us that night were all enslaved, their wills stripped. Vampires were not my enemies then, and your people are not mine now."

"Then... Explain, please, my love." Simeon took the hand Angel held out, his cool, strong fingers squeezing hard, giving him something to focus on.

"It is a matter of hate, but not mine for your kind.... How can you not hate... me? Why don't you hate me for what I did?" Finally voicing his innermost regret ripped a hole in his control, and his other hand came up, seeking comfort. The vampire pulled him forward, and Angel found himself in a powerful, all-encompassing embrace, shielding him from the world.

"Hate you? How could I hate you?" Simeon asked urgently, lips brushing the top of Angel's ear. Simeon hugged him, and Angel snaked his arms around Simeon's torso, letting himself cling.

"A combined forty-six humans died that night, between mundane humans and my family. I killed over a hundred vampires before the sun came up the next morning," Angel gasped out, burying his face in Simeon's shoulder. His voice was muffled, but he had no doubt Simeon could hear him. "Sentient, feeling, soul-bearing lives were ended by magic and flame, and I was the instrument of their final deaths. Twice as many vampires died that night, and none of them were there of their own free will. Vampires across the whole city, hell, all of New England hate and fear me for what I did that night. I scare them, Simeon. I see fear in their eyes when they look at me and hate. So much hate. I'm already persona non grata because I'm a necromancer, but my name is at the top of the Most Hated List. Your clan isn't as bad as it used to be, but I can still feel the fear and hate, even when I'm helping them. How can you not hate me, too?

I was raised in battle, in war, and I know in my mind that I had no choice, but I still did it. I killed over a hundred vampires, and did it with anger and vengeance in my heart."

"Angel," Simeon voiced quietly, so intensely his name was a rumble that shook his eardrums, "You did what you must, to survive. Don't carry their deaths on your conscience. Those sent after you and yours were dying regardless, poisoned by the magic used to bind their wills. The second death you gave them all was self-defense and mercy in one. Anyone with a clear mind and an unbiased heart would see and feel the same as I. It is a miracle that you and your brother lived. Never regret that, my love. I don't because you are here with me now because of it."

"This town wants me either dead or gone, probably both, and those that don't want me dead want to know my secrets for their own gain." He was stumbling now, mentally trying to rebuild his defenses, but it was a lost cause and Simeon knew it too.

"You have many enemies here in Boston, yes. That is true, I will not argue that with you. What I can do is tell you the truth. My truth. What I feel for you is so far from hate I cannot fathom you and that emotion in the same thought. My Master does not hate you, nor does he fear you. You, my love, are under his protection as much as mine, and he knows how I feel about you. You have nothing to fear from the vampires of this bloodclan, I swear it to you."

Angel turned his head and whispered against Simeon's neck. "And if your master changed his mind, and ordered you to kill me, or take me prisoner? To force from me the secret of my victory that long ago night?"

Simeon was quiet, and motionless as a marble statue, cool and hard. Not even a heartbeat breaking his immobile state. Angel strained, but eventually heard his vampire's quiet reply.

"Then I would defy my Master, and safeguard your life and freedom, even unto my own death."

Angel looked up and met Simeon's gaze. A hand's breadth apart, Angel searched clear emerald depths and found no deceit.

Every wall came down, toppled by that vow. He felt free, agonized and alive. Every breath hurt, and he ached, bone-deep, wanting nothing more than to have his arms around Simeon and never let go.

"Do you love me?" Angel whispered, no longer afraid to hear Simeon's answer.

"Yes, Angel. Yes, I love you."

"Kiss me then," Angel lifted up on his toes, angling his chin, lips a breath away from Simeon's. "Kiss me, and take me to bed. Please."

THE TRIP down the hall passed in a blur. Mouths fused together, Angel clung to Simeon as the vampire carried him to a bedroom. Angel landed on his back on a soft bed, the bedclothes cool and fresh-scented, spicy like cloves and chocolate, a hint of mint making him salivate and claw at Simeon's shirt, sliding his hands down to tug up the lower hem, needing fingers on skin.

Simeon rose over him, a knee opening Angel's thighs so the vampire could lower himself down, groin to groin, hard satin heat to cool stone length. Angel tore his mouth away and gasped for air, head back, hands tearing at Simeon's shirt and yanking it away, leaving Simeon's dark auburn hair in disarray and a smile on his pink lips. Lips that sipped from his neck, tongue laving in a smooth glide down to suck on his collarbone. Hands slid up his sides under his arms, pushing them up and over his head, his wrists caught in an iron grip.

A low whine escaped his throat, eyes blind with lust, Angel arched up into Simeon's touch when the Elder held his wrists with one hand and sent the other to work undoing his clothing. "Touch me, please."

He didn't realize he was speaking until Simeon chuckled and dropped a brief but firm kiss on his lips, stalling his whispered begging. His weather-proof sweater went first, then his shirt, and somehow Angel found his hands stayed put above his head when Simeon let go and knelt up on the bed, yanking off his boots and jeans. Angel gave a long exhale of relief when his boxer-briefs were peeled down his legs, Simeon manhandling him until he was naked and laying on his stomach. Hands still over his head, Angel gave a groan of approval when Simeon stripped as well, and lowered his naked form back down on top of him, pushing him into the mattress. A jarring shock of cold, hard flesh settled in his ass crack, then quickly warmed. Angel lifted his hips, trying to encourage the vampire to put his rock-hard cock to excellent use in his ass.

"You feel so good, Angel," Simeon said between wet kisses to his back and shoulders, teeth nipping his skin in stinging bites without drawing blood. Angel twisted and tried to spread his legs, needing to feel Simeon inside of his body, holding him down. The vampire was gradually warming, reflecting back body heat, making him feel like he was on fire. He writhed on the satin-smooth blanket beneath him, his cock leaving damp spots on the fabric, the shaft pulsing in time with his frantic heart.

"Simeon! Fuck me, now!" Angel surged up from beneath Simeon when the vampire clamped his jaws around the top of his shoulder, sucking up a deep mark. The danger of Simeon slipping up and actually breaking the skin merely sent his nerves aflame, the threat to them both serious and real, but it did little to calm his desire. He burned.

Simeon seemed as aroused as he, the man above him rocking his hips in time with Angel's panting breath, long cock sliding in sweat, rubbing over his hole, making him clench furiously.

Simeon's torture continued, his lover leaving stinging marks behind over his neck, to his other shoulder. His arms ached from being held above his head, and yet being held down and touched never felt so fucking good. Simeon was barely allowing him enough room to breathe, let alone trying to reciprocate. Usually, he hated having no control, but Simeon knew, *he just knew*, that he needed to have control stripped from him, his body adored and bruised in the most delicious of ways. Letting Simeon take over was as easy as breathing, and it amped him up even more that Simeon knew what he needed.

Angel turned his head, and Simeon kissed him, tongues dancing around each other, lips clinging. Angel ended the kiss by biting Simeon's lower lip, tugging on the soft flesh and growling, "Fuck me now, snack on me later!"

Simeon chuckled, a dark sound that made Angel's abdomen clench and his ass ache with need. Simeon let go of his wrists, powerful hands sliding down his back to his hips. Angel was lifted to his knees, ass in the air, knees knocked wide and fingers clawing at the blankets. He panted, biting at the soft fabric beneath him when a pop from a tube opening and a cool, wet finger on his hole signaled Simeon's intent. "Yes, please, yes."

"Shh, easy, you'll get what you want, I promise *a ghra*," Simeon whispered, thick finger piercing Angel's ass without hesitation, expertly twisting and landing right on his prostate. More lube dribbled down his crack, and Angel pushed back on the fingers working him open. Simeon had a hand on his lower back, holding him in place, taming his body's urge to buck up under the intrusion, seeking more.

Longer than he liked and sooner than he wanted, Simeon withdrew his fingers, and Angel looked over his shoulder to see the vampire slicking his cock, the deep pink of the fat head peeking out of the foreskin, shiny thick pearls of fluid dripping from the slit. Simeon wiped his hands on the bedspread, and grabbed Angel's hips, pulling him back as the broad head of his cock kissed Angel's hole. Angel tried to impale himself, but Simeon's unyielding grip held him immobile.

The glide in was torture. Slow, relentless, Simeon's cock filled him, going deeper, opening him wider than any lover before. Angel's eyes closed, and he fell forward on the bed, moaning as Simeon seated himself to the hilt, heavy balls snug against Angel's ass. The shaft in his ass made him ache, cool and foreign until his own body heat warmed the rock-hard flesh, making him squirm. It hurt, but in the best way possible, making him whine and twist on the bed as Simeon began to withdraw, giving him no time to adjust before Simeon surged back in with a snap of his hips.

"Fuck me!" Angel gritted out, teeth snapping on the bedclothes, fingers raking the blankets.

A feral snarl was his answer, and the bruising grip on his hips and the punishing rhythm surging against his ass took his mind apart at the seams. Body singing, nerves dancing, fire snapping behind his closed eyes, Angel submitted to his lover's fierce need, letting it drive him higher and higher. He barely noticed Simeon lifting him off the bed, pulling him so his back was plastered to Simeon's front, the vampire fucking up into him with short, powerful thrusts. His prostate sizzled and precum dripped from his untouched cock, balls tight, his breathing ragged and his heart ready to explode from sensory overload, Angel fell over the edge.

He screamed, head falling back to land on Simeon's shoulder, his eyes now truly blind as he climaxed hard. Spine bowed, legs shaking, Angel spurted across the bed, thick ropes of cum that fell with loud splats in time with his whimpers and gasps. Simeon shuddered underneath him, roaring as he slammed up into Angel, flooding him with heavy, wet pulses that seemed to fill every inner crevice.

Angel panted heavy, fast breaths that left him dizzy. Simeon cradled him close, gently lifting him off his still hard cock and laying him down in a tangle of limp limbs.

Angel dozed, occasionally jerking as his cock and balls twitched, aftershocks from his stellar orgasm echoing along his nervous system. He jumped when a cool, wet cloth skimmed along his ass and tender hole, cleaning him. His tried opening his eyes but only succeeded in cracking them a sliver, watching as Simeon walked naked around the room, picking up their clothes and moving out of his line of sight. Simeon came back after a moment, speaking on a phone in a low murmur Angel was too well-fucked to hear properly. Simeon hung up and came back to the bed. Cool arms slid under him, and Angel was quickly deposited under the covers, the dirtied top blanket pulled away and disappearing too.

Simeon crawled into bed beside him, arms pulling him close, cool lips pressing a kiss to his forehead. He snuggled, and sighed happily, utterly spent and exhausted. Angel had the mental presence left to make sure his connection to the veil was secure and thin, power seeping into him in a steady trickle before letting sleep take him under.

Angel woke with a start, sitting up so fast he made himself dizzy. Rubbing his eyes, Angel took in the room, a crystal chandelier hanging from the ceiling, set on low, providing more light than the heavily treated gray-hued windows. It was daytime, as best he could tell, since he could see outside, the view of downtown impressive, the partial view of the harbor clear. The treated windows made the room feel shadowed and gloomy.

He was alone, Simeon nowhere to be seen, the divot in the pillow next to his still deep, so the Elder was there until recently. He went back to admiring the view, or trying to.

Angel frowned, thinking Simeon was getting ripped off with the view since the glass was so thick and tinted, spelled and treated to keep the vampire from being exposed to the UV rays and radiant magic that would kill him. It was functional but horribly inconvenient. Though Angel's spells would not work here—his sunlight reflection wards and runes would only function if they were based on an Invitation, offered willingly by the mortal who resided within the warded home. It might work if Simeon had a permanent blood donor who lived with him, but what he knew of such arrangements was thin. He knew a vampire's weaknesses, but how the inner working of their society functioned was beyond him at the moment. He had no idea if blood donors and slaves lived with the vampires they fed, or if the humans had their own living spaces.

Sliding from the bed, Angel headed for the bathroom, feet sinking into the opulent carpet, muffling his footsteps. He used the toilet and hopped in the shower, sniffing the soaps. They were odorless, and he smiled. That meant Simeon's delicious scent was natural, and Angel couldn't help the wave of happiness that swept through him at that realization. He blushed, even though there was no one to see him acting like a teenager suffering his first case of puppy love.

Thinking about the Elder led him to thinking about the night before, and Angel stood under the hot spray, distracted by memories of how thoroughly he fell apart under the vampire's hands. Simeon had known what he needed, and even now, his ass aching and his shoulders bearing love bites, Angel still felt his lover's hands on him, the weight of his body, the taste of his kiss.

Shaking his head, Angel finished washing up and got out, drying off with a fluffy and soft towel before rummaging under the sink. He found a box of new toothbrushes and travel sized toiletries, and he raided the supply. It didn't look like anyone else had used the supplies unless Simeon replaced them often. Not wanting to think about how often the Elder had sleepovers with blood donors or even other vampires, Angel cleaned himself up, eyeing his messy hair in the mirror with a frown.

His hair was dark brown, but the ends were capped white and honey blond, and since it was so short, most thought him a blond instead of a brunet. His eyes were dark, a mix of green and brown, and his skin had a light golden tan regardless of the season. Thankful the toiletries included shaving cream and a razor, Angel shaved before setting his hair to rights.

He looked like his father. Angel was shorter than his father had been, Raine Salvatore over six feet tall, built like a dancer and elegant. Angel was shorter, built more like the swimmer he was in high school, but their coloring was the same and Angel bore his father's features.

Thinking about his father led his thoughts to August, and how the man's life was stolen from him.

"Who is Deimos?" Angel said, speaking to himself in the mirror. "Why now, after ten years, does he make his move now? I've been here the whole time in Boston. I never left, everyone who mattered knew where I was, who I am, so why now? What is happening in the world now that makes Deimos come after me? Something changed, and recently."

Angel washed his face, drying himself. He leaned on the counter and met his own gaze in the crystal clear mirror. "August said Deimos wanted the spell I used that night. No one living remains who knows how I managed it, and I've only ever told August, and even he had trouble understanding it. He never told, otherwise I would be dead right now, every vampire on the entire East Coast clamoring for my head. Deimos wouldn't have left August at my office and challenged me if he knew what spell I used."

"Yes, that is logical, *mo ghra*," Simeon said from behind him, and Angel spun heart racing. He was so intent on talking to himself he never saw Simeon come into the bathroom. Simeon smiled and kissed him before taking his hand and pulling him from the bathroom to the bed, where Angel recognized his own clothes from the night before, cleaned and folded. "Keep going, you were making progress."

Angel got dressed, thinking. "Well, in the last few months, I've had two people be overly interested in how I defeated the army that night. A young man who came to my offices under the false assumption I would share the secret with enough flattery and hollow praise, who I promptly sent off before I set him on fire, and now Deimos. The human was rude, and Deimos homicidal, so they may or may not be connected, but dismissing coincidence can get you killed. Has anyone here in the clan been asking about me too much? Maybe someone repeatedly inquiring?"

Simeon thought about it, and replied, "Not here, at least not in recent months. The Master's stance on how he wants you treated is well known, so anyone curious about you has been left unsatisfied and knows better than to approach you. Though William Bridgerton asked about you the other night at the welcome banquet. My Master deflected most of his questions."

"The unranked master from Atlanta? What exactly did he ask?" Angel said, and Simeon shifted on his feet, the usually controlled undead man looking sheepish. "Simeon, now I really want to know. What did Bridgerton say?"

"He inquired as to the clan's relationship with you, and if there was any animosity. Not an unexpected question, as he seeks to move himself and his fledglings here. He would want them safe, and an angry necromancer with the ability to destroy large numbers of us at once would be a dangerous neighbor to have."

"Yeah, okay, but I can tell that isn't all he asked," Angel said, eyes narrowed. "Spill."

"He asked after you specifically, your personality, what you looked like, and a fledgling showed him a picture. Bridgerton's reaction was…. interesting." Simeon looked angry, his green eyes flashing. Angel cracked a smile, and put a hand on Simeon's chest, rubbing firm muscles and enjoying every second of it.

"Interesting, or do you mean interested? Are you jealous? Did he think I was hot?" Angel asked, chuckling when Simeon growled and flashed a fang at him. "Ha! You are jealous!"

"You are mine. He cannot have you," Simeon hissed, yanking Angel forward and hugging him close. "You finally let me in, and I will not lose this chance to earn your love and my place in your life. Bridgerton can get his own necromancer."

"I haven't even met this vamp, and you're getting all caveman on me. Is he hot? Sexy? Should I be looking to upgrade?" Angel teased, snorting out a laugh when Simeon snarled again and lifted him off his feet, throwing him onto the bed and laying on top of him. Angel laughed, and Simeon huffed and started licking and kissing along Angel's jawline. He turned into the caresses, cock perking up, hands wandering down Simeon's shoulders and back. "I thought I agreed to be yours?" Angel murmured, eyes drifting closed as Simeon went about what seemed to be his favorite pastime, sucking up marks on his neck, this time right behind his ear. "I could've sworn I agreed to be all yours already."

"Yes, you did. All mine, *a ghra*," Simeon whispered, nibbling on his earlobe. "Did you have plans for the day, or may I show you again how much I desire you?"

"Aw man, not fair," Angel sighed, groaning. "I need to call Milly and see if the cops came by and if she's okay, and since my office is still a crime scene, I guess I have no plans other than tracking down a killer."

"Then call the lovely Millicent, and afterwards we shall spend the day creating more alibis," Simeon kissed him, deep and hard, making him moan and arch up, burying his fingers in thick auburn hair and humming his approval. "Unless you'd rather hunt down that killer now...."

"Shut up and kiss me!"

"So demanding."

The kiss Angel got was enough to make him forget his name. Full of tongue and chocolate, fangs and mint, Angel drowned in Simeon's kiss.

He was working his fingers down to unbutton Simeon's waistband when a chime went off, stilling Simeon atop of him. Angel pulled back and stared up at his lover. "What is it? What's that noise?"

"My master summons me," Simeon said, face closing off, and he carefully got up from the bed, pulling Angel up with him. "I must attend him."

"Shit. All right. I'll stay here then? I'll just find my cell and call Milly, see what's going on with her. Maybe order a pizza, I'm starving." Angel put his hands in his pockets, oddly nervous. He gave a thin smile to Simeon when the Elder cocked a brow at him. "What? It's not every day a guy starts a new relationship and then his boyfriend gets summoned by an all-powerful master of vampires. What if your master wants me to leave? And I swear to god, I sound like a kid freaking out over his first boyfriend and whether or not the parents like me. What the fuck."

Simeon interrupted his rambling by kissing him, strong hands curling over his shoulders. Angel stilled, tipping his head back and losing himself in the touch and sensations. Every time Simeon touched him, every kiss, it was getting harder and harder to hold on to himself, keep his focus and his desires in check. Simeon was wearing him down, consuming his control and becoming the focal point for all his wants. He had never once felt like this, and between feeling as if he were adrift on currents outside his control, and the need to place his heart solely in Simeon's hands, Angel was fighting with everything he had to survive from one moment to the next.

"*Leannán*," Simeon whispered as he pulled back, lips moving over

Angel's, making him shiver with need. "Just breathe, please. All will be well. I must go, though. I will be back. If you wish to call Milly, your cell is with your bag. It's on the coffee table in the front room. You left your bag in the limo last night."

Angel pulled back, licking his lips, Simeon's eyes tracking his tongue. He grinned, then blinked, focusing. "No one messed with it? My bag, I mean?"

"Please check if you want. If anything is missing, I will rectify the problem when I return. The phone on the table beside the bed calls to Housekeeping. Order yourself something to eat. I must go."

Simeon kissed him one last time and walked from the room. Angel watched him go, heart jumping, oddly worried.

His cell was where Simeon said it would be, in the huge living room on a coffee table. Angel put it in his pocket, intending to call Milly in a few minutes. His bag was there too, and he didn't hesitate to check the contents. Everything was there and looked unmolested. The sea salt and venom jars were beyond priceless, and it showed how fucked up he was the night before that he forgot all about them. He pulled out his athame and went back to the bathroom. He cleaned the blade, wishing he had holy water to properly do the trick, but tap water and a quick prayer was enough to cleanse the residual energy from the blade. He stuck the blade behind his belt at the small of his back, his long, heavy sweater enough to cover the hilt and the blade from casual observers.

Taking out his cell, he dialed Milly. It was late enough to be a decent hour to call since she got up late on days they weren't offering classes. With their studio a crime scene, neither of them were working.

"Hello?" Milly said, cranky.

"Morning, sunshine," Angel quipped, sitting on Simeon's bed, catching a whiff of their activities in the night. Angel smiled, and fell back on the bed, wincing when the hilt of the athame dug into a rib. He shifted, and listened to Milly grumble at him.

"Don't call me sunshine, young man," she snapped, obviously

upset. Angel bit his lip and tried not to laugh. "Your BFF Detective Collins was here earlier. Asshole woke me 7am."

"Did you turn him into a rat? I'd pay to see that," Angel said, thinking about it. Transformation spells were incredibly difficult and ran the risk of killing anything living, but it might be worth it to see Collins match his personality.

"No, and I'm regretting that now. They went to your apartment and tried to get past your wards. I saw a few detectives sporting your tracers, so I don't know if they managed to get in or not."

"If they tried hard enough they may have, though my tracers will stick to anyone who's determined enough to breach them. I wasn't woken by any sensory echoes from my wards falling, so I don't think they made it in."

"Hmmm," Milly hummed, and he could hear her clinking around, water running. "I, of course, had no idea as to your whereabouts if you weren't at home, and since I informed them I'm far too young to be your fucking mother and as such I have no idea what you do at night, I was able to tell them nothing. I'm assuming you had to go somewhere other than home after your adventure last night?"

"Ummm," Angel said, thinking. He could lie, but she routinely caught him out at it anyway. He was safe enough on the other side of town he could tell her the truth. "My old friend hadn't been autopsied, and I left evidence behind. We had to rectify that, and almost got caught. So now I'm.... Making an alibi at the Tower, actually. With Simeon," he added, as if his location wasn't a big enough clue to let her know what he'd been doing late last night.

Crickets. That must be what he was hearing through the silence on the line. Crickets, followed by a long, even exhale and a deep breath. Wincing, waiting for a lecture or a shriek, Angel was left flabbergasted when Milly merely said, "It's about time. Took you fuckers long enough."

"Thanks, mum," Angel sighed. "So glad you like my boyfriend."

"Stop it!"

Angel laughed and got back to his feet, cell pressed to his ear. He heard something in the front room, and he headed that direction thinking Simeon was back. "Let me know if anything happens, please? And the bad guy's name is Deimos. Sound familiar?"

"No, it doesn't," Milly said, humming as she thought. He heard a kettle in the background, she must be making tea. "I'll ask around?"

"Do it carefully, please. August is dead, I don't want to get a call from the cops saying they found your body. You could be next—the asshole wants to know how I survived that night and what spell I used."

He didn't need to elaborate—Milly understood. "As I don't know what spell you used myself, and have told numerous idiots that who've asked me in the last several years, I think I'm safe, but I will be cautious, dear. Give my best to Simeon."

"Sure," Angel said and hung up as he entered the living room. Simeon was back, and his lover wasn't alone.

"Hey, what's going on?" Angel asked. "And Milly says hi."

Simeon gave him a tight smile, fangs hidden, but stepped to the side. "*Leannán*," he said with a short bow, "May I present to you my esteemed colleague, Elder Etienne Gaston. Etienne, my *Leannán*, the necromancer Angelus Salvatore."

The Master of Boston was odd in some ways, like his near-total recluse status and the fact he only had two Elders. Most Masters of a city had several, sometimes up to a dozen, but here there were only two, Simeon and the dark-haired, slim vampire eyeing him like he was dessert.

"Hi," Angel said, not offering his hand. The vampire Elder was a couple inches taller than Angel, slim, and just as pale as Simeon, making his dark brown eyes stand out even more, his chocolate-brown hair brushed back into an elegant wave. "So what's going on?"

Simeon smirked at his abruptness, and the new vamp's eyes narrowed, probably in annoyance, but Angel couldn't care less. Angel saw a hint of fang before the new Elder got himself under control. He was hungry, he wanted to get fucked again, and he had a bad guy to burn to ashes, and being polite wasn't something he was all that skilled at anyways. Simeon was acting odd, but then he had never seen Simeon in the presence of an equal, always seeing his lover around lesser masters and fledglings, so it made sense he would act differently in the presence of someone with ostensibly as much authority as he.

The new vamp was very pretty, in a strong, masculine way, but Angel preferred the wild warrior with his dark red hair and tattoos standing at his side to the polished exterior of the other Elder, and his obvious lack of awe at meeting this new Elder came across fairly clear. Simeon took Angel's hand, and Elder Etienne rallied, smoothing out nonexistent wrinkles in his fine jacket.

"I have come to offer the sincerest welcome of our Master, and ask that you do him the honor of attending him for your repast," Elder Etienne said, his French accent smooth and heavy, but his words were perfectly understandable. As was his annoyance. "The police are reportedly searching for you, and our Master wishes to speak to you about such matters in person. As your connection to the bloodclan is widely known, I believe the police have correctly assumed you are here. My master wishes to speak to you before the police arrive."

"Shit," Angel swore and turned to Simeon. "Did I get you in trouble?"

"Not at all, my love. We should go, though, as my master has ordered brunch for you."

"Brunch. Sounds special. Alright, after you," Angel said, hiding his nerves. He wasn't afraid, not really—he was more worried about Simeon in this whole mess. Was he in trouble for dragging the clan into Angel's shitstorm? And why did Etienne come back with Simeon instead of his lover returning for Angel alone?

Angel followed Etienne out into the hall, the three of them walking to the elevator and its guard stationed outside the doors, this time, a human man, dressed identically to his undead counterparts. Angel kept his hand on Simeon's, and when they got in the elevator with its human guard and Etienne scanned his palm, Angel was additionally worried when Simeon made it a point to stand between him and the other Elder as if protecting him. Angel got a quick look at Etienne's face and the sneer twisting his lips before the elevator stopped at the penthouse.

A guard stood outside the doors in the hall, and two more stood down at the entrance to the penthouse suite. Angel walked down the hall at Simeon's side, Etienne in front and one of the guards following behind. He refused to be nervous, but he clutched a bit tighter at Simeon's hand.

The doors were opened by the guards, and they swept into a grand room, tall windows tinted the same as the ones in Simeon's bedroom, but their height allowed more natural light into the space, even if the view was just as boring in gray-scale tones. Even the vibrant hues of scarlet and burgundy, snow-white and rich cream were dulled by the oppressive nature of the view, despite the distance to be seen across the harbor and most of Downtown. Though absolutely minuscule compared to The Hancock's 60-stories of glass and steel, the Tower was placed so as not to be near any other taller buildings; its placement in one of the most historical areas of Boston prevented newer developments and taller buildings from devouring its view of the city. The vamps further protected their territory by buying the surrounding properties and having them all declared landmarks to some degree or another.

An unlit chandelier above his head caught the meager light and threw rainbow-hued spots across the walls and floor, and over the golden hair of The Master of the City. Angel met crystalline blue eyes that glittered as brightly as the ornaments above them and froze.

9
THE MASTER

Angel had only ever seen the Master of Boston once, from a distance across the grand floor of the casino buried at the base of the Tower. He had been leaving the room as Angel entered it, heading for one of the private rooms adjacent to the main playing floor where high-stakes games were played. A young vampire had bitten one of the servers, a woman who had a witch in her family tree close enough to poison her blood with latent magic. Angel was able to cure the vampire, and scold the undead in charge for not schooling both their younglings and their employees to avoid such mistakes in the future.

His one glimpse was insufficient to prepare him for the sheer magnitude that was The Master. Tall, Simeon's height at least, and broad across the chest and shoulders, muscles moved as a cat's would as the ancient vampire stalked away from the windows towards where they stood. Pale skin, unlined and smooth, glowed white as snow and just as pure, with deep pink, lush lips that revealed pristine fangs and shiny teeth flashed in a charming grin.

A scent as familiar as apple pie and pine, with a hint of lemon washed over him, making him breathe deep and hold it in to enjoy it better. He breathed out when his lungs began to burn, eyes meeting bright blue once again, and found his tongue incapable of forming words.

"Simeon," the vision spoke, accented with such a foreign influence that it left Angel floundering, "Is this creature of magic and allure your necromancer? Surely not, for one so young and beautiful to be so powerful."

At the first hint of bullshit, Angel snapped back to reality. The Master knew exactly who he was, and back-handed compliments did nothing but piss him off. He held his tongue, but narrowed his eyes a smidgen, taking a better look at the ancient undead in front of him. The Master was beyond attractive; he exuded an aura of raw masculinity and power that Angel could feel, cloying and purring as a cat would, trying to entice him into touching, to wanting. Angel had a thing for big men, but this creature before him was too much dangerous wrapped up in a tame exterior. Not to mention the charisma rolling off him in waves, trying to suppress Angel's will, left him royally pissed.

"Yes, Master. This is Angelus Salvatore. *A ghra*, the Master of Boston, Constantine Batiste." Simeon's words were pure courtesy, but the tension in the hand Angel held warned him to tread carefully.

"Angelus, greetings." Angel found his free hand in the Master's, without noticing how it got there. The fucker was fast and too slick. "Welcome to my home."

"Angel, please. Only my mother called me Angelus, and that was when I forgot to clean my room," Angel replied, trying to discreetly pull his hand away, but Batiste held him without effort. Cold, hard fingers that sucked in his own body heat, rapidly warming, and as the cold receded he could feel the smooth skin, the satin glide of perfect flesh. Too perfect, somehow, and it bothered him.

"Of course, Angel. And you are an angel, are you not? I can feel your power, it burns around you in a verdant halo, just under the surface," Batiste said, damn near purring. The ancient vamp could sense Angel's aura, meaning his own power was substantial. Not that Angel had any doubts, considering how easily he was almost swept under by the vampire's charisma. "Will you dine with me? Food has been prepared, and I am eager to see your enjoyment of what I have had arranged for you."

Holding back his retort at just how fucking creepy that sounded, Angel gave a tight smile and nodded once. "Sure, sounds great. Did you order something for Simeon, too? Poor guy must be parched."

Simeon stiffened, and Angel felt a minor tremor in the hands that held his, but there was no sign of anger or annoyance in the perfect face of the master. "I shall have something bought out immediately. Please, this way."

Angel finally had his hand back, and they were led to a small table underneath the windows, a single place setting with fruit, pastries, and what looked like a rasher of scrambled eggs and bacon. He was hungry and sat. Servants appeared, and while Batiste and Simeon sat, Etienne stood nearby. The servants put a goblet in front of both Simeon and the Master, and Angel got a hint of metallic heat on the air. Blood in the goblets, not that he expected anything less. A clear water goblet was placed next to his left hand, and Angel sipped, watching both the master and Simeon. The master gave him a charming smile and Simeon sat still, both hands flat on the table on either side of his goblet.

He piled food on his plate and dug in. The odds of being poisoned were next to none here—Angel could heal himself of anything deadly, eradicating the toxins with a rush of hellfire through his system, and the motive behind such an act wasn't obvious or apparent enough to be likely. Unless Deimos was a highly ranked vampire and in this room or preparing his food in the kitchens, and somehow able to hide his scent from Simeon, no one here wanted him dead... yet.

Not able to remember the last time he ate anything substantial, Angel went back for seconds, Batiste watching him the whole time, amusement stamped on his features. The servants left the room as silently as they entered it, and it was just Angel and three vamps, only one of them he was certain wouldn't try to either kill him or bewitch him.

Angel swallowed, and said, "Not used to seeing people eat food?"

"I am not, no," Batiste agreed, "I do not spend time with my donors outside of my own sustenance."

"So no wining and dining? You just have 'em come over for a snack and send them on their way afterwards?"

Simeon went extra still, if it was at all possible for someone to become so frozen that they all but vibrated with palpable tension while not actually moving, but Simeon managed it.

"You are not as I expected," Batiste said, drinking from his goblet. Not a drop of crimson to be seen on his lips, and Angel was watching with morbid curiosity. "Most humans dare not speak to me at all, let alone dare ask me about my feeding habits. Beautiful and daring, and quite powerful. Is your heart set on Simeon, Angelus, or can I sway you to my side? An Elder is truly powerful, but none are more powerful than a city master. To have a Master as your lover would keep your enemies forever at bay. I might even be able to help you find revenge on the few that escaped mortal justice."

Angel leaned back in his chair, hands crossed over his stomach. He put a leg out under the table and rested the toe of his boot on Simeon's foot. He got Simeon to send a glance his way for a nanosecond before the Elder went back to his impression of an undead statue. For some reason, Simeon was remaining out of this, and for a powerful Elder to be so cautious made Angel both infuriated and curious.

"We've only just met, and you're trying to get in my bed? You move fast for an old guy."

Batiste smiled, showing a sharp fang and his blue eyes flashing. "When I see what I want, I get it."

"So you want me."

"Oh, yes. Very much."

"I'll ask you exactly what I asked Simeon. Why now, after two years? I'm beyond certain you've had every step I've made in the last two years watched, so you've had plenty of time to come calling if you were all that interested. And I know you could have just as easily told Simeon to stay away from me, which means you know he's been courting me. What now? Did my choice to have sex with Simeon prove my supposed aversion to vampires was an assumption, and now you think the way is clear? Simeon's done all the work after all, and like you said, a Master is better than an Elder any day."

Angel was so mad a puff of smoke rose from his fingers, and he fought back the urge to let his hellfire out. A singed brow may make Batiste back off, but he had doubts he could kill the Master before he got to Angel.

Elder Etienne hissed, and flowed across the room, coming to stand right behind where Angel sat. Angel didn't react at all—he was not showing fear in here.

"My Elder objects to your tone, necromancer. Are you brave, or foolish?"

"Both, without a doubt. I'm full of flaws."

"Maybe less than you think." Batiste finally stopped staring at Angel, and sent his regard to Simeon. "My oldest child loves you. He calls you *Leannán*, in old Irish. Has he told you what that means?"

"No, but I'm guessing it's important."

"Yes, very. But as he hasn't explained, the way is clear for me." Batiste stood, and walked around the table, edging Etienne out of the way and coming to stand right behind his chair. Simeon was watching now, green eyes locked on Angel's face. Heavy hands came to rest on his shoulders, fingers curling in slightly, holding him in place. Angel let his own arms relax, his hands falling from his stomach to rest by his hips.

Angel now had a strong suspicion why Etienne came back with Simeon for Angel—they were planning this fucking sexual ambush from the start. And Simeon couldn't stop it. The Simeon he knew wouldn't let Angel be harassed like this unless he had no choice—and that meant there was a hidden motive to this all. Simeon wouldn't let his life be in danger, he knew that much, but maybe if he interfered Angel *would* be in danger then? Something was happening here that Angel couldn't understand, and not knowing what was going on pissed him off even more.

The hilt of his athame was not that far from his left hand, and if he needed to, he could grab it. Maybe not before he lost his head, but he could try. Whatever kept Simeon from interfering was not going to keep Angel from protecting himself.

Batiste leaned down, mouth by Angel's right ear. Again he got the scent of apples and spice, and he fought back his enjoyment of the scent. Charisma and sheer power rolled off the ancient vamp, and Angel gave the tiniest of shivers, Batiste's hands tightening when he felt it. Angel held Simeon's gaze and tried to keep his anger and increasing fear off his face.

"Surely a city master holds more appeal than a single Elder. You've tasted the passion found beneath a vampire's touch. Imagine how mine would feel. I could satisfy you, pleasure you, protect you and treasure you for the entirety of your life. No enemies could get to you while you enjoy the protection of my embrace." Each word from Batiste's lips tickled along his ear and neck, and Angel's whole body tingled with instinctive fear and the need to run.

Angel fought to control himself, to stay as relaxed as possible so as not to give himself away to the monster leaning over him.

"And what would you get out of it? You make no mention of love."

"I would get you, Angelus. Power and beauty, strength and danger in one gorgeous body. And love. Love is for mortals, humans who have nothing. What need have I for love when I have eternity? And I know you, Angelus. Never have you kept a lover, nor something so insipid as a boyfriend. You satisfy an itch, then move on, still listless and discontent. Let me satisfy you. I know you have not mentioned love to Simeon, so surely my bed holds more appeal. Let me send them away, and I can show you passion you've never known."

Angel kept his eyes on Simeon. He saw something in the emerald depths that spoke of worry, and a shadow of fear. Etienne moved closer, as Batiste scented at Angel's neck. He felt a tiny hint of fangs gliding over his skin. Things were about to get dangerous. Maybe a city master had the ability to survive magic poisoning, and Angel was about to join the menu.

Somehow the thought of sleeping with the golden Adonis wasn't at all that appealing. Simeon was wild, an untamed creature masquerading as a gentleman, and the touch of feral strength in the

Elder called to Angel. Wild he may be, but Simeon was also kind, patient, funny, and sometimes so sarcastic he made Angel wince—but he spoke of love with honesty and without fear. And Angel trusted him. Yet it was there in Simeon's eyes—Batiste was right, Angel had never mentioned love, or even how he felt to Simeon, and that worried Simeon, gave him doubt. Angel had said nothing, other than a mangled yes to an urgent plea, and given his lover no firm foundation on which to stand.

Angel sighed. He was such an ass.

"You're right, I haven't told Simeon I love him," Angel said, Batiste giving a growl of satisfaction in his ear. Angel slid his left hand back and under his sweater, and pulled the athame free, holding it out of sight. Batiste was nuzzling at his neck, right under his right ear, no doubt able to see Simeon's love bites. A hand slid down from his shoulder, over his chest, now getting way too close to his abdomen and below. Batiste was going for gold immediately, thinking Angel a sure bet. "I may not have told him I love him because I've never been in love before. Saying it before I'm sure I mean it would be as wretched as never saying it at all."

"Will you be mine then?" Batiste whispered against his flesh, making Angel tip his head to the side. Batiste's wandering hand stopped just shy of his waistband, fingers rubbing over his stomach, before slipping lower. The ancient vampire's fingers slid under his jeans, homing in on his groin. Angel shivered with repulsion, and bared his own teeth in a snarl.

"No." Angel pulled the athame up, faster than he should have been able to, but then a man, no matter the species, tended to get distracted when thinking with his cock. Angel pressed the tip to the bottom of Batiste's chin, calling his hellfire to the blade. It erupted in green flames, and Batiste froze. His cool hand was centimeters from grabbing Angel's cock, and Angel wanted nothing more than to light the undead fiend up like a torch. Etienne snarled, and made to leap at him, but Simeon thawed and jumped over the table, shoving Etienne into the window and holding him with one hand to the glass by the throat. Simeon looked back at him, worry now obvious on his handsome features. "Get your fucking hands off of me."

Batiste obeyed instantly, pulling his hand out of Angel's pants and holding both hands out to the side.

"I may not know if I love him," Angel gritted out, pushing with the blade, breaking skin. He made Batiste stand up, and Angel moved, the burning blade spitting and hissing like a cat as Angel maneuvered them so he could see both master and the two elders. Angel glared at Batiste, and raised his right hand, calling hellfire to dance around his fingers. Etienne hissed again, but Simeon choked him, silencing him. Batiste was smiling, even as blood dripped down the blade and began to burn, filling the air with a bitter odor. "I may not know if I love Simeon, but I want to. I want to love him with everything that remains of my broken heart. I agreed to be his. I am his, and I always will be. Now back the fuck off, or I show you just how nasty things get when I'm upset."

Batiste laughed. Angel had him at blade-point, and the bastard laughed. It snapped and coiled around the room, echoing oddly. Angel tensed, ready to fight, but all Batiste did was raise his hands, palm out and said, "Peace, necromancer. You have proven Simeon's claim upon your heart and affections. You may relax, and I will trouble you no more on the subject of switching lovers."

"Was this a fucking test? I have a knife to your throat and that's okay because you didn't mean it?" Angel hissed out, enraged. Simeon made a noise, halfway between a sigh and a strangled laugh. "You put your mouth on me, your hands on me, without invitation, and it's all okay because this was just a test? Fuck you!"

"*Leannán*," Simeon spoke for the first time since they sat down, his voice a sexy rumble that cut through Angel's anger better than yelling ever could, "All will be well now. You have made yourself very clear, and my master will apologize for his transgressions. Will you not, Master Batiste?"

"I sincerely apologize for doubting your devotion to my treasured Elder, and my methods for testing you. Please forgive me."

Batiste still had that cocky grin on his lips, but Angel was done fucking around. He didn't believe a damn word, but this standoff couldn't last forever. "Touch me again without invitation, even with something so innocent as a handshake, I'll burn you to ash without hesitation, and I could give two shits about your Master of the City title."

"Understood, necromancer," Batiste replied with a purr, smiling.

"Do you know who Deimos is?" Angel asked, intensifying the hellfire for a heartbeat.

"I do not."

It irked him to no end, but he believed Batiste.

Angel killed the hellfire, and dropped the athame from the vamp's throat, stepping away from Batiste at the same time. Simeon dropped Etienne on his ass and blurred as he came to Angel's side, taking him in his arms and burying his face in Angel's neck, breathing in deep. Simeon was shaking, and Angel stilled, battling back his anger. Simeon was deeply upset, more so than he'd ever seen the vampire before. Angel tucked the athame back into his belt, and hugged Simeon back, lifting up on his toes to get a better hold around Simeon's neck.

Angel glared at Batiste over Simeon, the ancient vampire merely grinned back at him and dabbed at the cut on his chin with a snowy white handkerchief. Etienne hovered over his master, but Batiste ignored him, returning to his seat at the table and sitting down.

"Hey," Angel murmured, rubbing the back of Simeon's neck. "You doing okay there?"

Simeon lifted his head, and smiled down at Angel. "You wish to love me?"

"Yes," Angel said quickly, disregarding their audience, not that Batiste was paying them any attention now. "I may love you already, but that's outside my experience so how about I get back to you on that?"

Simeon chuckled, and kissed him. Angel closed his eyes and leaned into Simeon, humming as Simeon delved deep, exploring Angel's mouth and taking his time. Simeon broke the kiss, and said,

"I will show you my love until you recognize your own, and you can tell me with surety that you love me."

"Sounds like a plan," Angel replied. "But maybe you can tell me what *Leannán* means?"

"This ought to be interesting," Batiste said dryly, chuckling.

"How about you tell me when we aren't surrounded by assholes," Angel said, and he flipped off the Master. Etienne twitched and Angel flipped him off as well. Batiste smirked. A thousand-year-old vampire smirked at him.

"Come sit, my love, and finish your meal," Simeon said and tugged him back to the table. He wanted out of here, but until he knew for certain that Deimos wasn't in the Tower and that the police weren't going to arrest him, he was going to have to stay here in vamp HQ for now.

"Not so hungry anymore," Angel said, and his thoughts got derailed when Simeon pulled out Angel's chair, sat in it himself, and then tugged Angel to sit in his lap. "We have too many people watching to be playing at Santa and his Naughty Elf."

Simeon snorted out a laugh, but tucked Angel close to his chest and held him there. Angel sighed with exasperation, but let Simeon have his way. The expression on Simeon's face was pure satisfaction, and the smug twist to his lush lips made Angel growl, and nip at them. Simeon gave him a delighted glance, and kissed him in return, taking his time, as much staking his claim as pleasing them both.

A dark chuckle came from across the table, but Angel ignored it, taking his time with the kiss. He was discovering that after years of avoiding intimacy that he was severely starving himself of some really great sensations, chief of which was how it felt to be held and adored. He'd never realized that he wanted such a thing, but he was becoming to love it, and it was in this undead man's arms. Simeon gently nipped his lower lip as they broke apart, and Angel sighed, his residual anger seeping out of him. He was never going to trust the Master, but he wasn't homicidally angry anymore.

Angel put an arm around Simeon's neck, adjusting himself on his lover's lap. He spared Etienne a glance, and the chilly expression on the other Elder's face told him he would have to be cautious there. Batiste was smiling as if he hadn't just had a knife to his throat and his hands down Angel's pants. "Explain what the fuck that was. Now."

Batiste threw back his head and laughed. "You are the bluntest creature I have ever had the pleasure of encountering. You charge in, be damned the consequences, and you set the world aflame. No wonder my oldest child loves you so," Batiste waved a hand, and servants appeared again, clearing the table and depositing a thick leather portfolio on the table in front of the Master. "Tell me, necromancer, what do you know of mating rituals among supernaturals?"

Angel looked at Simeon, "You said we weren't magically mated, dammit!"

"And we are not, *Leannán*. I promise, all you swore to me was to be mine, but you can always take it back. I hope you will never want to, but you and I are not bound," Simeon vowed to him, cupping his chin in one cool, big hand, smoothing a thumb over his bottom lip. "I would never trap you like that, I swear."

Angel humphed, but relaxed again, glaring now at Batiste. "Quit fucking around."

"So fiery. A shame I could not turn your head," Batiste mused, but he went from annoying to business-like in a nanosecond, opening the portfolio. "I merely asked as I wish for you to understand how momentous an occasion this is for my darling Simeon. We vampires are capable of romantic love, just as we were when mortal. The exception is the means by which it happens."

"Master, don't. Let me explain it to him," Simeon interrupted. Angel looked back to him, frustrated and getting annoyed, again. Simeon held him closer, cradling him, and Angel was even more annoyed he liked it.

"Someone explain. How the fuck is this hard?" Angel frowned, glaring. Simeon rubbed a hand over his back, soothing.

"My master means to tell you that while we can love, once we turn, we can only ever fall in love once to such a degree that we call another mate. My heritage calls such a one *Leannán*. I can love friends, my sire, my fellow fledglings, even donors, but I have never been in love. I am over four centuries old, and you are the only person I have ever been in love with," Simeon said. "And you have my heart in its entirety. I call you *Leannán*, as I have no other before you. After centuries of never letting anyone in as I have you, Master Batiste fears that I will not survive loving you."

"So we *are* mates?" Angel asked, getting riled up again. Nothing but talking in circles.

"No, we are not. But...the possibility to become mates is very high, and I wish for nothing more than to call you my mate, my *Leannán* in truth, and have you return the sentiment. Right now I am all yours, but the bond is incomplete. It takes more than instant lust and love at first sight. It takes prolonged contact, exchange of emotions, and developing a rapport of trust and love and willingness to sacrifice. A mate bond for our kind takes a long time. Sometimes weeks or months—sometimes years. And it can be broken before the final pieces are in place," Simeon hurriedly explained.

"Sounds less like mating and more like an engagement period before marriage," Angel said, fucking butterflies in his stomach, mouth dry. "With magical and spiritual ties instead of legal or religious ones."

"Yes, that is the most accurate comparison," Simeon agreed. His smile was wary, and Angel could feel the tension in the vampire's big body beneath him. His vampire was waiting for his reaction to this *Leannán* situation, but the avid gaze of the master vamp nearby was bugging the shit out of him.

"So what was the whole switching lovers bullshit?" Angel demanded.

"I was testing your level of devotion to Simeon. He is already too far gone to recover from your loss if you decide that being his mate in the future is too much for you. He won't die from a mate bond being left incomplete, but he will never love another. I wished to make sure you would not destroy my most treasured child," Batiste interrupted, rifling through papers and photos in front of him. Etienne hissed, but everyone ignored him. "The Celt is a feared warrior, and much of this clan's power comes from his superior skills and strengths. Having him laid low by a broken heart is not something I will allow."

"What the ever loving fuck..." Angel rubbed his face, thinking hard. He looked back at Simeon, their faces inches apart. Simeon was watching him, emerald eyes clear, without a trace of doubt. "You really know how to box someone in, don't you?"

"You aren't boxed in, my love. You have all the freedom in this relationship, all the control. I swear you're not trapped."

"No, I'm only responsible for your mental and emotional wellbeing, and if I screw you over and turn my back on you, or if we just don't work out long-term, I haven't just messed with you for a few months while you get over a bad breakup—I've broken your heart forever. That is a huge responsibility."

Angel found himself in the air. The room blurred, and suddenly he was standing on the far side of the room, overlooking the northern part of the city, the overcast day appearing drearier through the heavily-tinted glass. Simeon cupped his face, holding him still, eyes locked on each other.

"Is that what you fear? Hurting me?"

"Fuck, Simeon. You tell me I'm your one and only, literally, and how can I not be afraid of hurting you?"

"You won't, *a ghra*. It's not in you."

"I suck at interpersonal relationships. My brother hates me, who by the way I need to make sure is still alive, and I have one friend. My students all think I'm an asshole, and they'd be right. I've never had a relationship that lasted longer than an exchange of top versus bottom, and I don't know what I'm doing," Angel said, holding onto Simeon's wrists with both hands.

"Neither do I, Angel. I've never been in love before."

"Then we're the blind leading the blind?"

"I prefer to think of it as finding our way together."

"I will say I told you so if this goes sideways."

Simeon smiled at him and pressed a kiss to his forehead. "I have faith in us, *Leannán*."

"The police are on their way up," Simeon said, walking back to his side from where he'd been speaking quietly to Master Batiste and two other vampires, one of which was wearing the most expensive suit Angel had ever seen before in his life, and that was saying something. The other vamp had an unassuming air about him, marking him an assistant to the wealthy vamp. They had both shown up after Batiste sent Etienne away for them, the Elder not returning. "A Detective Collins and two uniformed officers."

It took Angel a moment, but it clicked fast enough. One detective—questioning. Three cops, two of them uniformed officers for backup, meant they had either a warrant for his arrest or plausible cause to toss him in handcuffs. And if he went to jail, Angel had no doubts about how long he'd last behind bars. "They're here to arrest me."

"Then can try, *a ghra*," Simeon said, flashing his fangs with a grim smile. "We shall see what they want first."

"There's a Collins leading the charge," Angel said one eye on the door to the penthouse. The cops should be there in a few minutes. "Every encounter I've had with the cops in the last few weeks has gotten steadily more aggressive. I may yet walk out of here in handcuffs."

Angel looked at Batiste, and there was no doubt the Master and the two new vamps heard every word. "Is the Master going to break his seclusion and stay, or is he leaving the establishment of my alibi to you? You've got the clout to back me up. You okay lying for me?"

"Lying is the least I would do for you. You did what was necessary to find the truth behind your friend's murder. I don't care about the legalities of human customs; I care about keeping you safe."

A commotion broke out in the hall, voices raised through the door. Batiste straightened, the portfolio from brunch tucked up under his arm. Angel stood with Simeon along the windows just as a thick cloud cover took a firm hold over the horizon, and the lights came on in the penthouse.

The doors opened, the cops surrounded by angry vampire guards. Detective Collins was bristling with anger and annoyance, and Angel could guess it had something to do with the fact the vampires were carrying the cops' weapons.

Angel didn't know much about the inner structure of vampire society, but he knew enough about how vampires interacted with human society—the top two highest ranks of vampires, Elder, and Master, were considered a type of sovereign and independent authority, and few human laws pertained to them, but the ones that did were set in stone and would bring the attention of the human authorities, typically in the form of the federal government if violated. The Master and Elders then placed laws upon the clans underneath them, maintaining control and making it possible for humans and vampires to interact in their daily lives without anarchy. If a human joined a clan, then they fell under the authority of the master and the Laws of the Bloodclans and were no longer subject to human laws. There were few exceptions, and this structure was copied amongst the supernatural community—which is why the Blood Wars raged on for so long—the human casualties weren't high enough for the human government to step in until it was too late.

Practitioners existed in the gray areas—they were human but supernatural, and the level of accountability and responsibility changed depending on the particulars of each practitioner's situation and family. There was a Council of High Sorcery, but it was based in Europe, and they rarely looked across national boundaries unless the infraction was severe. *Like raising the dead...*

Detective Collins saw Angel, as if he were a compass and Angel true north—and ignored the ruckus around him, pointing.

"Salvatore! You're coming downtown to the precinct; you've got some shit to answer for!"

He may not have his gun, but he still had his cuffs, and Collins pulled them off his belt and tried to get through the mess of people in the doorway. Hissing rose as the cops tried to bulldoze their way through the guards, shouting and threats rising. Things were disintegrating quickly, and Angel hadn't even said a word yet. For once, this couldn't be pinned on his big mouth, and he grinned, which only made Collins shout louder.

Years ago, the night Simeon and Angel met, the Elder contained the lower echelon of vampires at the Halloween party through an exercise of power Angel had never experienced before, or after. He knew it was Simeon, as it smelled, even tasted and felt like the Elder, and it was potent enough that Angel could still recall it years later. But what he felt rise in the penthouse now eclipsed Simeon's power as a hurricane would a gentle rainfall.

Power swept across the floor, an almost tangible wave of energy that felt like the cold touch of ice and tasted like the sharp bite of hard cider, reminiscent of apples and spice and chilled orchards forced into slumber by the advent of winter. Hairs all over his body rose and his breathing stilled, and Angel froze, eyes wide. Voices cut short, and movements were aborted as Batiste made his presence known.

Collins dropped his arm and stepped back, the guards relaxing. The expression on Collins' face made Angel snort, as he finally had a prime example of what it looked to see someone so shocked as to be called 'shitless'. It was clear the cops had made no effort to think about who else would be present, and to Angel that was the height of stupidity—they were in vamp HQ, in the penthouse of the Tower—who else other than the Master would be present?

Collins gaped like a fish, and Angel finally couldn't hold in his laughter. His instinct for self-preservation must be faulty as the incredulous looks he got from both the vampires in the room and Collins just made him laugh harder, bent over, hands on his knees, dissolving into giggles. Simeon put a hand on his shoulders, and Angel finally relaxed, wiping his eyes. A few weeks' worth of stress escaped in those spare moments, and he felt better, a wide smile on his face.

"Welcome to my home," Batiste said graciously as if Angel didn't just have a laughing fit. The Master waved a hand, gesturing to some plush armchairs nearby. Collins awkwardly pocketed his cuffs, but he apparently realized just who he was standing in front of if the red crawling up his neck was any indication.

The cops were herded to the chairs, Collins and the two uniforms bracketed by the vampiric guards. Collins coughed into his hand, and his eyes bounced around the room, sweat gathering at his temples. "You are the, um, Master? I'm sorry, I don't know your name...sir."

Batiste glided across the floor, every action less human, too elegant for a mortal to pull off. Feet stayed on the floor, but he may as well have been flying for the resemblance to a human he maintained. Angel found himself transfixed, a mouse in front of snake, and he gripped Simeon's hip, holding on. His heart jumped, and the other humans in the room were just as affected. Batiste gave Angel a single flick of his blue eyes before sitting just as graciously as he walked, and to see the effect Batiste had on humans was startling.

They couldn't look away—and Angel was fighting the desire to stare just as hard at Batiste. Simeon's presence at his side grounded him, and he was very grateful for it as he watched the humans fall under Batiste's charm. Batiste sat, unbuttoning his suit jacket, leaning back and looking for all the world to be a dignified prince or esteemed CEO, elegance and power gilded in luxurious hues.

"I am Constantine Batiste, Bloodclan Master of Boston. How may I assist the finest BPD has to offer this evening?" Slick bastard served them up and had them eating out of his palm, the cops were swept under.

"I need...we are here for Salvatore," Collins was able to get out, slow blinking. Angel couldn't tell if Batiste was deliberately trying to charm the detective into submission or if the human just had zero resistance to the sheer power oozing off the ancient undead.

"He is right here." Batiste gestured at Angel, who stayed exactly where he was. He didn't trust Collins not to jump him and cuff him, and good luck keeping things from going nuclear then. "Mr. Salvatore, as a consultant for the bloodclan, has use of our lawyers," Batiste gestured now to the well-dressed vamps standing off to the side, "Is this a matter that requires counsel?"

"A body was stolen from the city morgue last night. A murder victim's body, one that Salvatore identified as one August Remington, former teacher of the high arts here in Boston," Collins said, and with each word he was able to speak more clearly, his control returning, though his eyes were still locked on Batiste. "The coroner, a highly trained wizard in his own right, said it was done by a sorcerer. Magic was used during the theft."

"My condolences on the theft, Detective. Bodysnatchers in Boston? Disturbing. And to Mr. Salvatore as well, as I understand the deceased was a friend of yours?" Batiste gave Angel a vague smile, politely cool. Angel nodded though obviously Batiste knew everything. "And why do you need to speak to Mr. Salvatore?"

"We need to verify his whereabouts—there is some concern necromancy may have been the motivation for the body theft," Collins now broke away from Batiste's allure and stared hard at Angel. "And he was the one to identify the body."

"As I understand it, Detective Collins, Boston has the highest concentration of magical practitioners in New England. Some reports even place Massachusetts at the top of the list in terms of natural born practitioners for the entire country—that means there are thousands of sorcerers in this state. How does this then translate to Mr. Salvatore being involved in the theft of a murder victim's body?"

"Like I said, we suspect necromancy. Salvatore is the only necromancer in the city."

"And your proof of necromancy? You do have proof?" Batiste asked, smiling. There was none. Angel knew this, at least he hoped he left no clue behind, though he was certain he hadn't.

Collins was quiet, eyes darting between where Angel stood half in Simeon's embrace and Batiste. "Last night, witnesses placed Salvatore and an unknown man leaving his apartment on foot, heading in the direction of the city morgue. The unknown individual's description fits the man...umm, vampire, standing with Salvatore now."

"Yes, he was in the company of Elder Simeon," Batiste said, lip curling up in a charming grin that revealed a hint of fang. The detective gulped. "They were on a...what is the word humans use these days? A date? The bloodclan limo picked them up at the Commons after their walk."

"And what time was that?" Collins demanded.

"Just after sunset I believe. They then came here."

Angel and Simeon broke in about two hours after sunset. They may have seen him leave his place after sunset, but they hadn't managed to follow him to the morgue. Simeon would have sensed the cops stalking them through the city streets. Humans weren't capable of that level of stealth against a vampire. If Batiste maintained their alibi, then the break-in couldn't be pinned on them. Angel held still, face blank, waiting.

"Were they here the whole night?"

"I cannot ascertain that personally. Simeon, my child?"

"Yes, Master?" Simeon replied, the sexy rumble of his voice not just affecting Angel but Collins as well. The detective gave an infinitesimal shiver, and Angel bit back a grin. Simeon tended to make people want him, no matter their persuasion.

"Were you and Mr. Salvatore here all night?"

"Yes, Master. We spent the night in my suite." Simeon sounded smug as fuck and deeply satisfied, and Angel actually blushed at the heat in the Elder's words. He leaned into Simeon, rubbing his hands up the Elder's chest and shoulders, relaxing even as he burned with need. Simeon gave him a smile and a kiss, giving their audience an example of their middle of the night activities.

"So rude to inquire, my apologies, my child. And I had breakfast with the pair this morning just after dawn. Is that sufficient to satisfy your questions?" Batiste asked Collins.

Detective Collins knew he was getting played. He may be distracted by Batiste and Simeon's sexy undead vibe they both were rocking, but the cop wasn't completely fooled.

"I still need to question Salvatore. A body is missing."

"And that body is one of a murder victim, who, from descriptions provided by Mr. Salvatore as he was the man who found the body, was slain by a vampire. Slain as any would be when they are not palatable to our kind. Yet I don't see you inquiring after the whereabouts of my children when this poor man was slain. You come in here asking about his body, when the poor soul is past all caring what happens to his earthly remains. Why are you not asking me to provide proof of my whereabouts when August Remington was killed? Or any of my children, for that matter? No need," Batiste said, standing abruptly, making the humans jerk in alarm. "There is no need for you to ask where the members of my bloodclan were the other day during the murder, as they were all here and accounted for."

Batiste wasn't done. The portfolio, which he'd had all morning, suddenly landed in Collins' lap, the detective reflexively grabbing at it to keep it from spilling. Batiste stood over Collins, predatory and cold. "In that file are six murders. Committed by a rogue vampire, one that BPD has done nothing to find. All mentions of the killings have been kept from the press. Family members would be up in arms if not for threats from BPD to remain quiet about the killings. In the last two weeks, six people are dead, and just as many are missing from the deceased individuals' families. The victims were fed upon, killed, and then a family member was taken from the murder sites. Those taken were all young, healthy and without heavy emotional entanglements such as spouses or lovers."

Collins gaped. Angel was shocked.

Anger kindled in his heart. Indignation, disbelief, righteous fury —he felt it all. There was a rogue, most likely Deimos—since the odds of two vampires going about killing people in one city ruled by an omnipotent a leader as Batiste made that scenario unlikely—and the cops were literally doing nothing. Nothing at all to stop it. The corruption in the room was enough to make Angel sick to his stomach.

"There is a rogue in Boston. A rogue that is siring fledglings," Angel growled out, taking a step from Simeon's side. He was so enraged he was shaking. "That's the behavior of a rogue vampire siring new baby vamps. Gorge themselves just before they sire a new vamp. That's why there are people missing from each murder scene! There is a rogue vamp in this city and you aren't trying to stop it!"

Simeon grabbed his about the shoulders, holding him back. Batiste nodded, looming still over the cops. "There is indeed a rogue in this city. He or she may be siring newborns. And they will have no control. They will kill indiscriminately once they rise. More humans will be killed. I will not have my city descend into madness, turning the populace against my bloodclan, which is what will happen."

Collins sputtered, but nothing came out. Batiste reached down, and yanked the detective to his feet, making him clutch the portfolio. Batiste leaned in and spoke quietly in Collins' ear though Angel could hear him clearly.

"You come here on a literal witch-hunt. You come for my necromancer, and do so contrary to your sworn duty. No proof but hatred fueled by old prejudices that should have died in the Wars. Someone is trying to kill Angelus, yet you seek to throw him behind bars where he would surely die," Batiste stalked Collins back towards the door, driving the cops ahead of him. "A rogue hunts the streets of Boston, killing and turning innocents by force. The police do nothing, and those who would do something are silenced. If the police do not act, I will. Under my authority as Master of this city, I have hired Mr. Salvatore to find the rogue and bring him to justice, whether by blade, sorcery, or death at my hands. Any attempt to stop him will be treated as an act of aggression on the part of BPD."

Batiste paused and gave Collins such a feral smile that the detective paled whiter than a corpse.

"The Mayor is attending my gala tonight, and I will be discussing the matter with him, so it is in your best interests to get to work."

Batiste, with the guards at his side, all but chased the police from the room, the doors closing.

"Get out, and resume your sworn duties."

The door shut.

10

UNEXPECTED FESTIVITIES

"I'm your what, again?" Angel asked, sitting on Simeon's bed, watching as the vampire removed his shirt, fingers flying over the buttons. Pants quickly joined the shirt on the floor, and Simeon prowled toward the bed.

"*Leannán*," Simeon purred, and Angel grinned. Simeon stopped on the edge of the bed, eyeing Angel, lust and need and a depth of emotion that made his heart race. "Love, soulmate, beloved."

"And what does a *Leannán* do, exactly?" Angel toed off his socks, hands going to his waistband as he stripped himself quickly, clothes ending up back on the floor twice in less than twelve hours. They had nowhere to be for the rest of the day—most of the bloodclan slept during the day, despite the treated windows, and the first thing Angel wanted was to see Bridgerton and his entourage—but they slumbered, and even Angel was cautious of waking sleeping undead. There was some sort of gala tonight—why they couldn't just call it a party was beyond Angel—and that would be his best chance to see the new vampires in town.

"A vampire's lover in general or my *Leannán* in particular, *a ghra*?" Simeon asked, whispering as he climbed the bed, catching Angel by an ankle and holding him still.

"Yours... what does your lover do?" Angel gasped when Simeon bent down and kissed the arch of his foot, nipping, making his leg jerk in Simeon's strong grasp. Angel moaned when Simeon repeated the process but on his ankle, then the back of his lower leg.

"My lover, my soulmate.... if he would be my mate... would let me treasure him," Simeon whispered, and his eyes began to glow, emerald green flames that burned as embers in a banked fire. "My *Leannán* would let me cherish every moment he gifted me, every smile, every taste of his lips..." Simeon crept up the bed, spreading Angel's legs, encouraging him to wrap them around his lean waist. Angel pulled him closer, their hard cocks, one cool the other burning with heat, sliding over each other, making them both groan.

Simeon lowered himself atop Angel, who opened his mouth in welcome when a questing tongue tasted his lips. Angel undulated his hips, causing a rapidly heating, rock-hard cock to slip between his ass cheeks and glide over his hole. Simeon growled, and took the kiss deeper, feeding the rising passion between them. No thoughts left for words now, just them and the need to connect, to be as close as they could possibly be.

Angel rolled his hips again and again, and Simeon shuddered with need, growls reverberating through his torso while Angel kept up the torture. He wanted, needed, had to have Simeon inside of him, and this fire burning between them was too new for it to be tempered by patience.

Angel bit Simeon's lower lip, making Simeon jerk in his arms, and Simeon reared up, kneeling on the bed, fangs lowered completely and eyes wild and glowing. Hands gripped his knees, opening his legs, holding him still. Simeon bared his fangs, cock standing proud and flushed, leaking a clear line of fluid from the tip that dripped down the inside of Angel's thigh. Simeon reached out and took Angel in hand, stroking him, ownership in every flick of his wrist. Angel gasped, and lifted his hips, arching into the hand that worked him without mercy. Simeon's other hand slid down the back of his leg, fingers seeking out his ass, slipping between his cheeks and growing straight for his hole, blunt fingertips rubbing over the puckered flesh.

Angel stilled, eyes wide, mouth open, lungs unable to work as Simeon did it again, stroking his cock in to time to the slow, steady and very proprietary touch over his hole.

Simeon chuckled, a cruel sound that made Angel shiver. Angel reached out, frantic to pull Simeon down on top of him, in him, to get Simeon to hold him down and fuck him senseless. Simeon dodged his desperate hands, and leaned over, hand searching in the blankets. Angel heaved a fast breath in relief when Simeon's hand came up with the bottle of lube.

"Please," Angel gasped out, arching his hips, reaching for his own cock, desperate for a tight grip on his aching flesh. "Make me feel like I'm yours. Hold me down, I need to *feel* it."

He was losing his mind, he had to be. He'd never begged in his life.

Simeon must have seen something in his expression or heard it in his voice that spoke to the depth of his need, since he was soon covered by hard muscles and long limbs, Simeon's weight pushing him down, legs wider. He locked them about his lover's lean waist, hooking his heels and lifting his hips. There was no finesse, no cautious and careful preparation; in the barest of thoughts, Simeon was inside of him, stealing his breath and will. Hot and cold collided, and he shook, overwhelmed.

Simeon captured his mouth in a kiss that was all tongue and harsh lips, his hips rocking. Angel cried out, reduced to wordless sobs. Simeon moved, each thrust inside ruthless and deep, ever so fucking deep, leaving Angel no place to escape in his mind as Simeon systematically reduced him to aching, whimpering passion.

Hands scored Simeon's shoulders, Angel searching for a lifeline, but he had no moment to catch his breath, no second to gather himself and do more than *feel*—Simeon took him over, wholly and totally, left no part of his body untouched by his masterful hands and obliterating rhythm of his hips. The thick cock spearing him, impaling him and holding him down moved relentlessly, and Angel cried out with each thrust and withdrawal. He felt stretched thin, ready to snap and burst into a thousand pieces of raw pleasure and sweet aches.

"So tight around me," Simeon whispered in his ear, his big hands now wrapped under Angel's shoulders, holding him in place as he increased the pace of their fucking. "Hot and tight, you fit me perfectly. So perfect, my *Leannán*."

Every shiver, every tingle, and buzz along his nervous system began to coalesce, to slowly pull in from his extremities and gather in his center, rumbling down his spine to settle heavy and expectant in his groin. Angel whined, and he bit the hard, wide shoulder above him when he came with a deep shudder.

His body clamped down on Simeon, who thrust harder, shoving them both across the bed, sheets tearing beneath clawed fingers. Angel tasted the tang of mint and chocolate and cool sweet spices across his tongue, and Simeon lifted his head, screaming out his release, cordons in his neck standing out in relief and fangs bared. Angel came again, and his head fell back, exposing his own neck, Simeon's blood running from his lips. He could feel Simeon shuddering atop him, the strange and welcome coolness in his depths signaling his lover's release, making him gasp with each heavy pulse into his core.

Simeon's cry still echoed about the room, pinging in his ears, the last thing Angel heard before darkness swept over his eyes and a sudden and unexpected wave of pleasure chased him into oblivion.

HE RARELY SLEPT AFTER SEX. In fact, he could say honestly he had no idea when the last time was that he passed out after having an orgasm—though the first time with Simeon made him do the same. Whether it was having sex with a vampire, or having sex with Simeon that made him pass out he had no idea, though he had a feeling it was more about the man than the supernatural creature.

Angel sat up, the covers falling from his chest. A swipe of his tongue across his lower lip confirmed his blurry memory of biting

Simeon so hard the vamp bled. The surface of his tongue bloomed with a chocolate sweetness, a cool hint of mint chasing the taste down his throat. Angel blew out a shaky breath, and looked at the clock beside the bed. But for the blood still on his lips, he was clean, no lube or spunk in sight. It was just after sunset, though he couldn't see out the windows—they were all obscured by thick red curtains, and a single light from across the room let him see he was alone.

"I'd like to wake up next to him just once," Angel muttered as he slid from the bed, grabbing the sheet as he went, wrapping it around his hips and gathering the excess around his arm like a badly done toga.

The door opened, and Angel stopped, as startled as the human in the doorway.

"Um, what the fuck?" Angel said, annoyed someone would just waltz into a bedroom without knocking. There was no reason for bad fucking manners—and the excuse he could see hovering on parted, pouty lips on the presumed blood donor wasn't going to stand up under his doubt. "Ever heard of knocking?"

The human man stepped over the threshold, bowing in the half-light from the single lamp. Angel saw shiny, pale silver marks along the sides of his neck, and it clicked for him what, not who, this person was—blood servant. The man's words next confirmed it. "Elder Simeon is attending to the Master, but bid me to come assist you. Your clothes have been laundered, though Elder Simeon has sent new apparel from the clan tailor for you to wear tonight at the gala."

"He did what? I'm going to the party thing? Oh, wait... fuck. What the hell is going on?" Angel gaped. This wasn't some rags-to-riches bullshit movie trope—he had his own clothes, and no one was dressing him. "Why does no one call it a damn party like normal people and why can't I wear my own clothes?"

"It is a formal black tie event, sir. Elder Simeon left you a note, I believe?" the blood servant didn't seem at all phased by Angel's bad mood, though not surprising as he made a living from feeding vampires from his jugular. Not much rattled people crazy enough to do that on a daily basis. Angel glared, but went looking for a note. He found it on Simeon's pillow, the handwriting elegant and reminiscent of ages past.

Bridgerton will be at dinner tonight before the midnight gala welcoming him to the clan. The gala will be the only opportunity to meet all the new additions before Bridgerton moves to his new accommodations. His people will be there. This is our best chance to see if Bridgerton or his people are Deimos.

"I guess I'm going to a party," Angel groused, looking down at the sheet around his waist. Angel sighed and gave the blood servant a tight smile. "Where's my new clothes at?"

The servant bowed again, saying, "I shall fetch them immediately, sir. Dinner is in less than an hour."

The blood servant left, and Angel crumpled the note, summoning a burst of hellfire and burning it to ash in his hand. If he had his way, the vampire known as Deimos would be ash himself soon. All Angel needed to do was find him. He let the faint breeze from the central heating system blow the remnants away, and he headed for the bathroom, dropping the sheet as he went.

THE LAST TIME he was in clothing this fancy, he was burying his whole family. Angel fussed with the black silk tie, not enjoying the stranglehold it had on his neck. The black tuxedo and pristine, snow-white shirt and black trousers were so finely tailored he was afraid to breathe and rip some seams.

Shaven, dressed to kill, and hungry, Angel waited impatiently for his date to arrive, feeling foolish and excited all at once. Here he was, planning on attending a damn ball in order to identify and kill a murderer, and he was nervous about Simeon's reaction to how he looked.

There was no point in thinking he would bother catching Deimos and handing him over to either the police or the Master. The police were clearly not to be trusted, and the Master may find his hand stayed by the identity of the killer, depending on who Deimos turned out to be. There was no doubt in Angel that Deimos was here, now, in the Tower. Too many changes in the last week that were all connected and true coincidences really weren't all that common. Especially not in his world.

The door opened, and Angel forgot how to breathe. Simeon walked in and took his hand, staring down at him with an affectionate smile on his lush lips, and his green eyes were lit up, shone off to advantage by the rich hues of his smoky gray tuxedo and jewel-toned tie. His auburn hair was swept back in a high, smooth wave that showed off his high cheekbones and even complimented the woad-colored tattoo peeking over the back of his collar on his muscular neck. A diamond tie-pin glimmered, and the single gold ring on Simeon's third finger glowed with a deep, large emerald.

Angel meshed his fingers with Simeon's, and they stared at each other in awe. Simeon hummed his approval, leaning down and gently biting Angel's jaw before kissing away the slight sting, moving his lips around to Angel's mouth and kissing him softly. Angel moaned, head tipped back, and arched into Simeon's arms, rubbing his front all along the vampire's, needing more contact.

"Can we just stay here? Let's do that," Angel breathed out, as Simeon rumbled out a laugh and hugged him tightly. "You can sniff out a killer from here, yeah?"

"I shall be scenting them all discretely tonight, my love, no fear on that. If I can scent the killer, I will immediately tell you. Though we have a place to be, *Leannán*. I wish I could remain here and show you just how much I adore how handsome you are in that tuxedo," Simeon kissed him again, a firm press of lips that made his hurt, but Angel wanted another. He liked hard, firm kisses, and Simeon knew it. "Come, my love, we have people to impress and hopefully, someone to kill."

"Gives a new meaning to the expression, 'dressed to kill'," Angel laughed out, accepting Simeon's arm as his lover lead them out into the hall.

"I believe that was the original meaning, *a ghra*," Simeon replied, chuckling.

"Shush, don't ruin this for me," Angel chided and surprised himself by blushing when Simeon brought their joined hands up and kissed the back of Angel's knuckles.

The ride down in the elevator was odd, as there were double the guards present, cramping the space. The guards wore tuxes too, both vampires and humans on duty. The only way to distinguish between the two species was that while they were all huge, only the vampires moved with an innate grace that no human could pull off. Armed, and intimidating, Angel gave the guards he encountered a cheeky grin, making them alternately flinch, glare, or ignore him.

The elevator dropped them off on the ground floor of the Tower. The casino was on this floor, along with several conference rooms, private rooms for a myriad of purposes, and a large, grand ballroom replete with a stage for live music, a DJ booth, balconies along the walls, and open bars on each wall. Tables ran along the outside of the dance floor, and Simeon led him through the milling throng of humans and supernats. Angel recognized local celebrities from the news and papers, some football players, and the mayor of Boston and even a few senators. Wealth dripped from the crowd in copious waves of gems and silk, luxurious fabrics and designer clothing. Waiters prowled around the room, serving flutes of champagne and crystal glasses of hard liquor. The ceiling above was lit up by three large chandeliers, blazing like miniature suns.

The vampires were easy to pick from the crowd, as were the other supernats present. Angel was surprised to see several fae, the reclusive species rarely seen in metropolitan areas, but he saw, at least, three of them mingling in the crowd. The slightly pointed ears and the inhuman beauty were dead giveaways, as were the forest hues to their clothing. Werewolves, the hirsute behemoths along the walls, the least likely of wallflowers congregated together and everyone else gave them a wide berth. They were safe—it wasn't a full moon for another week, so no one was going to rage out. Lesser known supernats moved through the crowd, and Angel couldn't resist double glances at some of the more surprising guests.

What got to Angel the most was the way Simeon moved through the milling crowd. The Elder moved as if there were no on else present, as if they were alone and the path clear before them. Total ownership of his space and purpose drew countless eyes to them as they walked across the grand space. As they approached, vampires bowed and backed away, murmuring greetings to their Elder. Humans looked nervous, or even frightened, all of them moving out of the way as well. Angel could see which were blood servants and which were guests, the bite scars and fresh scores on necks making the distinction obvious.

Simeon took them to the top of the room, where a long, dark oak table with seating for at least twenty people stood, covered in candles and silver platters. Simeon took Angel straight to the head of the table, where Batiste stood, surrounded by a well-dressed crowd of vampires and humans, each vying for his attention. They parted before Simeon and Angel, and Angel soon found himself across from a tall, swarthy vampire, whose natural skin-tone resisted even the pallor of his vampiric nature. Dark, long hair tied back in a braid, with a short, neatly trimmed full beard, the other vampire looked to Angel as he imagined a pirate would back in the 1600s. There was even a jeweled earring in the vamp's left ear, a tiny skull carved from a blue gem that dangled from the scarred lobe.

"Necromancer Salvatore, may I present William Bridgerton, lately of Atlanta, our newest clan member," Batiste took Angel's free hand, holding it in both of his larger, colder hands, and giving him a small dip of his head before turning to Bridgerton. "William, it is an honor to present to you Angelus Salvatore, Boston's singular necromancer and the *Leannán* to my esteemed child, Elder Simeon. I believe you met Simeon the other night at dinner, yes?"

Bridgerton's eyes were locked on Angel, his full lips twisted into a mocking grin, more aggression than welcome in his eyes. Bridgerton gave Angel a brief nod of acknowledgment, then his eyes went to Simeon. "We met, yes. Very briefly before your Elder appeared to get important news and left us in a hurry. Can I assume it was about your beloved accepting your courtship, as I could swear no one mentioned that Angelus Salvatore was bonded to a member of this clan?"

"I am standing right here," Angel quipped, and gave a small zip of power to the hand in Batiste's grip, making the Master let go of his hand. Angel gave Bridgerton a narrow glare, all but daring the old vamp to say something else. "My personal relationship is none of your business."

Shocked hissing and nervous shifting from the crowd around them told Angel he was treading on dangerous ground, but he wasn't worried. He wanted to know if anyone of the numerous vamps standing at Bridgerton's back was Deimos—and as Simeon hadn't reacted at all to Bridgerton, then that meant Bridgerton wasn't their vamp.

"Angel has recently accepted my courtship," Simeon replied, and his hand gripped Angel's harder for a brief second before relaxing.

"I must offer my congratulations then," Bridgerton said, and Angel caught a hint of accent in the older vamp's voice. British, or something close. Bridgerton grabbed a drink from a passing servant, holding up the glass of what looked to be carbonated cranberry juice…until Angel's nose twitched. Designer blood drink. Everyone who had a drink briefly toasted them, and Angel glowered at Bridgerton, ignoring the murmured compliments tossed in their direction. "It's a shame you left when you did, Elder Simeon. I was about to declare my intent to challenge for a position as Elder of this clan when you left so early. But since you are here now," Bridgerton smiled, predatory and grim, turning to Batiste and bowing, "I will be challenging for a position as Elder, Master Batiste."

"I had a feeling you would be. Though you are aware I will not be opening a new position if you go through with your challenge? You will have to fight, and defeat, either Etienne or Simeon for the honor of being an Elder." Batiste replied, appearing bored, though Angel was fighting back the urge to hex Bridgerton where he stood and burn him to a crisp.

He wanted to be an Elder, and somehow Angel didn't think the contest was to first blood. From the way Etienne shifted nervously, and how Simeon gave Bridgerton a single brow lift and hugged Angel to his side, it was obvious which vampire was not going to be challenged. Etienne glared at Bridgerton, who completely ignored him, finishing his drink.

"I would wish you luck, but I cannot. I would suggest you rethink your intentions since you cannot properly ascertain the dangers you're taking on with such a task as an Elder challenge," Simeon cautioned. "Neither Etienne nor I are lacking in skills."

Bridgerton chuckled, and sent a lazy glance over Etienne, the Elder hissing back.

Batiste interrupted the deeply intense moment by moving towards the table.

Everyone seemed to take their cue from that, people sitting across the room. Dishes clinked and silverware echoed across the space, and Angel found himself sitting between Batiste at the head of the table, Simeon on his right, with Bridgerton directly across from him, Etienne on Bridgerton's other side. How Etienne could sit next to Bridgerton and not lose his shit Angel had no idea. Vampires in general had to be stone cold bastards to not show any emotion after casually discussing killing each other.

The rest of Bridgerton's entourage was seated at the table, and Angel wished they hadn't sat so soon, since he wanted to talk to some of these people, see if Simeon recognized their scents.

Angel looked as carefully as he could at the vamps and humans across the table, but none of the vamps stood out. He couldn't hear them well enough to distinguish voices, not that he was sure he could recall Deimos's voice from the stairwell as the vamp had been in fullblown bloodlust at the time, fangs warping his voice and mouth.

Dark brown eyes, so dark they were nearly black met his, and the human gave a jerk, his face going blank of all expression before he looked down at his plate and ate. The young man was younger than Isaac, probably twenty or so, and his neatly messy hair was dirty blond and thick. Angel kept watching, and the young man dared a glimpse up at him, saw him watching, and startled again, this time knocking his glass over. Water spilled on the table, and the young man awkwardly mopped it up with a linen napkin.

"I don't know anyone," Angel said aloud, looking away from the awkward young man, suspicion fussing at the back of his mind. He knew that boy. Somewhere, somehow, he knew that boy at the other end of the table. Angel jabbed at Simeon with his elbow, and Simeon gave him a raised brow, confused. "Introduce me to some more people," Angel said, and nodded his chin at the boy, who was now staring back at Angel, face paling, eyes wide.

"Of course, *a ghra*, though I do not know everyone here. Some of our guests belong to Bridgerton," Simeon said casually, and he directed his next comment across the table. "Mr. Bridgerton, would you do the honors of introducing us to your friends?"

"Certainly," Bridgerton replied with a smile that told Angel he was anything but pleased. "My companions," he said, pointing to two vampires on the other side of Etienne, who nodded as they were named, "Ellora Sumar," a dark, nymph-like woman who looked like she was fifteen but acted far older, and "Douglas Eschard," an older vamp who was reborn undead in his fifties, "both who have been members of my household for the last century, and my blood servant Rachel Evans."

"Who's the boy?" Angel asked, and Etienne bristled, but Batiste answered.

"That young man is Etienne's newest toy. Daniel, I believe is his name?"

Time stopped, made a funny hiccup that stole the air from his lungs and sent his skin aflame in awareness. Angel slowly turned his head, the conversations around them falling into the background, his mind taken up in a refrain of horrified recognition.

Daniel. He did indeed know the boy at the table, and the young man knew him, too.

Macavoy.

Daniel Macavoy, son of Leicaster Macavoy, only ten years old when his whole family conspired and committed the mass murder of the Salvatore clan.

Simeon growled beside him, sensing his alarm, but Angel was too busy staring at Daniel. The young man at the end of the table stared back, so pale he was likely in danger of passing out.

And Angel saw in him the rude, abrasive young man at his door months ago, demanding to know how Angel killed a hundred vampires in a single night, alone and without help. Angel had sent him away, not even bothering to learn his name or why he so earnestly wanted to know how to kill vampires *en masse*. Daniel swallowed, and got up from the table, rattling the chair and table and mumbling apologies to the people seated next to him. Daniel wasted no time, taking off like a shot between the tables.

Angel pushed back from his chair, dodging Simeon's hand and ignoring the voices calling after him, demanding answers. Angel followed Daniel, tracking the young man as he wove through the crowd.

"Daniel! Stop, dammit!" Angel called, pissed off. He just wanted to talk. He didn't even know Daniel was still in Boston—and how the hell was he a blood servant? He was the son of two powerful sorcerers; Daniel's blood was pure poison to any undead. "Daniel!"

"Stay away! He said you wouldn't recognize me, I'm sorry! He made me do it!" Daniel cried over his shoulder, running between two tables for a side hall. Guards saw them coming, and people were yelling behind them. "Leave me alone!"

"Daniel Macavoy, get back here, dammit!" Angel yelled, sprinting hard. The guards at the door made to grab Daniel, but he backpedaled away and rammed right into Angel. Angel caught him about the waist and tried his best to hold the boy still, but Daniel was taller than him and weighed more. Daniel broke free and swung wildly at Angel. He ducked and held his hands up. "Daniel, stop, goddammit. Is it Deimos? Is Bridgerton Deimos?"

"What? No!" Daniel was panting, sweating, eyes darting around the room as both vamps and guards circled them, guests rudely kicked out of their seats. Simeon was approaching, Batiste, Bridgerton, and Etienne close on his heels, forcing their way through the crowd. "Stay away from me!"

A *thump*, a powerful tide of energy echoed between the space between Daniel and Angel. Angel knew what is was, and from the gasps in the room, he wasn't the only practitioner in the room to feel Daniel tap into the veil. Blue energy crackled around Daniel's shoulders, his aura flaring, becoming visible as he fed raw veil-power into his core.

"Daniel! I just want to talk to you! Stop it!"

He got his own shields up just in time. A ball of blue fire roared across the space between them, crackling as it fell in spurts of flame to the floor, his shields breaking it apart. "Get out of the way!"

Screams and shouts came from the guests as Daniel threw spell after spell at Angel, the boy clearly panicked and terrified. Eyes wild and hands shaking, Daniel screamed at him in bad Latin, his lack of training making him even more dangerous. A haphazard curse came screaming at him, and Angel caught it, his shields absorbing it before it could ricochet off their surface and hit someone in the crowd.

"Get out of here!" Angel screamed at the confused onlookers, getting Simeon's attention and pointing at the people standing around watching. "He has no idea what he's doing! Get them out of here or someone is going to die! Move it!"

Simeon nodded and began yelling orders, and Angel kept his hands up, pushing out with his shields, covering the fleeing crowds behind him as Daniel tossed spell after spell at him. The boy was barely holding onto the veil, power surging in badly maintained waves that swelled and fell in near chaos. Their impromptu duel was nothing but raw power and instinct. Fires broke out across the room, along the walls and on the ceiling, tables melting and glass breaking.

Daniel was casting with everything he had, draining himself and leaving his control over the veil disintegrating. Angel kept his shields up and made them less reflective, stickier. Spells came at him, landing with sharp whines and hissing, the air thick with ozone and heat, and his focus fell to the boy in front of him. Daniel was sweating through his suit, and the boy fell to his knees as Angel pushed out, ready to pull a fucking risky as hell maneuver. All he had to do was get close enough, and he could turn his shields inside out and drop them over Daniel—trapping him inside, under Angel's control, and the boy would likely knock himself out with his own spells. It was like flipping a teacup over on top of a spider, and he had to do it quick enough not to get bit.

He was only a handful of feet from Daniel when the boy stopped, a hand on the floor holding himself up, and he seemed to understand that everything he was trying to do wasn't even getting through Angel's shields—Angel had him outclassed. He hadn't even needed to draw on the veil to protect himself from Daniel. The boy may be a sorcerer, but his training was woefully lacking, and Daniel was coming to realize that. The boy gave a frustrated scream, and Angel saw a ring of vampires approaching, encircling the boy, fangs barred and claws out.

Something was driving the boy, instigating his fear to such heights that his first reaction to being recognized by Angel was to attack, even in a room of innocents. Daniel was terrified—but the question was, who scared him the most? Angel, or Deimos?

"Daniel. Please listen to me. I am not your enemy; I will not harm you. Please, please stand down," Angel pleaded, even as he twisted his wrists, prepping his shields for the flip. There was no way Daniel would recognize the motion, not with his training as bad as it was.

"You're a Salvatore! You hate us all! You want me dead!" Daniel cried out, tears joining the sweat on his face. "He said you would kill me if you knew I was here!"

"Who said, Daniel? Who are you so frightened of?" Angel asked, crouching on his heels, hands still up, palms out, ready to flip his shields if he must. He could pour his will inside and break Daniel's, as he would an out of control student lost in the veil, and knock the boy out. He made his voice softer, kinder. "Daniel, I am not your enemy. You were a little kid back then, and I have never blamed you for anything. Let me help you."

The vampires were coming closer, Simeon, Batiste, and Etienne directly behind the exhausted sorcerer. Angel met their gazes, and gave an infinitesimal shake to his head, asking them to stop. They all did, Batiste holding up a hand to get the other vampires approaching to halt as well. Etienne was the last to stop, crouching about ten feet from Daniel, ready to pounce.

Angel met Daniel's eyes, trying his best to convey his honesty. "Daniel, I will not hurt you, I promise."

It made his chest hurt, actually hurt, to see the hope in Daniel's dark eyes. The boy was ready to collapse, and Angel pressed just a bit more. "Daniel, who is Deimos? Is he the one who you're afraid of?"

Daniel bit his lip, but nodded, and Angel cheered inwardly in victory. "I can keep you safe from him. Who is he, Daniel? Is he here right now?"

"Yes," Daniel answered, falling forward, whispering. Angel could feel him trying to let go of the veil, the ambient power in the room spiking as Daniel fumbled his control.

"Easy, Daniel," Angel cautioned. "Let me help you let go of the veil. You know I can do that for you, yeah? Then you can tell me who Deimos is, and this will all be over, okay?"

"Okay...." Daniel breathed, the boy ready to pass out. Angel dropped his shields completely, lunging forward as Daniel collapsed before catching himself, forcing himself back up on his knees. The vampires hissed in concert, creepy and disturbing. Etienne inched closer, and Angel glared at the Elder, wanting him to back off.

Angel was two feet from the boy when Etienne lunged, screeching. Angel was knocked away, falling on his ass as Etienne landed on top of Daniel, jaws wide as he bit the boy on the neck. Daniel screamed, blood running over his lips, the sound strangled. He clawed ineffectively at Etienne's back, trying to get free as the vampire ravaged his neck.

"No!" Angel screamed and blasted Etienne in the back with a green ball of fire, making the vampire rip away, throwing Daniel to the floor. A small, dark gray jar bound in black twine fell from Daniel's jacket and bounced a few feet away, clattering on the hardwood floor. Etienne roared in triumph when he saw it, and leapt, smashing the jar with his hand.

"Fuck!" Angel threw another ball of fire, but it was too late—Etienne blurred away, and the other vampires converged. Angel lifted

Daniel in his arms, and with a burst of kinetic energy, pushed the vampires all away from him and Daniel. He kept an eye on the broken jar, the black smoke emanating from the fractured pieces, setting fire to floor in a set pattern as the spell released itself.

Daniel's blood, running from his neck and out across the floor, met a trail of smoke, and the spell flared to life, a circle combusting around the remnants of the jar, and a void of black puddled and swirled in the center. Angel put a hand over Daniel's neck, the boy unconscious already, trying to stem the flow of blood from his injury. Daniel had released the veil the second he lost consciousness, his mind open to Angel.

Angel reached for the veil this time and raised his shields around him and the boy dying in his arms. The spell unspinning itself in front of him was more dangerous than anything the boy had cast before—and now Angel knew who summoned the demon that attacked him.

"Angel!" Simeon called to him, trying to get to him through his shield, bashing at it with his hands, light flaring out and crashing from the points of contact. "My love, take the shield down!"

"Simeon, get back! Trust me, and get back!" Simeon cried out, unwilling, Batiste grabbing him and yanking him away.

A horrible roar of sound, and an intense and fiery burst of light crawled from the depths of the black void—a many-clawed hand snapped through the abyss, lodging on the wooden floor, and the demon on the other side of the void pulled itself through in response to the set summoning spell that had been trapped in the jar. Dark gray and green scales, splashed with random yellow spots adorned the beast, and it straddled the void, its tail slipping free just as the portal closed with a horrific snap.

It roared, raising to an impressive ten-foot height, its many tongues flailing over hundreds of teeth, the demon's voice frighteningly familiar. "Angelus!"

"Angel!" Simeon screamed, the terror in his voice breaking Angel's heart and threatening to destroy his focus. Batiste kept his hold on Simeon, who screamed in defiance and tried to break free.

He could handle this—he had to, or the boy would die, and the demon would kill Angel.

Angel sent his will down, into the boy, who was dying. Daniel Macavoy was hovering on the brink of death—and that was where Angel was strongest. He could not heal scratches or bruises or broken bones—but a mortal wound, a killing blow—that Angel had dominion over, and he used his affinity now. He could not bring someone back from death, at least not as they were in life, but as a revenant like August or a zombie or wraith—but a soul on the edge, between life and death and not fully departed, Angel could and would pull them back. The death magic answered him, and Angel sealed the torn arteries, fused the sundered flesh, poured veil-drawn energy into the failing body in his arms, and he called Daniel's soul back from the brink. And while his spirit and Daniel's communed, the transfer of power total and complete, Angel saw into the boy's mind and heart, and knew the truth.

Angel lifted his head, and his hand came up, covered in Daniel's blood, wet and sticky and full of power.

The demon scored the floor, its long tail smashing tables and chairs, tossing aside the foolish vampires attacking it like raptors would a t-rex in those sci-fi movies Isaac loved so much. Ichor dripped from its red mouth, and Angel saw the scars along its snout from their first encounter. Simeon yelled at the vampires, their bodies broken and slashed, but they backed away, waiting on Angel.

Angel kept his hand up, and spread his fingers, sending out his will. As he healed Daniel, he stole from the boy the original name of the beast before him, summoned unwilling across dimensional voids to kill for his master. Angel gently lay Daniel down, the boy still wounded and drained, though he would live if Angel got him to a doctor.

Angel stood, and stepped over Daniel. He took one step, then another, focusing his will on the beast, and it backed away, lowering to all fours like a cat, its form changing and twisting, torn apart by the energies that held it here in Angel's world, away from its home. The *geas* upon the beast was what drove it to violence and madness; Angel would end its suffering.

"Eroch, child of the void," Angel intoned, stepping forward, measured steps and calm, even breaths focusing his will. "Eroch, hear me and obey."

"Angelus!" It hissed, a thousand voices tumbling over themselves to form his name, and its eyes narrowed, flaring yellow. Spittle dripped from its fangs, and Angel could feel the beast push back against his command through the tenuous connection between them. "You must die, angel of death."

Its voice was weakening, its will eroding, but not fast enough. If Angel couldn't tame the demon, the *geas* would overwhelm the beast and send it after Angel, and anyone in its way.

"Eroch! Stolen child, enslaved soul of the void, hear me and obey!"

"Nooooo!" It screamed, neck twisting, lowering down on the floor, and Angel dropped his shields, needing no interference between the demon and himself. It was such a risk to take his heart thundered in fear, but he must win, he must make it answer to its name.

Simeon yelled at him, and Angel was thankful Batiste was the stronger of the two, keeping Simeon from harm.

"You will answer me!" Angel screamed, throat hurting, and he pulled more of the veil into himself and set it crashing along the weak link to the beast. It screamed in turn, collapsing to the floor, and it submitted at last.

Silence fell, and Angel rushed forward, the deafening quiet muffling everything, even his own breaths. Angel kept his hand up, and his will on the beast and Angel scuffed the circle on the floor, kicking apart the broken pieces of the jar that had held the complete summoning spell. It was an impressive yet foolhardy example of spell-casting, a masterpiece composed by a fool who did not know any better. It may have been Daniel, it may not, but Angel now had the beast under his control and did not need the haphazard summoning circle to stop it.

He could not send it back; not with the geas attached to it still, and from the memories he'd seen in Daniel's mind, the boy had not placed the geas—it did not take magic to do so, as all a sorcerer had to do was summon a demon, any demon, and allow anyone present to give the beast its first command, the geas. Once done, the geas would remain in place until the demon was killed, which was almost impossible, or the one who gave it the *geas* was dead or willingly absolved the demon from its task.

What Angel could do was change the shape of the *geas*. The task for this beast was to kill Angel—he was the focus, the lodestone for the demon's task. All he had to do was change the task, and keep the focus on him.

"Eroch, child of the void, hear me, and be at peace. Peace, child of the abyss, I lift from you the pain, the torture. Be thyself, free from bonds of violence. Hear me, and become as you should be," Angel whispered, standing over the beast, its size huge and dwarfing him. It gave a keen, a hollow wail of pain, and shuddered.

It shrank. Gray scales shimmered, turned a deep emerald green, a wave of verdant light flowing over its hide as it became smaller, limbs shrinking, the dreadful beast softening, the pain leaving its body as it twitched and chirped.

From murderer to devoted companion. Angel was still the focus of the demon's task, but the task was new.

Angel knelt, and with a slow, careful breath, picked up the small dragon, its yellow eyes blinking slowly, so tired and exhausted. Without the *geas* upon it demanding it commit murder contrary to its innate nature, Angel's control over it granted the beast its free will. The demon resumed the wild shape it held in its home dimension. The tiny dragon was the size of a housecat, emerald and scaled, with four legs and two small, perfect wings upon its shoulders, its tail twice as long as its body and winding around Angel's arm. It chirped, frightened, confused, and Angel sighed, exhausted himself as he got to his feet.

Angel was still the focus of the demon's task, but the task was new. Angel soothed Eroch, the tiny dragon so confused and lost, and he felt horrible himself. He was still its master—and the dragon may now be itself, but it was still just as trapped.

"Forgive me, Eroch, child of the wild skies," he whispered, and the tiny head lifted to look him in the face, and it nodded, curling into him, eyes closing. He would give it peace and protection until he could kill their mutual enemy.

He held Eroch gently and turned to the rest of the room.

Shock was the least of the expressions sent his way. Dumbfounded and frightened were the most prevalent, the vampires and the few brave remaining souls in the room all staring at him. All but one, at least.

Simeon shook off Batiste, the Master just as shocked as the rest of the room, and Angel smiled as his lover approached. Simeon stepped over the debris and the scorched floor and took Angel in his arms, sleepy dragon and all.

"You are a marvel," Simeon whispered in his ear, clutching him close.

"I love you too," Angel said, and laughed, utterly exhausted.

Batiste approached, as Simeon pulled back and gave Angel a sweet smile, his lover's eyes shadowed by worry and affection.

"Daniel Macavoy is now mine, Master Batiste. I claim him as my apprentice," Angel stated, his words ricocheting around the room, stilling all movement. "As per our agreement, anyone I claim as mine is under my protection and immune to violence from you and your people."

"Are you certain, necromancer? Such a one would be as a viper in your home—certain to poison you at its first chance," Batiste said, glancing to where Daniel lay unconscious, before turning his gaze to the slumbering beast in his arms. "Though any man who can turn a demon into a pet may not need to worry about such trivial things as betrayal."

"Let me worry about my house. You should be worrying about yours," Angel retorted and smirked at Batiste. "Etienne is Deimos."

11

LOVE IN DEATH'S EMBRACE

"Be careful with him, dammit!" Angel scolded the blood-servants who carried Daniel into the spare room in Simeon's suite. They put him on the bed, and removed his burnt and bloodstained clothing, stripping the boy down to his underwear before pulling the covers up to his chin.

"The doctor is on his way," Simeon said, entering the room and coming to Angel's side. "We have one on call for emergencies."

"Blood loss something the doctor probably sees a lot, then?" Angel said, hoisting Eroch up to his shoulder, the tiny dragon winding his tail loosely around Angel's neck before going back to sleep. "I need to talk to Batiste."

"He's still here," Simeon replied, leading the way back out to the front room. Batiste was standing at a window, staring down at the streets, and even nine stories up the flashes of red and blue from the ambulances and police cars below reached up into the suite, glancing off the ceiling.

"Tell me why Etienne is Deimos," Batiste demanded, and even Angel heard the order under the steely words.

"I saved Daniel. He was dying and was I able to slip inside when his defenses were down. It's something I can do with my students if they get lost in their magic—I subsume their wills, and while I was healing Daniel, I was reading his mind," Angel explained, stroking Eroch when the dragon chirped in fear, responding to Angel's mood. "I saw Etienne approach him, take him from his home and bring him here as a new blood slave. He never actually drank from the boy, just made it look like Daniel was his newest toy. Somehow he fed the boy lies, said I was solidifying my power base here in the clan, and would be coming after what was left of my enemies once I was in good with the vampires. Etienne charmed the boy—he is poorly trained, not surprising considering his family is persona non grata here in town, much like my own, and he lacked for anyone to teach him. Leicester is a drunk and a recluse, and couldn't give Daniel a proper education. Etienne was able to sway Daniel, and convince him I was going to kill him if I bonded with Simeon before taking over the clan."

Angel glanced at Simeon, who gave him a small smile, and Angel took the hand Simeon held out to him. "How long have you all known Bridgerton was coming?"

"He sent queries six months ago about joining my clan," Batiste answered, turning from the windows, hands in his pockets, watching Angel. "Why?"

"How long has Etienne been a part of your clan?" Angel asked instead of answering, and Batiste tightened his jaw in annoyance, but he replied.

"Nine years. I made him an Elder eight years ago," Batiste snapped, impatient.

"Where did he come from?" Angel asked though he knew the answer. He'd seen it in Daniel's mind. He wondered if Batiste knew, though.

"Etienne is from France," Batiste said. "He came here from Paris."

Angel shook his head and sighed. "You made Etienne an Elder because his ability to charm humans and supernats is uniquely powerful, didn't you? Etienne rarely needs to fight—he can charm his enemies into submission. Anyone not as strong as him he can make into puppets. Much like you, actually."

Batiste was quiet, listening.

"Etienne is the legate from Providence, the vampire who betrayed his clan and sold them to the Macavoys. That's how he got Daniel to trust him so fast, and why his charms lasted so long on the boy—Daniel knew him already. So Etienne's twisted tale of the evil Angelus Salvatore had more weight behind it. Etienne took the role of another vampire coming here from France, and joined your clan, hiding in plain sight. He was able to charm his way to the top. That was working, right up until you moved your clan to Boston."

"And we began our relationship with you," Batiste murmured. "Simeon began his long courtship, and you came here more and more. Every time you came here, Etienne...Deimos ran the risk of exposing himself."

"Yeah, but he wasn't worried about me, not at all—my aversion to talking about the tragedy is well known, and you'd already ordered your clan to leave that topic alone. He was hidden, and one undead slot away from the top of the pile. Deimos was content to stay there, right up until you started fielding inquiries from Bridgerton to move here."

"What does Bridgerton have to do with Etienne trying to kill you?" Simeon asked, and Angel squeezed his lover's hand, reassuring him.

"Think about it. Bridgerton is an arrogant ass. He wants to come here, to a clan that is the sole powerbase for vampires in the city, and only has two Elders. Atlanta is one of the biggest cities in the country, and the city has multiple clans in it. Too much competition, right?" Simeon and Batiste both nodded, following along. "So Bridgerton comes here. He makes no attempt to hide his plans. I bet the both of you, and Etienne, discussed the likelihood that the guy would challenge for Elder, yeah?"

Simeon gave a short nod, and Batiste bristled, but he agreed.

"The only thing Etienne... Deimos has as a weapon is his super charm. Bridgerton is old, scary old, and while Deimos is old, I can bet Bridgerton has him outclassed. He wouldn't be able to keep the new guy from challenging him—I mean, that was the consensus downstairs, I saw you all. Bridgerton came here to challenge and kill

Etienne for his place as Elder, and he has nothing to defend himself with."

"So why the boy? Why try to kill you? Why any of this?" Batiste snarled at him, and Angel rubbed his face, chuckling.

"You already know the answer. Tell me, Batiste, why are you so comfortable with Simeon bonding with me, why allow me to stay in this city unmolested? Why build a relationship with me at all? Why do you want me in this clan?"

Batiste snarled quietly, backing away, returning to the windows and looking down again, then out to the city. Angel waited, but he got his answer. "I want you in this clan because you are powerful. No other clan will move against me, no one will challenge me, while I can claim you as one of my people. With you, and the secret you hold to our mass destruction, this clan is unassailable."

Simeon hissed and hovered over Angel. He rubbed Simeon's chest, soothing his lover. "It's alright, Simeon. I knew this the second he tried his bullshit this morning."

"He is mine, Batiste. You cannot have him," Simeon warned his master, and Angel grinned, impressed.

"Don't worry, I swear he won't try anything stupid. Blind as he may have been to Etienne's duplicity, I have a feeling your master isn't a total fool. Douche, sure, but not a fool."

"Get to the point, necromancer! I have a clan to restore to order," Batiste snapped, still staring out over the city.

"Long story short—Etienne gets to Macavoy in an attempt to get a sorcerer he can control. The boy tries, unsuccessfully, to become one of my students to learn how I killed so many vamps. Deimos wanted Daniel to learn the mystery spell, and then with Daniel under his control, he was either going to solidify his place as Elder or even make a move for clan master. Daniel fails to get me to take him on, not surprising since he acted like a little shit—probably fear talking, but I took it as attitude. Meanwhile, Simeon and I are getting closer, and Etienne's chance to get to me is slipping away. He goes out to the city, and falls back on his backup plan—building his own clan and killing me. If I die, then Simeon is left devastated and weak, and

Bridgerton would be likely to challenge Simeon instead of Etienne." They nodded, Simeon frowning fiercely.

"He is the rogue in town, which all three of us suspected. Slow and stupid, but with enough numbers he could get himself a fairly strong bulwark between himself and Bridgerton. Deimos goes after Greg Doyle, using Daniel, to test just how secure the promise is between myself and Simeon, even Batiste. I bet the only vampire to ask too many questions about me, to raise any complaint has been Etienne, yes? He wanted to see if he could get away with killing me or taking me, and what the clan's reaction would be if I either ended up dead or missing."

Simeon was listening, a frown on his face, but he was nodding. Batiste had turned from the glass, now watching his as well. "Meanwhile, Daniel is freaked out. He decides to try and break Simeon and I up—if I give my allegiance to Simeon, then any chance Etienne has of learning it from me by force or subterfuge is gone. My powerbase gets added to Simeon's, and Etienne loses any chance he had against Bridgerton, and Daniel thinks my way is clear to enact my evil plan. They decide to try and kill me, since by this time, they already have August, and torturing him isn't getting him to talk. Again, I die, Simeon is weakened, and Etienne has a better chance of Bridgerton challenging Simeon instead of him."

Eroch chirped, and snuggled closer.

"It's the whole premise, 'if we can't have the secret weapon, no one can!' and they send the demon for me. I banish it," Angel said, petting Eroch where he slept on his shoulder, Simeon and Batiste both glancing at the slumbering dragon for a second. "They try and get to me through August next. Thinking I'd go insane after watching my old mentor die and throw away caution, Deimos kills him in front of me and waits for me to blunder into his trap. Instead, Milly keeps me from losing my shit, and I retreat."

"Why didn't I recognize his scent on August's body?" Simeon asked brow wrinkled in confusion.

"Daniel warped Etienne's scent. It's not permanent, it returns eventually to his natural aroma. It's why no one was able to learn who the rogue was killing around town, and why you didn't recognize Etienne on August. Daniel has also been using his few family connections to rile up the Collins and the police—he's been telling them lies, fed to him by Etienne, claiming I'm about to take over the city in a mad scheme for power. The Collins control the police, and they were ordered by the heir to the Macavoys to not hunt the rogue vampire. The Macavoys may not have the power they once did a decade ago, but they have plenty of sway with their kin. It's why the cops have been after me too."

"Why claim the boy as yours, then?" Simeon asked him, his thumb rubbing over the back of Angel's knuckles.

"Because that boy has next to no family left—he was orphaned, same as I was, and while his father may live, he hasn't been an actual parent to Daniel in ten years. That boy was left vulnerable, and Etienne took him over and abused him. Daniel began to realize over the last couple of days that Etienne, or Deimos—was full of shit, and was just using him. Daniel is terrified, and he has blood on his hands by helping Deimos and his mad schemes. That kid needs saving, not punishment."

"Etienne will face my punishment. He will not escape his crimes," Batiste said, and Angel was cheered by the rage on his face.

"Good, because I'm going to kill the motherfucker. I made a promise to an old friend," Angel vowed, and Simeon grinned, a feral smile that sent hit throughout Angel.

"Where is he, Daniel?" Angel asked the boy, who was pale and weak, though awake. His eyes were nearly black, dark circles under them, his lips almost blue. The doctor had come and gone, attaching a unit of blood to an IV that ran into Daniel's arm, replacing what he lost when Deimos ripped out his throat. If Daniel had peace and quiet and plenty of sleep, he would recover. Physically at least—Angel's mind shied away from the memories he saw in Daniel's mind, the horrors Deimos committed on the vulnerable young man merely reaffirming his desire to kill the rogue Elder.

The scars were still there, angry red and vibrant. Angel was no healer—he may be able to heal mortal wounds, but he rarely had the chance to use that part of his affinity. Not many people lay dying in front of him on a regular basis. He would have done what he could for August, but his heart stopped before Angel even opened the door, placing him just past Angel's reach. His own heart hurt thinking about it, but at least he could save Daniel.

Eroch was still about Angel's neck, but he was awake, watching with bright yellow eyes, making little chirps and squeaks, commenting on everything around him. Angel had a feeling the little dragon had never had a chance to see this dimension without pain and a *geas* warping him, blinding him to the world, and the tiny creature was inquisitive and charming. Daniel barely reacted to the wee beastie, and Angel had to reach out and take Daniel's hand to get the boy to look at him.

"Hey, kiddo," Angel said, and Daniel focused on him, licking his chapped lips and blinking, eyes clearing. "There you are. It's okay, you're safe. Deimos is gone, fled. The demon is no longer under your control or Deimos. I know everything, except where the bastard is hiding. Can you tell me?"

Daniel opened his mouth, and whispered, "Home." His eyes shut, and he fell back asleep. Angel let him, standing from his partial crouch beside the boy's bed.

"Home, huh? Whose home?" Angel mused, and he walked from the room. It was dawn—and he was exhausted. He needed sleep and food. Simeon waited outside the doorway, and Angel went into his arms gladly, accepting the strength offered so freely in the vampire's embrace. Eroch chirped, and climbed from his shoulder to Simeon's, sniffing at the Elder like a cat, his tiny snout poking at the vampire's face.

Simeon held totally still, and Angel laughed, reaching up and taking Eroch back into his arms. "No climbing on the boyfriend,"

Angel said, and Eroch chirped sadly, but Angel held him securely, hugging the tiny beast. "Shush, no cuteness overload please."

"Is that thing safe?" Simeon asked warily, eyeing Eroch with caution.

"His name is Eroch, and he is fully sentient. Just not in any way humanoid, so don't go applying our behavior to his, and you'll be fine. He's not a pet, but a friend," Angel said, heading for Simeon's room. Guards lined the hall and even more were in the front of the suite, guarding Angel and Daniel equally, insuring Etienne... Deimos, hell whoever he was couldn't get back in. "Eroch will be fine. I need food then sleep, then we're off to kill the evil vampire."

"Do you know where he is? Did the boy tell you?" Simeon asked, and Angel nodded as they entered Simeon's room. He let Eroch go, who jumped from his arms and flew to the bed, crawling under the blankets and disappearing.

"I have a really good idea where Deimos is," Angel replied, stripping down to his underwear, heading for the bathroom. He took care of business and came back out moments later, and headed right for the food cart a blood servant was wheeling into the room. Simeon was shifting on his feet, and the servant was waiting, both of them looking at Angel.

"Oh," he said, and it clicked. Simeon was hungry, too. Angel could not feed Simeon—his blood was poison, and the Elder had to eat. "Um, Simeon, if you need to eat, go ahead. You want me to leave? Or I can stay, either one, up to you two."

The blood servant gave a relieved bow and walked out of the room, Simeon following. They were gone maybe five minutes, Angel staring at the door when it opened and Simeon returned. His clothing was intact, and he was discreetly wiping his mouth with a handkerchief. He stopped when he saw Angel staring, and the door swung shut behind him. "Does it bother you, *a ghra*? My need to feed on humans?"

"I won't lie. It does, a little bit, but only because I'm not used to it. He offered willingly, right?" Angel said, meaning the servant.

"Yes, I do not force-feed from humans. They offer their blood, in exchange for a safe place to live and an increased lifespan."

"How increased?" Angel asked, grabbing a sandwich on a plate and heading for the bed.

"A blood servant gets another fifty or sixty years added to whatever age they are when they begin to feed us. Repeat exposure to our saliva when we bite halts all aging, and when it begins to wear off, we either turn the human into one of us, or we let them go, depending on their wishes."

"Damn, sounds like a sweet job. Where do I sign up?" Angel quipped, and Simeon relaxed, smiling.

"I was afraid you would not be able to accept this part of my nature," Simeon revealed, undressing. "Many humans have trouble with it."

"I'm not really all that human," Angel said, taking a big bite of his sandwich, moaning happily at the flavor. He chewed and swallowed. "And you went and broke the law with me, and helped me raise the dead. If anyone needs help accepting his significant other, anyone would think it would be you."

"Your gifts don't bother me, *a ghra*," Simeon said, naked and resplendent and so gorgeous Angel had to force himself to finish eating. "You are a marvel, and my love for you grows deeper every day."

"Great answer," Angel smiled, and set aside his now empty plate, crawling into bed, Simeon following him in.

Simeon pulled the covers over them both, and Angel found himself draped over Simeon's chest, head resting on his lover's muscular shoulder, staring up close at several of his woad tattoos. The ancient designs were as wild as the man, and Angel grinned. Even when his life was full of danger and death and old rivalries, he was happy. He couldn't recall the last time he was happy.

Angel was nearly asleep when Simeon startled, moving his legs. Angel heard a reproachful chirp from under the blankets and smiled, just before he fell asleep.

ANGEL DREW his weather-proof sweater on over his head, yanking down the thick garment. He tried to fix his hair, but gave up on it, reaching for his bag and athame. The blade spun easily in his hand, the weight familiar and reassuring. It had once been his father's, and it was one of the few items he took from Salvatore Mansion when he and Isaac left.

Eroch chirped at him from the bed, stretched out on the blankets, waving his wings. Angel gave him a smile, and said, "Stay here, my friend. I'll have you freed before dawn, okay? Just relax, and you'll be home soon." The dragon chirped, and began rolling happily in the blankets.

Angel moved to the door, meeting Simeon at the suite's door. Daniel sat on one of the couches, freed from the IV and moving about. He was still weak, but improving, the scars on his neck still raw looking and bright red. Angel met Daniel's gaze, who promptly ducked his head and looked away, and the boy would have blushed in shame if he'd had enough blood left in his body to do so.

"Daniel," Angel said, making the boy look at him. Daniel lifted his eyes back to Angel's, and he gave him a short nod of approval. "You are not in danger here. You'll be safe, and you and I will talk when I get back."

"Will you be back?" Daniel dared to ask, worried, his dark eyes nearly black with swirling emotions.

"Yes, I will. I am going to kill Deimos; do you understand?" Angel asked, making his plans clear. "He's gone rogue—he has to die."

"I understand," Daniel said, his voice soft and thin. The boy curled in on himself and buried his head in his arms. Angel sighed but turned for the door anyway.

"Angel?" Daniel called just before they stepped into the hall.

"Yeah, kiddo?" Angel called back, half turned, to see Daniel peeking up through his thick bangs.

"Is Isaac still alive?" Daniel asked, biting his lip. "Did you find him yet?"

"Isaac...what do you mean?" Angel asked, taking a step back towards Daniel. "Is my brother in danger?"

"I think Deimos kidnapped him the other night."

"What!" Angel shouted, every hair on his body standing straight up, his breath stalling in his chest. He forced himself to breathe, and pointed at Daniel. "Explain!"

"Deimos tried getting to him before Remington, but Isaac only goes to the clan bars where everyone knows who he is and no one will bother him, and Deimos couldn't snatch him without drawing attention to himself. He even tried to get in his place, but the wards kept him out. So he took Remington instead," Daniel said, curling tighter in on himself. "But the other night he said Remington was a bust, and he was going to get Isaac to force the truth from you. He disappeared a couple nights ago, and he came back smelling like smoke and his hands were burned."

"Oh fuck," Angel swore, and tore away, running for the elevator. Heart racing, pulse thumping in his ears, Angel pulled out his cell and dialed Isaac's number.

"Angel, does he have your brother?" Simeon asked urgently as they got in the elevator, the door shutting with a ding. Simeon got them moving, scanning his palm and hitting the button for the garage.

"Come on Isaac, answer the fucking phone," Angel gritted out, wishing he could pace but he felt trapped and helpless in the confines of the elevator. The phone rang out in his ear, over and over, unanswered. That was not unusual, as Isaac ignored him on any given day, but this time he was tormented by what-ifs, images of his baby brother torn apart, his eyes dull and lifeless, blood spilled across the floor of his unkempt apartment.

"Breathe, *a ghra*," Simeon said, gripping the back of his neck, squeezing hard. Angel sucked in a deep breath, and redialed Isaac when it went to voicemail. "Calm yourself. Losing control will only endanger yourself and your brother."

"He isn't answering. He never does when I call, so use your cell. Here's his number," Angel said, turning his cell so Simeon could see his brother's number on his screen. "Call him, see if he answers. We need to get to his place, now."

The elevator finally stopped in the garage, and Simeon dialed his cell as he took Angel's arm, both of them sprinting towards a low, sleek black car. Simeon tossed Angel his cell, and he held it to his ear, his chest growing tight as it rang unanswered, over and over.

Simeon brought the mechanical beast alive, and with the tires screaming, they leapt out from beneath the Tower, heading for Isaac's apartment.

※

Angel sprinted up the stairs, too impatient to wait for the elevator in Isaac's building. Angel burst through the door in the stairwell, running full tilt for Isaac's door. The hall was dark, the lights flickering. Isaac lived in a fairly posh building, and the shared spaces were always well-maintained, so the bad lights were new. Angel dug out his keys, and tripped.

He flew forward, Simeon's hand grabbing him by his upper arm and stopping his descent a foot from the floor. Angel gasped, staring down at the dead eyes of Gregory Doyle. Simeon lifted Angel back to his feet, and they both looked down at what remained of Isaac's erstwhile boyfriend. Greg was torn to pieces, an arm ripped from his body, torso sundered, and blood was dried and pooled beneath his body. Several bags of groceries were spilled across the floor, a milk jug punctured and the milk mixed with blood. A pizza box was wrecked, and the contents were strewn across the hallway.

Scorch marks littered the walls and floor, and even the corpse. Which was bloated, flies and bugs crawling upon it, and the food was well on its way to rotting in the warmth of the hallway. Isaac lived alone on this floor—the only traffic through here was his brother, and Isaac rarely left his place except to head to vampire bars. The groceries on the floor were the first he'd seen any evidence of since Isaac moved out.

Angel put a hand out and rested it palm flat on the door of Isaac's place. The wards hummed, intact, and he sent out a tendril of thought, seeking his brother on the other side.

Nothing.

"He's not here. They never made it back into the apartment before they were ambushed," Angel said, backing away from the mess in the hall. He gave Doyle one last look of regret, and backed away. "Doyle's been dead for at least two days. Deimos has Isaac."

"Are you sure? Should we not check the apartment?" Simeon asked him though he followed Angel as he jogged back down the hall, back to the staircase. "How did no one find the body?"

"Isaac is gone. Whether Deimos has him or not, I can't tell, but my brother put up one hell of a fight," Angel huffed out, taking the stairs down three at a time, Simeon keeping pace. "Isaac and Greg have that floor all to themselves. No other tenants, so there's no reason for anyone to get off on that floor. It's a closed building, so no one wanders around."

"How do you know Deimos has him, or that he's not in there still? I thought your brother was a mundane mortal," Simeon said, and they left Isaac's building and ran for the car. They got in, and Angel pulled out his cell and answered Simeon as he dialed 911. As much as he disliked Gregory Doyle, Isaac had loved the man, and Angel couldn't leave his corpse to rot in the hallway with the spoiled milk and pizza.

"He doesn't practice, hasn't since he was a kid. I sent Isaac to public school with the human kids after the Wars, and taught him at home. He's still fully trained, I made certain of that before I let him move out. Isaac is a sorcerer, just like me," he said, hitting Send on his cell. "Deimos is in for a world of hurt if he has Isaac."

"How so, *a ghra*?"

"My little brother's affinity is for fire," Angel said, and Dispatch answered his call. "I need to report a murder and potential kidnapping."

Angel gave Dispatch the barest of details, then hung up. Simeon gave him a glance, and Angel took a deep breath, centering himself as best he could. He reached for the veil, charging himself and his reserves past his normal levels, spindling the power inside of him, until his fingers tingled.

"Where to, *a ghra*?" Simeon asked, turning the ignition and waiting for directions.

"Salvatore Mansion," Angel answered, and buckled himself in. Simeon was startled, but pulled out into the evening traffic, heading south.

Daniel had said, "home." And that was where Angel would go.

※

The long street was lined by tall, straggly pines and barren deciduous, dormant with the onset of winter. Simeon parked the car outside the community gate, and they got out, approaching the wrought iron fence and stone wall.

The community was ostensibly still inhabited, but the main gate had moved to the other side of the community, letting the few remaining residents the ability to come and go without having to drive by the Salvatore Mansion. Set back a few hundred yards from the road, Angel got glimpses of his familial home through the trees as they walked down the pothole pocked street, the sidewalk cracked and reduced to rubble in many places. Old scorch marks from pyres and melted slag from what was once street lamps made puddles and ripples across the ground, like lava cooled to obsidian.

"Have you never been back?" Simeon asked, his voice hushed. Angel stepped around a scorched and melted section of asphalt, kicking aside some pieces of charcoal that may or may not be a piece of some burnt-out car, hell, even a bone.

"I took some things from the house, packed up Isaac and myself, closed up the house, and left," Angel replied his athame in hand, glad he left the bag in the car. They would need to move fast, and Angel wouldn't be taking the time for structured casting.

They were walking down the main avenue where most of the vampiric army sent for the Salvatore family was destroyed. Where he killed them. Angel paused, breathing in deep, the fresh air familiar and poignant with memories.

"My love?" Simeon whispered, standing at his shoulder, blocking the meager wind. Memories ate at Angel, and he had to regain control, or there would be no rescue and no vengeance meted out tonight.

"My father didn't teach me when I was done with school, that was August. But one thing he did teach me when my affinity for death was confirmed was an old family fable," Angel exhaled roughly, tears threatening to run down his chilled cheeks. This was no time for him to fall apart. Remembering his father's words like a lifeline, Angel rested his forehead on Simeon's shoulder, breathing slow and deep.

Simeon put his hands over his shoulders, giving him something to focus on, rubbing and soothing. "What was the fable, *a ghra*?"

"It's too long to tell the whole of it, but the moral is fairly simple. That the life of a necromancer is a complicated, twisted path, strewn with pitfalls and steep inclines, dangerous decisions and prejudice. We are feared for our powers, as much as we are needed. Necromancers make the best priests, the strongest healers when all hope is lost, and yet we are the most skilled at killing, causing misery and pain and death. We commune with the dead and ease the soul's passage, taking up priestly vows as often as we stray from the path and raise armies of undead. He said my life would follow the same path as those that came before me, and that my story would depend upon me. The tale is a cautionary one, called the necromancer's dilemma, but he called it the necromancer's dance—he was dancer, and his metaphors followed suit," Angel whispered, lifting his head, wiping at his eyes, closing them for a moment as he recalled his father's face, how he sounded in that long ago conversation. "He told me my dance would be no less fraught with peril and choices to make, and he hoped I would make the right decisions."

Angel breathed in, held it, and let it go, slowly, his calm returning. He was on his family's land, home at last, and it was time to finish what was started all those years ago. Deimos betrayed his people, and sent them for Angel's, and they were all dead as a result.

"I never intended to survive that night," Angel said, stepping back from Simeon, meeting his lover's concerned gaze, strength returning to his voice, his heart beating with purpose. "I had no idea what I was doing, and with what I thought was my last breath I cast a spell that was meant to put an end to the death around me. I tried to die, and ended up killing my enemies instead. But tonight I intend to survive, and I have a purpose. Deimos dies, Isaac gets home in one piece, and I sleep for a week after this."

"Excellent plan, my love," Simeon smiled, and Angel walked on, his calm returned.

"Is Isaac here?" Simeon asked as they came up to the house's driveway, following the gravel and stone road toward the old mansion, rising from the unkempt gardens like a lost castle in the wilderness.

"He is," Angel affirmed. "He's still alive, too. The land recognized him."

"Can you sense if Deimos is here, too?" Simeon asked, and the Elder was watchful, cautious, eyeing the surrounding wild growth and the shadows under the trees. "Does the land know you?"

"The land knows me," Angel whispered back, his awareness stretched out across the width and breadth of his heritage, feeling the near-dormant pulse of the land that saw the birth and death of six generations of Salvatores. Isaac's presence was a brilliant red glow, a single flame that shimmered amidst several deep pits of cold void—fledglings. "Deimos is here, as is...five, no six...six newly risen fledglings."

"I can handle them," Simeon stated, absolute conviction in his voice. "They cannot withstand my power."

"Even against their sire's will?" Angel asked, and he gestured with the athame, guiding Simeon away from the wide, tall windows in the front of the mansion, heading towards the side door to the garden that would take them into the depths of the house.

"Etienne has attempted many times in the last decade to sire fledglings bound to him, and each time he failed. Another master had to take them in hand, or they were killed," Simeon informed him, and Angel grumbled.

"Great, so they will be wild. Any idea if you can handle that many at once?" Angel asked, approaching the door cautiously. There was no point in trying for stealth—a vampire's hearing was sharp enough to hear Angel and Simeon out at the gate.

"I have done so before, *a ghra*," Simeon said, a feral smile on his lips.

Angel made the door, the thick wood panel set with stained glass his mother's favorite, and he pressed his hand to the metal doorplate, feeling it warm under his fingers. The door unlocked with a soft snick and swung inwards.

The study was dark, the furniture standing out in the shadows like ghosts under their dust covers. Angel stepped inside, Simeon at his side and Angel closed the door, the solid thump echoing through the house. Subterfuge wasn't an option when against enemies who could hear his heartbeat from across the house.

Angel sniffed and sent Simeon a wry glance when the heavy scent of mint and chocolate filled his nose. Simeon was vamping out, eyes glowing, fangs bared, and his claws grew to sharp points on his fingers. He was about to ask why when hissing echoed in the room, and Angel flared the athame awake with hellfire just as the shadows moved and dark figures leapt from the corners.

Simeon moved so fast Angel could not see what happened, only that a fledgling lay broken at the Elder's feet, and another slammed against the wall, falling unconscious to the floor. The shadows moved again, and he brought the athame up, scoring the ribs of another fledgling, claws reaching for his face and neck.

The fledgling screamed a high-pitched wail that left his ears ringing. His hands flared with hellfire, the flames responding to the rush of adrenaline in his system, and the fledgling blurred as it ran, screeching as it disappeared into the depths of the house. Simeon cursed, and ran his hands over Angel's face, looking for injuries.

"I'm fine! Keep moving. I fucked that one up but it can still function," Angel said and ran for the door to the rest of the house.

"Where is Deimos, can you tell?" Simeon asked, his voice slightly warped due to his fangs.

"He's upstairs somewhere, with Isaac," Angel said, and he ran for the stairs, counting on Simeon to see the fledglings coming before he could. The central staircase went from the middle of the house and wound its way all the way up to the third floor before smaller stairs took their paths to the individual turrets at each corner of the mansion. Isaac's red flame sparked somewhere above them, and Angel had a sinking feeling he knew exactly where his brother was.

Angel ran upwards, leading the way, Simeon guarding his back, light from the burning athame casting its glow on the walls, and off the pair of eyes just at the top of the stairs. The wounded fledgling crouched, black blood dripping down the stairs, and it was warped past any semblance of humanity as it bared its fangs at them. Simeon roared a challenge, and the fledgling leapt. Angel dove to the side, and Simeon caught the newborn vampire in his arms, restraining it, its impact nothing against his superior strength. A sharp, wet crack came from the vampire's torso, and the fledgling went limp, its spine broken. Simeon dropped it, and it rolled down the stairs, landing in the grand foyer.

Angel crawled up the stairs to the landing, and paused, breathing hard. Simeon was putting out waves of pheromones, making Angel's body twitch with the instinctive need to flee, his lover in full hunting mode. His eyes were a brilliant green, burning as brightly as Angel's blade, and Angel figured their chances of success were pretty damn good.

"Deimos!" Angel yelled, ready to end this and go home. "I want my brother back, fucker!"

His words echoed off the stone walls, silence his answer. Isaac burned somewhere ahead, and Angel pointed the way, Simeon going ahead of him this time. They took the hall to the right, and Angel's guess for where Deimos put Isaac was accurate.

During the attack that night so many years ago, Angel saved Isaac by dragging his little brother into the family panic room. His entire family but for Isaac had all been downstairs in the dining room when the attack came, and the older members of his family activated the estate wards, but not fast enough. The wards were always on, the ones at the boundaries of the property, but they were soon submerged by the sheer numbers of undead. That night the wards around the house rose in a haphazard manner, leaving gaps in the protections big enough for the horde to stream through, overwhelming his family in sheer numbers. Raine Salvatore had driven most of them back, and after Isaac was secured in the panic room, Angel had joined his father in beating the vampiric army back, until only Angel was left standing, having drawn the unthinking undead away from the mansion and his little brother. It was there he made his last stand and cast his spell.

The mourning fire spell, cast wide and without discretion and fueled by the veil, had obliterated everything carrying death magic, feeding voraciously upon the ancient magic in each of the undead. They were an endless conflagration of pyres, burnt into his memory. He still did not know how exactly he managed it, nor if he could duplicate it. The concept of using a funeral spell as an offensive tactic had never crossed anyone's mind, and Angel was lost as to how he managed it.

He awoke not long after, and dragged himself back to the house and upstairs, to the panic room, keying in the code that would open the door. Isaac was inside, catatonic with grief and fear, curled in a corner of the room. His brother was just coming into his powers, but Isaac had enough skill to know when each of their family fell, and Angel did not need to tell Isaac they were orphans.

Isaac was now in the same room, the hidden panel open as Angel had left it all those years earlier, his little brother propped up in the same corner, trussed in iron shackles, eyes shut, a trail of blood running from one temple.

"Shit!" Angel swore, and Simeon entered the room, heading for Isaac. "No, wait!"

Before Angel could say trap, a heavy weight slammed into Angel's back, sending him careening down the hallway. A deep hiss and a rumble echoed down the hall as Deimos hit the door latch, and the panic room door slid shut with a resounding thunk, trapping Simeon inside.

"Angel!" Simeon's roar was full of rage and despair, muted by the heavy door. The panic room walls and door were over a foot thick, made of steel and stone, and impossible to break through. There was a release inside, but with Isaac knocked out Simeon would have to waste time searching for it.

Deimos chuckled, his dark eyes burning from within, and Angel crawled backwards, looking for his athame, having lost it in his tumble. He didn't need it, but it helped.

"I am going to kill you," Angel swore, using the wall to get back on his feet. He felt odd—lightheaded, dizzy. He must have hit his head when Deimos sent him rolling down the hall.

"I think, necromancer, that I am going to kill you. With you dead, I can kill Simeon, and I will get the spell from your darling little brother," Deimos hissed, all traces of French accent gone, his ruse as Etienne over. The vampire stalked down the hall, backing Angel away from the panic room. Angel stumbled, his legs forgetting how to work. "If you were taught it, then so was he."

Many had made that mistake, thinking the spell he used was hereditary, but Isaac didn't know. Isaac hadn't wanted to know.

He tried reaching for the veil, but his control slipped away from him, and his mouth was dry, his eyes heavy. "What the fuck did you do to me?" Angel whispered, falling back against the wall, grasping helplessly for anything to keep him upright.

Deimos stepped closer, into the light from one of the windows in the hallway, and lifted his right hand. Claws fully extended, and dripping in blood. Angel's blood.

He felt it now, a streak of icy flames along his back and ribs— Deimos had slashed his back open, from hip to shoulder, each claw leaving a deep groove through which he was bleeding to death. He could save himself if only he could focus, but his mind was slipping away.

Angel fell to the floor, blinking slow, panting heavily as he bled out.

He was going to die, in the place where his family died before him. Simeon was still alive, the hallway reverberating with sound as Simeon tried to bash his way free. Isaac would be safe as long as Simeon survived—Deimos was no match for the Elder.

Claws hovered in his narrowing vision, stroking over his face and neck. "It is a shame I cannot drink from you, necromancer. I would taste my victory," Deimos whispered, chuckling. "Simeon never got to taste you. His bonds to you as his *Leannán* never set in, did they? He never thought to have you drink from him, too busy chasing me. Too late for love to save you."

Love.

Angel closed his eyes, heart slowing, body growing cold. His last thought was to be of love. That wasn't such a bad thing, not at all. He never thought he would have it, never sought it out. But he was glad, so very thankful to have been given a taste of what love would have been like, a life spent in Simeon's arms. He would never know what it would feel like to be a vampire's beloved, Simeon's *Leannán*, and that regret burned in his heart.

He never thought to have you drink from him.... but he had. Angel did drink from Simeon, biting his flesh as he came from a powerful orgasm, his lover's blood rushing down his throat. As Angel knew his own blood, and could sense and control any undead that drank from him, Angel went looking for the traces of his lover in his body. He sank deep into his mind, his body dying around him, and there, his own life-force dimmed, Angel saw the thin tendrils of Simeon's blood, his essence, twined around his soul. The beginning of a bond was there, nascent and unformed, but enough for Angel to see what would have been, and help it along. Without the pain of dying distracting him, Angel used the power of his own life on the brink of death, and reached for Simeon, that bastion of strength and support and undying love he sensed just out of reach.

He knew it worked when he found a cool, minty presence in the void, full of despair and grief, and bitter rage. He tied a bond around that cool beacon that glimmered in the black, and called.

Simeon.

Shock, confusion.... then hope, obliterating all in its path, love on its heels. That love poured into Angel, and he took it in, melding it, molding it with his magic, and Angel opened his eyes, pushing the power he received selflessly from his lover out into his own body, and took a breath.

He was no longer in the hallway, the fledglings standing over him having dragged him into a room, circling him and whining like the feral beasts they were without a master strong enough to make them retain their humanity. Angel breathed in again, and out, and sent his magic to the mortal wound in his back, sealing the claw marks in fire and magic. Simeon kept sending him strength, the Elder a bottomless well from which to draw, and Angel breathed in, gathered Simeon's essence, and released it.

The fledglings fell as one as if their strings were cut. They lay limp and unmoving on the floor, and Angel carefully pushed himself to his feet, eyes searching for Deimos.

His blood had soaked his clothing, and he squished as he walked. He was in his parents' bedroom, and Angel growled at the sacrilege when he realized Deimos had set up residence in their room.

"Deimos!" Angel screamed, rage and righteous fury finding one voice in his own. "Deimos, you bastard!"

The door crashed open, and Deimos gaped at him, eyes darting from the three fledglings incapacitated on the floor, and back to Angel, the vampire unable to understand. Angel roared out his fury, reaching for the veil at the same time Simeon sent him another burst of power, a horrific crash sounding through the house as the panic room door lost its battle with the trapped Elder.

Angel raised his hand, Deimos hissing, and the vampire leapt at the same time he cast, a writhing bundle of pure fury and flame arching across the space between them. A blur swept through the room, and Angel found himself in Simeon's arms, the Elder moving him out of the way as Deimos crashed to the floor where he had been standing.

Angel's hellfire moved as snakes, stabbing into the vampire, consuming his undead flesh in green flames, eroding him from the inside out, thin wails of anger and pain clawing at Angel's ears. Angel fed his hellfire snakes more power, and Deimos died a fiery death, reduced to ash and fractured bits of scorched bone.

Simeon clutched him close, and Angel threw his arms around his lover's neck, holding on for dear life. "I love you."

"I love you too, *a ghra*."

Angel lost track of how long they stood like that, leaning on each other, emotions careening from the bond between their spirits. It was thin but strong, and Angel embraced it with care, knowing he had the power to sunder it, just as he had the power to forge it, and he would need to tend it with love and respect for it to grow stronger.

"Angel?" He lifted his head from Simeon's shoulder and looked to the door.

Isaac stood there, bloody and bruised, but free of the iron that muted his powers. Isaac hovered in the doorway, as if uncertain of his welcome, but when Angel moved toward him, his little brother ran at him, the brothers colliding in the middle of their parents' bedroom, holding each other tight.

12

NEW BEGINNINGS

"Move it another foot to the right," Angel directed, and Simeon pulled the heavy steel bedframe across the floor, settling the king-size bed in its new spot.

"I do not understand why we are not staying at the Tower, *a ghra*," Simeon complained, for the thousandth time.

"We are not living at the Tower for many reasons, chief of which is Batiste is a douchebag, and he won't stop making eyes at Isaac," Angel retorted, grabbing the new sheet set and snapping out the fitted sheet, tucking it around the mattress, Simeon helping. "And Daniel hates it there. I don't blame him for what that asshole Deimos made him do. Not to mention Bridgerton is insufferable as an Elder. That vamp oozes arrogance. He gives me heartburn."

"Yes, but with the four of us in this one apartment...." Simeon mused, brows furrowed as they made the bed.

"Who said you were moving in with me?" Angel said, straight-faced, and got a pillow in the face for his quip. Angel laughed, Simeon grinning at him in return. "Look, there's room. Isaac is back in his old room," his brother having given up his apartment after Greg's murder and his abduction, "Daniel gets the study down the hall I never used, and you and I are in here. Sure, kinda a snug fit, but you like it that way," Angel grinned at Simeon and winked, his lover growling, flashing him a fang.

"You two stop flirting and get out here! Lunch is ready!" Milly yelled from the kitchen, Daniel and Isaac laughing. Angel grinned, and jogged out of the bedroom, Simeon following.

"Milly, it's not lunch after sunset," Angel argued, grabbing a bowl of clam chowder and a handful of oyster crackers. He settled in at the island, Simeon getting a cleverly disguised blood unit bag from the fridge and a straw. It looked like a juice bag but held a whole pint of O negative, Simeon's preferred vintage.

"Close enough," Milly retorted, tossing a cracker at Angel. He caught it in his mouth and grinned, which made Milly snort out a laugh. "Eat up boys, tomorrow we have a long day ahead of us at the studio. Try number fifty million to get the Serfano boys to shield."

Daniel groaned, moping, but he ate his chowder anyway, fending off Eroch as the little dragon kept trying to steal the crackers out of his bowl. Angel had offered to send Eroch home, the *geas* lifted from the little dragon when Deimos died, but Eroch had merely chirped at him, and went back to sleep on Angel's pillow. Angel had a sinking feeling he had just picked up his first familiar, but as they went, a dragon was kind of the pinnacle of sidekicks. He had no idea what to do with the wee beastie, but he was good company on nights Simeon had to fulfill his duties as Elder and Angel didn't want to trek to the Tower to see his lover.

Daniel was officially listed as his apprentice, and with Batiste and Simeon's backing the young sorcerer was avoiding punishment for his part in Deimos's schemes by serving Angel, at least until Angel repaired the broken and incomplete education Daniel had in the higher arts.

Isaac, for all that he acted carefree and fine, carried a heavy weight of grief in his heart and eyes, and it made Angel grieve along with his little brother. Angel never did like Gregory Doyle, but the man's love for Isaac had been a constant, as true as his alcoholism and perpetual laziness, but real all the same. Angel and Isaac were nowhere near where they should be in terms of actually fixing their relationship, but some of Isaac's walls were down, and Angel was trying to learn how to listen as a brother, instead of as a reluctant parental figure. Angel had hope they might end up in a good place.

Daniel had gotten the Collins to back off, and with Angel finding the rogue vampire and killing him, the Mayor of Boston had offered Angel an official job as a consultant to the BPD. Angel took it after careful consideration and a fully vetted contract, giving him the choice to help or not, at his discretion, and his fee was hefty. Batiste had made the town's brass very unhappy, and Detective Grant Collins was sent on a long sabbatical, ordered to think about his priorities. Angel's liaison was Collins' old partner, the always charming Detective James O'Malley, who hit it off splendidly with Simeon, the two men speaking in Irish every chance they met.

A knock came at the door as Angel was rinsing his bowl in the sink, and Simeon went to answer it. "Simeon! So good to see you," Detective O'Malley said, greeting the Elder, the two Irishmen shaking hands and murmuring to each other in a fluid string of words Angel had no hope of deciphering. O'Malley laughed and nodded at Angel as he approached the door.

"Got a case we could use an outside opinion on," O'Malley said in lieu of a greeting, lighting a cigarette. "Several dead bodies stomped into jelly, pentagram burnt into the floor, and a really big hole in a wall."

"Sounds like someone summoned a demon," Angel replied, leaning on Simeon, his lover hugging him close. "Either that or they resurrected a mammoth."

"So that mean you coming?"

Angel looked up at Simeon, who nodded, reaching for Angel's bag and repaired weather-proof sweater. Angel took them, Simeon grabbing his apartment keys from the wall.

"Milly, I'll see you at work tomorrow," Angel called as he stepped into the hall. Eroch gave a chirp and jumped into the air, winging his way to Angel, landing on his shoulder. Milly rolled her eyes and waved, and the boys went for second helpings of chowder, ignoring him. Simeon followed him out into the hall and shut the door, and Angel waited patiently, listening.

His wards activated, Daniel a second behind Isaac as his brother and apprentice made sure their home was protected while they were out.

O'Malley led the way, and Simeon took Angel's hand, the bond between them flaring brightly before it settled with a gentle glow. "Ready, *Leannán*?"

"Ready, my love," Angel said, following the detective.

THE STORY CONTINUES in *The Necromancer's Dilemma*, Book Two of The Beacon Hill Sorcerer.

AFTERWORD

Thank you! I hope you enjoyed the book. Please consider leaving a review on Amazon, Bookbub, or Goodreads. Reviews help other readers decide to take a chance on self-published books. Reviews help indie authors like me continue to write and bring new books into the world.

—Sheena (SJ)

Want more options to help support my writing? Join me on Patreon!

ALSO BY SJ HIMES
AN INFINITE ARCANA SERIES*

THE WOLFKIN SAGA
Wolves of Black Pine
Wolf of the Northern Star

BEACON HILL SORCERER SERIES*
The Necromancer's Dance
The Necromancer's Dilemma
The Necromancer's Reckoning
A History of Trouble (Collection)
Mastering The Flames

WEREWOLVES OF BOSTON*
Wolfsbane

REALMS OF LOVE
The Solstice Prince

SCALES OF HONOR
Knight's Fire

STANDALONE TITLE
Saving Silas

Find all my titles in audiobooks on Audible!

ABOUT THE AUTHOR

My name is Sheena, and I have more pen names than I probably should. I write as SJ Himes, Revella Hawthorne, and Sheena Himes. I reside in the mountains of Maine (closer to Canada than I am to fresh lobster) on a 300 year-old farm beside a river in the woods. My companions are my furbabies: Wolf and Silfur, two cats who love me but hate each other, and Gingersnaps, my Barn Cat Turned Reluctant Housecat. I write romances with an emphasis on plot and character development, and almost all my characters are LGBTQ+ and that's on purpose. I am nonbinary and my pronouns are they/them.

To keep current on what I'm working on and where to find me on social media, go to my website:
www.sjhimes.com